FLIGHT
OF THE
NORTHERN STAR

FLIGHT
OF THE
NORTHERN STAR

By

James A. Jack

iUniverse, Inc.
Bloomington

Flight of the Northern Star

This is a work of fiction. All of the characters, names, incidents, organizations, and dialogue in this novel are either the products of the author's imagination or are used fictitiously.

iUniverse books may be ordered through booksellers or by contacting:

iUniverse
1663 Liberty Drive
Bloomington, IN 47403
www.iuniverse.com
1-800-Authors (1-800-288-4677)

ISBN: 978-1-4759-7051-7 (sc)
ISBN: 978-1-4759-7052-4 (ebk)

Library of Congress Control Number: 2013900220

Printed in the United States of America

iUniverse rev. date: 01/29/2013

From that first flight in the twin,
to our 'night over the Everglades';
lunch on the island;
a gas station hot dog on Thanksgiving;
and now this project,
you've helped me through it all,
this book is for you—my quilter, my co-pilot, . . . my wife!

The author wishes to acknowledge the following individuals

    * Kelly Thompson—editing

    * Kenneth Carter—editing and content advice

    * Mr. Dale Thornton Jr. and the employees of McDonalds store # 19231 for their hospitality during hours of writing and waiting for my son.

CHAPTER 1

Victor Stone quickly downshifted as he attempted to wipe the dust from his goggles. He pressed the accelerator to the floor and flicked the steering wheel to the left. His beloved MG-B shot out from behind the pesky Triumph TR-4 trying desperately to cut him off.

Upshifting, Stoney gained enough of a lead to move over in front of the Triumph—at last! A huge grin of satisfaction peered through the dust and dirt that covered his face.

Looking ahead to the next curve, he knew he would have to downshift and use the emergency brake to slide the car sideways around the curve to avoid losing any speed in the loose gravel. Every year Stoney ran this race up Pikes Peak in his MG-B sports car, and every year that Triumph managed to stay ahead of him. *Not this time!*

Stoney thought confidently as the car responded to his inputs and slid around the curve.

Stoney was accelerating out of the curve when he began to hear a strange beeping sound. Glancing around the car's instruments, he saw nothing that looked out of place.

What was that beeping?

It only got louder as Stoney prepared himself for the next curve. The beeping grew louder and louder still, until the piercing noise disrupted the rapidly changing landscape in his windshield. All that remained was blackness, and Stoney realized he wasn't in the MG but instead was lying in bed in a darkened room.

Several seconds passed before he realized it was the alarm clock beeping. He looked over at the clock. His fuzzy brain read the numbers *4:00 a.m.* He reached over and slapped the snooze button. What seemed like only seconds later, the routine repeated. Only this time the cognitive side of his brain realized the alarm was not going to give up its constant vigil, so he sat up on the side of the bed, reached over and turned it off.

Stoney glanced out the window, and he confirmed what he already knew: It was still dark. Stoney's intense love of flying did not include the *before sunrise* part.

Sitting there in the dark, he worked to get the fog of sleep out of his brain. As it cleared, he reflected on how early mornings were just part of a pilot's normal routine. It was funny how the mornings seemed to come a lot earlier as he got older. He picked up the TV remote and punched in the channel number for the BBC early morning news show. He had stayed here, at the Empress Hotel in Victoria British Columbia, enough times to know the channels by heart. This hotel was where all of the Atlantic Pacific Air crewmembers stayed before their flight across the vastness of the northern arctic to London.

The fuzzy picture finally resolved into view revealing a commentator interviewing an expert on U.S. and Soviet relations. Ever since the dawn of the Cold War, the status of relations between the two Super Powers was of interest to everyone on the planet and Captain Victor Stone was no exception.

The flickering light from the television danced around the darkened room as he wondered how his life would be different if he had taken that job with Trans World Airways instead of APA.

He could have been flying TWA's newest Boeing 707 jetliners instead of the piston-powered Lockheed Super Constellation. With TWA, he would have been a glorified bus driver, but with APA, his job was a little more important then just getting passengers from here to there.

He had taken the job with APA for two reasons: first, he dearly loved the Super Constellation aircraft; and second, he was not only flying passengers around, but he was also helping his country in its intelligence war with the Soviet Union. Stoney had been the youngest pilot recruited by the "owners" of Atlantic Pacific Air which was part of a special U.S. intelligence program called 'Northern Star'.

The CIA and the NSA had formed a joint task force or in U.S. government terms—a 'Program Office'—that ran the Northern Star program, and indirectly, Atlantic Pacific.

During Stoney's maturation as a pilot, he had been required to fly on numerous occasions with FAA check pilots who evaluated his skills and approved his applications for various pilot ratings. His flying skills were so admired by those check pilots that word had gotten back to Cecil

Richards the chief pilot for APA, who eventually flew out to Stoney's home airport in Durango, Colorado, to recruit him.

After a check ride of sorts, Mr. Richards offered Stoney a job flying APA's regular commercial routes. Within a couple of years he transitioned to the special Northern Star routes and shortly thereafter received a promotion to captain of a Northern Star Super Constellation.

Glancing at the bedside clock, he realized he needed to get moving or he would be late for breakfast with his crew. He took the responsibilities of his job seriously, and he expected no less from his crew. He walked into the bathroom and turned on the light. The blinding white light hurt his eyes until they adjusted to the brightness. Standing in front of the mirror, he looked at his square jawed stubble covered face and saw his sky blue eyes staring back at him. Stoney smiled at himself. *I get to fly again today*, he thought and rubbed his eyes. *Just wish it wasn't so early!*

At six-foot, two-inches with close-cropped blond hair and a body honed from years of rock climbing and deep powder skiing, Stoney was ruggedly handsome and would have been at home on the cover of any outdoor sports magazine. After lathering up his face, he carefully shaved with the straight razor his father had given him.

Stoney had just started flying for Atlantic Pacific Air when he received word of his parents tragic death in an avalanche while skiing in Colorado. His family had been very close and each year they would go to Steam Boat Springs and ski the fresh deep powder in the back bowls. That particular year, he wasn't able to join them since he was in APA's co-pilots school. The news had devastated him and he came very close to dropping out of the class effectively ending his commercial flying career before it had a chance to start. Fortunately, cooler heads convinced him to stay and for that he was grateful. Each winter he skied as much as his schedule would allow and he went rock climbing each spring. Rock climbing was something his father had always wanted to do, so Stoney took it up as a way to keep their memory alive. Both his parents loved the outdoors which is why they had settled in Durango just after marriage. Growing up in the shadow of the Rocky Mountains, Stoney had grown to love the outdoors as much as they had.

Once finished, he walked over to the shower and turned on the water. While the shower warmed up, he shucked off his shorts, walked over to the toilet to take care of business, then climbed into the steaming shower. The hot water ran over his body and got his blood pumping, as it drove the remaining sleep from his mind.

As he dried off he thought back to the flight up from Los Angeles and the rough running number three engine. It had been running fine for most of the flight when it started to act up.

His flight engineer had been slow to diagnose the problem and still couldn't say exactly what had happened even after they landed. The problem had come and gone, and nothing they tried would make it reappear. These thoughts occupying his mind, he walked to the main room and unconsciously began to dress.

There was a light knock at the door. Stoney answered it and found his co-pilot, or First Officer, standing there in his APA uniform, flight case and over-night bag in hand. "Come on in Steve; I'll be ready in a couple of minutes."

Steve Valdochi, a trim young man of medium height, dark brown hair and a Midwestern accent said, "I checked on Lee and the Stews; they'll meet us downstairs in the restaurant. Lee will be running late though, I had to really bang on the door to wake him up."

Stoney and Steve had become quite good friends over the several months they had been flying together. Stoney admired Steve's ability to quickly analyze situations and find solutions when problems arose. Stoney had been concerned when APA management had assigned him such a young First Officer, but he soon discovered that Steve's age had no bearing on his abilities.

One of Steve's traits, Stoney really admired, was his ability to separate business from friendship. When they flew together, Stoney was in charge and Steve had no problem with taking orders. Steve was well on his way to his captain's stripes, and Stoney was determined to help him get there. As he grew to know him, Stoney slowly came to realize that in many ways Steve was a reflection of himself not that many years ago.

As Stoney was putting on his shirt and tie, Steve asked, "What do you think of Lee? I know he has a reputation as a first rate Flight Engineer, but on that last run it took him awhile to answer your question on our fuel usage. When number three started acting up he acted as if his brain had suddenly vaporized. I hate to think what would have happened in a real emergency where we really needed him to react."

"I know it seems that he has trouble sometimes," Stoney said. "However, he has some serious family issues that are weighing heavily on his mind. At first he seemed to be keeping the right perspective on family versus his job, however, I have noticed things are starting to get out of control and I'm going to strongly suggest he take a leave of absence when we get back. He's got to solve these problems or he will be grounded. Unfortunately there was no one to take his place on this trip so that will have to wait until we get back."

"What kind of issues does he have?"

"I can't say since Lee told me in confidence during our last layover. Let's just say, that if he doesn't take my hint I am going to recommend he be *forced* to take that leave of absence."

After putting on his uniform coat, Stoney picked up his hat, flight case, and over-night bag, and headed for the door. They walked down the stairs instead of taking the elevator, as was Stoney's custom. They continued across the lobby and entered the restaurant. As they entered, the hostess asked if they would like to leave their bags with her instead of taking them to their table.

"Great!" they replied, setting their bags down near the coat rack then heading to the table with the young ladies wearing APA's blue and red uniforms. Maria had auburn hair and was of average height and Stoney had not failed to notice, during a couple of layovers, that her curves filled out a bikini nicely. Virginia, on the other hand, was a tall blond with long shapely legs which she loved to show off by wearing stiletto heels whenever she could.

"Good morning, ladies!" Stoney said.

"Good morning, guys; hope you slept well," replied the Stews.

As they took their seats at the table, Stoney noticed that Virginia seemed to be giving Steve "the eye" a bit more than usual, and Steve seemed to have a special smile for Virginia who was the Head Stew. Last night, Stoney would have sworn he heard "the noises" coming from Steve's room, which just happened to be next door to his.

After Steve and Stoney sat down, Virginia said, "It was really hard to get up this morning. Guess I must have stayed up later than I thought."

Maria just giggled, and everyone noticed Steve had that "I've been caught" sheepish grin on his face. To break the ensuing silence Maria asked if anyone had plans once they reached London.

Virginia said, "I am planning to do some shopping. I desperately need some new shoes and skirts. The ones you find in London, if you know where to look, may cost a little more than in L.A., but they last so much longer and are in the latest European styles that haven't made it to the U.S. yet. Maria, do you want to go with me?"

"I would love to, but I am meeting some friends that live outside London, and they are going to show me the town. Would anyone else like to join us?"

Virginia said that she would like to so she would put her shopping off until the second day. Everyone on the crew was grateful they always had a two-day layover on these international flights in order to get their internal clocks reset and get plenty of rest before the return trip.

Lee Wyne, the Flight Engineer, walked up to the table. "Sorry, I am so late folks, guess I stayed up too late last night and had trouble getting out of bed."

"No problem, Lee; glad you made it down," Stoney said. He had always thought that Lee was a little odd even though he was a decent flight engineer.

Lee was of medium height with a slight build and tended to stay by himself and not socialize much with the rest of the crew. Stoney had not learned much about him even though they had spent many long hours in the small confines of the cockpit. Captain Stone had made it a point to treat everyone on his crew the same, so he had looked past Lee's idiosyncrasies; still Stoney had thought it was odd that Lee had confided to him about his marital problems during their last trip to London.

The waitress came, and everyone ordered breakfast. Stoney and Steve said that they would enjoy seeing London with Maria and her friends. However, Lee declined saying that he had some business to attend to for a friend, but he would meet everyone for drinks in the hotel lounge that evening. Everyone said they would miss him, but they understood. Finally, breakfast came and Stoney told everyone to "eat up" since they were running a little late, and the crew bus would soon be arriving to pick them up.

With the bill paid, everyone headed out through the lobby and to the crew bus that was waiting. As they walked out, Stoney and Steve stopped by the hostess station to pick up their cases.

Stoney, out of the corner of his eye, happen to notice Steve looking inquisitively at his flight case. "Steve is everything all right?" he asked.

"Something about the case felt different when I picked it up. It must be my imagination, guess I'm still half asleep."

"Well, get those cobwebs out before we get to the plane," Stoney said as he climbed into the crew bus.

Silence filled the bus as it made its way to the airport. Stoney had made this flight many times and was running through it in his mind. One point of concern was that pesky number three engine. Hopefully, the maintenance folks had found something as they worked on it through the night. He was not happy about taking a plane load of passengers and crew across the barren arctic with a possibly suspect engine. Grounding the airplane was an option, and as the captain, he had the authority to do so,

9

but he would not make any decisions until he had all of the available information. *If I have to ground the plane, there will be hell to pay but I will never jeopardize the safety of my plane, crew or passengers in order to satisfy management,* thought Stoney.

Inside the restaurant, the hostess asked one of the servers to watch her station while she went to the ladies room. No one paid any attention when she stopped by the pay phone and made a short phone call. Completing her trip, she returned to her station and made sure all was in order for the passengers of APA Flight 28A to eat breakfast before departing for London. It was still early, but she wanted everything to be ready for the early risers. She was new at this job and wanted to make sure that she performed her job well during her probation period. This was the one job where she could interact with both the passengers and the aircrew of each APA polar flight during its layover, and that was important to the person she had just called.

CHAPTER 2

Several months ago, Tom Train a senior level executive with NSA, had presided over a formal briefing to his joint bosses the CIA Director as well as the NSA Director on the status of the sensor upgrades to the Northern Star Program. Dieter Kauffman, the WWII ex-Nazi genius who developed the submarine detection system assured him it would be easy to integrate the upgrades into the Northern Star Constellation airframes with no major modifications. Train had used this information to seek approval to proceed.

At the conclusion of the briefing, he received a green light for the installation; however, they did shorten his timeline to get Northern Star #28A, the chosen prototype, outfitted and back on line. When the Directors eliminated the additional down time, Tom had stressed the need to stick to the original timeline and perform the additional testing he felt was necessary since the upgrade was effectively a complete redesign. In the end, he was overruled.

As the U.S. government's senior executive in charge of the program, Tom was well aware of the impact to Atlantic Pacific Air's passenger schedule to have one of its primary aircraft out of service for an extended period.

Tom, the APA managers, as well as their advertising agency had been able to build up the allure of APA's London routes by offering flights from San Francisco to London's Heathrow airport over or within view of the North Pole. These advertisements touted APA's Northern Star Constellations as the most luxurious aircraft in the skies. Their efforts resulted in full bookings for each flight, no less than six months in advance. Tom knew that cancelling a flight would be a major blow to their revenue stream as well as customer relations.

Initially the directors of the CIA and NSA had been skeptical of the whole concept of using passenger airliners to snoop for Soviet submarines. The directors were fully aware that the United States and the Union of Soviet Socialist Republics had signed treaties limiting the number of military aircraft flights over and around the poles. The idea was to reduce the likelihood of a sneak attack using intercontinental bombers. The treaties governing military flights had exempted commercial aviation since it was in the financial interest of both countries to keep those planes flying.

As such, the CIA had become aware that the Soviet Airline, Aeroflot, had outfitted its commercial planes with cameras and sensors to detect American submarine forces as they flew the polar commercial routes. The U.S. was behind the power curve, and the National Security Council wanted that gap closed ASAP. Tom and his CIA counterpart, Glen Burton, had managed to convince the directors that, like the Soviets, the U.S. could use commercial airliners for covert intelligence gathering, and, in fact, Dieter Kauffman had developed a sensor system that was ready for installation in an aircraft.

Both of the directors knew of Dieter's reputation in the field of radio frequency engineering, so there was no question about his equipment's capabilities. The directors finally gave Tom and Glen the approval to procure one aircraft as a demonstration of capability. Tom, Glen and Dieter had immediately decided upon the Lockheed model L-1649 Super Constellation. The tri-tail arrangement of the vertical stabilizers provided the perfect place to mount the three long-wire antennas needed by Dieter's sensor system.

They purchased an aircraft, installed the system, and obtained authorization for a single over pole flight to demonstrate the sensor's actual capabilities. The test had been an overwhelming success. Real sensor data in hand, the directors had briefed the President's National Security Advisor as well as the Congressional Intelligence Committee and shortly thereafter they received full authorization to proceed.

Tom's program office, through dummy corporations, had purchased a small upstart of an airline and through "creative financing" had transformed it into an international carrier. During that transformation, they had renamed the airline to Atlantic Pacific Air. APA Immediately began to bid on intercontinental and polar routes, and once they won those routes they began to purchase additional Super Constellations.

Engineers from both Lockheed and NSA modified several "Connies" to house the three trailing wire antennas as well as the associated radio and sensor equipment to implement Dieter's submarine finder system. Tom and Glen had decided not to mount sensor equipment in a few of the Constellations as part of the operational security—a shell game to keep the KGB guessing. Only a select group of people, namely the technicians, associated support personnel and the APA flight crews assigned to the Northern Star Program knew about the modifications.

Since the exact purpose of the program was highly classified, each aircrew member assigned to the program had to pass a Top Secret level background check and was placed into the Defense Department's Personnel Reliability Program (PRP). For security reasons, only the aircraft captains had in-depth knowledge of the installations and the associated security measures engineered into each aircraft but even the captains didn't know everything.

On the outside of the aircraft the only indications of the modifications were the three bulges at the base of each vertical stabilizer where it attached to the "boom" and the removal of the rear passenger doorway. The design engineers removed the two lavatories normally found in the rear of the aircraft and installed a new one in the front of the aircraft. The removal of the lavatories, the galley and the rear passenger door had created enough room at the rear of the aircraft to house Dieter's equipment.

The addition of the sensor equipment as well as the antennas (actually large reels of wire with associated winches) made the Northern Stars heavy in the tail.

To offset this dangerous condition, the Northern Stars had a new galley installed in the front of the aircraft. Additionally, they moved the baggage storage areas and other miscellaneous equipment toward the front of the aircraft to re-balance it. Unfortunately, the added sensor equipment and the newly installed luxury interiors had increased the empty weight of the aircraft so much that the Northern Stars could only carry twenty passengers, their luggage and an aircrew of six verses the standard commercial configuration that seated between sixty and one hundred-five passengers.

To make up the revenue difference, APA had installed new interiors to make them ultra chic and modern. The airline catered specifically to the very wealthy who did not mind paying a significantly higher ticket price to travel in such luxury. APA's policy was to treat each passenger as royalty which added to the desirability of the flights. The non-sensor equipped Constellations were modified to be identical to their sensor equipped cousins. Outside or inside there was no way for a layman to tell them apart.

As part of the luxury experience, the actual trip itself was broken down into two parts. The purpose of this was to simulate the old train or steam ship trips of the past. This did not subject the passengers, who could afford the ticket price, to the extremely long flight hours between San Francisco and London. The passengers boarded one of APA's smaller aircraft in San Francisco for the flight to Victoria British Columbia. They spent the night in the luxurious Empress Hotel where they experienced a traditional British "High Tea" and went on evening excursions to see the local area. During the entire experience, the staff treated the passengers like royalty and as such, APA's Northern Star Super Constellation flights were always booked.

The revenue from the flights allowed APA to cover the operating costs of the airline. The NSA and the CIA only paid for the cost of the special equipment, research, development, and installation of the special equipment as well as the required alternate airfields located along the Northern Star polar routes.

NSA/CIA had built these airfields to satisfy the FAA's requirement to have emergency runways located along the flight routes in case of an emergency. If something happened to the aircraft, they would be a short flight away from one of these alternate airfields where they could land safely and await repairs. NSA/CIA felt the cost of these airfields were justified since they did not want a Northern Star landing at just any airfield because of the sensitive equipment they contained. The captains were under strict orders to adhere to that policy unless lives were at risk.

APA enticed pilots to fly the Northern Stars and endure the peculiar security restrictions by giving them perks unlike any other international airline. Some of these perks included staying in the luxurious Empress Hotel and covering all meals. Normally, airline flight crews would stay in a low cost hotel and would pay for their own meals.

The U.S., in cooperation with Canada, Great Britain and British Columbia, had set up tightly guarded hangers where they could perform maintenance on the Northern Stars as well as download information collected during the flights. All of the maintenance personnel at these facilities were NSA/CIA employees. These friendly governments were willing accomplices since they received intelligence, from the CIA, based on the data collected by the Constellations as payment for their discretion.

Tom was proud of the contributions his program had made to National Security over the years. Each flight across the pole took approximately ten hours and during eighty percent of that time, the sensor technician was monitoring his equipment in search of "prey."

CIA had, through its counter-intelligence network, obtained information that the USSR was greatly concerned about the "hit" rate of the Northern Stars, and this was a grave concern to the Soviet leadership. As such, the leadership had tasked its intelligence community to devise a way to counter the American's capability.

The security measures put in place to guard the Northern Star secrets had caught several Soviet KGB agents over the years as they tried to infiltrate the program. Tom knew the Soviets would not just give up and as such he had tasked CIA to closely monitor the Soviet threat.

Tom had been pleased that the upgrades to 28A had gone as well as they had. Unfortunately, during testing it became clear that Dieter had made a mistake in his calculations for the needed electrical power. To fix the problem, Dieter directed the installation of new larger generators on all four engines, and Dieter had assured Tom the electrical wiring could handle the additional power requirements without the need for a complete re-wiring of the aircraft.

✪

Two days before Northern Star Flight 28A's departure from Victoria, B.C . . . .

Tom Train was in the NSA gym playing handball as he usually did during his lunch hour. Over the public address system, he heard his name saying there was an urgent phone call for him at the front desk. Tom thanked his partner for the game and hurried to take the phone call.

"This is Tom Train," he said into the receiver.

"Mr. Train, this is Rudy Smith, and I have a classified matter to discuss with you."

"Ah Rudy, no problem, I'm at the gym so I'll call you when I get to my secure phone, in say thirty minutes?"

"Thanks, sir; that would be great."

Tom hurried to the locker room and quickly cleaned himself up.

I wonder what has Rudy all upset? he thought. *The upgrades went fine, and last I heard, the test flights had proven the upgrades worked better than we had hoped.*

Arriving at his office, he sat down at his desk and dialed Rudy's secure phone number. After several rings, Rudy's voice said, "Rudy Smith."

"Rudy this is Tom Train, please turn your security key now."

"Yes sir Mr. Train, turning it now."

Immediately after turning his security key Tom heard the high pitched tones similar to those a computer telephone modem makes when trying to connect to another computer. This continued for about twenty seconds after which he heard a "click" and the tones faded away indicating the line was secure from eavesdropping.

"Rudy what's up?"

"Sir, we have run into a problem with 28A. The number three engine is periodically running rough, and we don't know what is causing it. We have inspected every inch of the engine and fuel system, but we cannot find a problem nor can we cause the roughness to happen. It is a very intermittent problem."

"Rudy, do you think we should ground the plane?"

"Well, sir, since we have tried unsuccessfully for several hours to recreate the problem, I am of the opinion the aircraft is safe to fly. I would ask that the flight crew monitor and log all systems statuses during their sensor run."

"I will give the go ahead to return the aircraft to service. However, once we hang up here I am going to call Dieter Kauffman and ask his opinion; unless you hear from me personally, release 28A on schedule."

"Will do, sir," Rudy replied, and the line went dead.

Dialing Dieter's secure number, Tom waited for him to answer.

"Dieter Kauffman here," said a voice laden with a thick German accent.

After completing the security encryption procedure once more, Tom said, "Dieter, I understand 28A has a rough running engine; what are your thoughts on the issue?"

At the conclusion of the call, Tom had a bad feeling in the pit of his stomach, but as he had explained to Dieter, he could not cancel the flight without proof of a problem. He knew that Captain Stone and crew would pick up the aircraft in Los Angeles the following morning and head for Victoria. The day after that, with a full load of passengers and crew, Northern Star #28A would head out across the Arctic for London.

Chapter 3

Upon arriving at the Victoria airport terminal, Stoney told Lee to head down to the maintenance area to see what, if anything, the mechanics had discovered about that number three engine during the night. Stoney had "squawked" it when they had arrived the previous afternoon knowing that would cause the maintenance crews to work all night to solve the problem before take-off time the next day.

"Lee, I will join you in maintenance as soon as I check in with the Ops Office. I will want a full report when I get there."

"I'll see what they found and meet you there," said Lee as he headed off to the maintenance area while Stoney, Steve and the Stews headed to the APA Operations Center.

"Good morning, Captain Stone and ladies," said the head of APA Operations as the team entered.

"Good morning, Gus, how are things looking for our flight?" said Stoney.

"The weather is not looking too bad, so it should be a good flight. I'll let Stan fill you in on the details."

"Stoney, Maria, and I are going to head down to the aircraft and make sure all of the catering is complete, and everything is set for the pax arrival," said Victoria.

"Great, we'll see you there in about forty-five minutes. What time are the pax due?" asked Stoney.

"Oh-eight-thirty," she replied.

"That's fine and unless we find something amiss, we should make our nine a.m. push-back time," Stoney said.

With that, the Stews headed to the aircraft while Stoney and Steve went to find Stan the weather guy.

"Steve, check with operations and make sure the aircraft was serviced with fuel, oil and emergency oxygen while I get the weather brief. Meet me in the flight planning room when you're finished."

"Yes, sir," Steve said and walked away.

"Good morning, Stan," Stoney said, entering the weather office.

Stoney had known Stan since the day he had started at APA as a First Officer, and they had been good friends ever since. Stoney held Stan's weather briefs in high regard. One thing he had quickly learned about the commercial flying world was to know which weather briefers knew their business; Stan was definitely one of those.

"Good morning, Stoney."

Both Stan and Stoney walked over to the large weather depiction chart tacked up on the wall.

"Looks like you will have fairly clear weather all the way to London. There is however a stationary weak low pressure system that is over the pole that may decide to slide south. It seems to be a fairly weak system, but those polar lows can be deceiving."

"Don't I know it; couple of years ago, we had a polar low that was reported to be weak that did slide south, and boy did it get nasty at altitude. That weak low turned out to be a very strong low, and the winds that it kicked up almost caused us to divert into Ireland for fuel. We ran out of de-icing fluid, and the turbulence was terrible," Stoney said.

"Well, I don't think that will happen this time. This one is fairly weak, and the winds are only about forty knots at your altitude. There is a high pressure ridge over Europe that I think will keep the low from sliding south for a couple of days. When you head back over from London, there may be an issue, but at least you should have a good tail wind," Stan said.

"By the way, please add current weather and forecasts for all of the alternate airports along our flight path to the standard weather package. We've had a rough running engine, and I want some options if it decides to act up. Steve will stop by to pick up the package when he finishes flight planning," said Stoney.

"Will do," Stan said. "I don't think there will be any weather problems should you have to divert. I'll get you the most current weather that I can, however, keep in mind that the alternate airports do not report any weather conditions so all I will have are area forecasts. I'll get that additional information together as soon as we finish here."

"That's fine," Stoney said. "Just want to have as much information as I can get. Really appreciate the effort on this one. I need to go and see how Steve is doing on the flight plan and give him these updated winds aloft numbers. Thanks again." Stoney gathered up the information Stan had already put together and headed to the flight planning room to look for Steve.

Stoney knew from his days as a charter pilot and flight instructor that flight planning is one of the most important aspects of safely getting from one point to another. Actually, it should be incorporated into any mode of transportation from hiking to travel by boat. The planner gathers as much information as possible about a specific flight and uses that data to make decisions about what route to take, what areas to avoid, and creates an alternate plan should an emergency or some other situation arise that causes a deviation from the original plan. All of this planning is an essential part to the successful outcome of any flight. Fuel planning is one of the most critical phases of flight planning since there are no 'service stations' in the sky.

Fuel planning was especially important on cross-polar flights since the options should you run low are very limited.

The number of commercial airports in that part of the world that can handle an aircraft the size and weight of the Northern Star was also limited. Additionally, the security protocols prohibited landing at one of those except in cases where loss of life could occur, instead APA trained its captains to use the APA maintained alternate airfields which were available for emergencies but so far none of the Northern Star flights had needed to use one and Stoney was determined to not be the first.

"Steve, here are the winds aloft numbers. Looks like we'll have a little bit of a tail wind going to London with little to no turbulence, there is no telling what the return trip will be like since it will be several days from now. The pax should have a nice view of the pole as well since the visibility should be good and the cloud cover minimal," Stoney said as he handed Steve the weather information.

After taking a quick glance at the wind information Steve said, "I agree; let's see how the numbers work out."

Steve retrieved his flight computer from his flight bag and went to work crunching the numbers. Watching Steve twist the outer ring of the flight computer brought back memories of his days as a flight instructor teaching his students how to use the specially modified circular slide rule. The actual computers of the day would take the entire aircraft to carry, and the airplane would be so terribly over weight that it wouldn't get off the ground. Past, present, and future pilot trainees would all learn how to use that special device which could fit in a pocket. Taking the weight of the aircraft, to include the basic airplane, the fuel load, oil load, baggage load, and weight of the passengers, the distance to travel, the speed of the airplane through the sky and the speed and direction of the winds aloft, Steve calculated their fuel burn and speed across the ground, and finally their time en route.

Entering the last numbers into his navigation log, Steve announced, "We'll have a two hour reserve of fuel when we reach London and that puts us well within company and international regulations."

"That looks fine," Stoney said. "Did you check on the actual fuel and oil load as well?"

"Yep, both fuel and oil are full and all of the luggage is on board. The Stews reported that all catering is complete, and the pax are in the lounge waiting to board," Steve replied.

"Make sure you have all of the chart updates and then meet me at the aircraft. I'm going down to maintenance and see what Lee has learned about the engine. As soon as I get to the aircraft we'll let the gate agents know so they can start the boarding process. Also, make sure to see Stan before you leave and get the additional information I requested; he'll know what you need." Leaving the rest of the operations duties to his FO, Stoney left the operations center and headed downstairs to maintenance.

When Stoney walked up to Bert's office, he paused in the doorway to listen in on the conversation between Bert and Lee.

"We have gone over that engine, the entire fuel system, the electrical system, and the ignition system and cannot find any reason that engine would run rough. I even called headquarters to inquire about the effects the recent upgrades may have had, but they could not provide any guidance or suggestions. I can only conclude that it must have been a little condensation in the fuel or a small piece of dirt that temporarily caused the carburetor to run lean," Bert said.

No one had noticed Stoney standing at the door.

"The engine did run rough for several minutes and then it seemed to clear itself up. None of the other engines had any issues at all, so I am a little suspect of the condensation in the fuel thought," Lee said.

"Good morning, Captain Stone," Bert said, noticing Stoney for the first time "We were just discussing your engine issue."

"Yes, I heard. I'm a little concerned that you didn't find anything. I don't like fix-actions for squawks that have no action when it comes to key equipment and over polar flights. Please call Dieter Kauffman, at home if you have to, and talk to him about the issue. I don't want to load the pax until we are absolutely sure there aren't any issues with the aircraft. Don't dally on the phone call; they are probably getting restless in the terminal by now. If anyone at headquarters gives you grief, then use my name to get what you need. In the mean time, I'm going to call Mr. Train and see what—if anything—he may know. Where is the closest secure phone?"

"There is a secure phone two doors down on the right. Here is the 'magic key' to make it work," Bert said, handing Stoney what looked like a plastic child's toy car key but was in fact the encryption enabling device for the phone.

"Thanks Bert, I'll be back in a minute."

As Stoney left to find the secure phone, Bert picked up his phone and once again dialed the number to headquarters.

Stoney found the phone, inserted the key and dialed Tom Train's secure number. After the initial pleasantries, Stoney voiced his concerns, but Mr. Train politely told him to continue the mission as planned and to have the sensor technician keep accurate logs during the flight to assist with narrowing down the potential cause of the anomaly. Stoney continued to highlight his concerns about rough engines and polar crossings, but his argument did not alter Mr. Train's decision. Finally resigned to the inevitable, he said, "Yes, sir, we'll continue the flight and take extensive readings. I will have the flight engineer work closely with the sensor tech to gather that data."

"Good luck and fair weather during your trip," Tom said. "Contact me when you reach London."

"Will do, sir; good bye." Stoney hung up the phone, withdrew the key and went back to Bert's office. When he walked into the office, Lee and Bert were discussing the call to Dieter, and they explained to Stoney that they had no additional information to add to the discussion. Stoney relayed his conversation with Tom Train.

"Lee, Train wants us to collect as much data as we can during this trip. Make sure to get with Brad to coordinate your data gathering efforts before we depart," Stoney said.

Brad Tillison worked for NSA but during his time with the Northern Star program, he also reported to CIA. He was the sensor operator for aircraft number 28A and was joining the flight here in Victoria. There was no reason for him to be aboard during the flights to and from L.A. so Brad, like the maintenance personnel, lived in Victoria.

For outward appearance sake, Brad was "employed" by APA and wore its uniform. His "public" job was an assistant flight officer. However, during the majority of the trip he would disappear into the rear of the aircraft and would not be seen again until just before landing and on many trips he was never seen by any passenger. If anyone ever noticed the sensor technician disappearing into the back of the aircraft, they were politely told that it was the long range communications area.

The assistant flight officer's station was located back there, and his job was to keep the aircraft in contact with ground control while over the polar area since normal air traffic control facilities did not exist along the route. The job of position reporting and communications with Polar Air Traffic Control actually belonged to the First Officer but it made a good cover story for the assistant flight officer's disappearance for most, if not all, of the flight.

Lee walked out to the aircraft, climbed the stairs, and entered the cabin. Stepping into the galley he said "Hey, Virginia; have you seen Brad this morning?"

"He's back in his closet with the crypto guys; do you need him?"

"I need to talk to him a minute, can I use your intercom to call and ask him to come up front?" Lee knew it was against regulations to walk down the aisle and enter the secure room. Only the sensor operator, the aircraft captain and cleared technicians could enter the room at any time. For security reasons, the rear section of the plane was off limits to almost everyone when the secure room was not sealed shut.

"Sure thing," said Virginia as she handed Lee the intercom phone and returned to setting up the galley.

Lee heard the familiar buzzing in the handset. Eventually, the buzzing ceased, and he heard a click as the distant handset was picked up. "Brad, here," came the voice on the other end.

"Brad, this is Lee; can you come up front? We need to talk."

"Be there in a minute; we're just finishing the crypto load." Lee heard a click in the handset as Brad hung up the intercom.

As Lee waited for Brad, he reflected on what was going on in the secure room. Brad was usually in the aircraft before the aircrew arrived to ensure all of his sensitive equipment was set and ready to go. Additionally he had to load information into the encryption equipment since it automatically encrypted all flight data which it stored for download and the "crypto key" changed daily.

Within a couple of minutes, Brad and one of the crypto technicians walked up the aisle from the secure room. After thanking the crypto technician who headed out the main door, Brad turned to Lee and said, "What's up?"

"HQ wants us to log any and all data related to the electrical loads and such during the flight. They need the data as part of their research to determine why the number three engine was running rough. I'll keep a log of the data from my instruments up front, but you'll need to keep a more extensive log then usual on your stuff," Lee said. "HQ has no idea why the engine occasionally runs rough. They have not been able to recreate the problem, and the mechanics here don't have any ideas either. I think they are shooting in the dark by looking at the electrical loads. But you know how it is; when the engineers can't fix a problem, we have to do extra work to help them out."

"Well, it's not like I have nothing to do back there!" Brad said. "No promises, but I'll see what I can do."

"I thought all you did was sit back and read Play Boy while locked in your hole!"

At that comment, Brad, with a big grin, playfully punched Lee in the arm and said, "How else do you think I keep up on my 'reading' and world events?"

Stepping through the aircraft's main door, Stoney said, "Good morning, Brad; has Lee filled you in on the latest from HQ?"

"Good morning, Stoney. Yes, he did. Not sure what those data heads at HQ think they are going to get, but Lee and I will keep continuous logs during the flight."

"I want you to pay particular attention to the load on the electrical buses before, during, and after your sensor equipment is fired up and running. Mr. Train at HQ said something about electrical loads while I was talking to him."

"That's funny," Lee said, "Dieter didn't say anything like that to Bert when we were talking to him. I would think he would have said something if there were concerns about the electrical system."

"Lee, you know those engineering types, they don't like to speculate to their customers, so Dieter must have said something about it to Mr. Train but chose not to say anything to you since he wasn't sure," Stoney replied. "Is everything ready to go?"

"Yes, sir," both men answered.

"Well, let's get this show on the road. Steve should be here any minute. Virginia, are you all ready for the pax?"

"Yes, Captain; ready when you are," said Virginia.

"Great, please inform the gate agent that we are ready to go."

"Can do, sir."

"Guys, guess it's time to go to work!" Stoney said, and with that Brad headed to the secure area at the rear of the aircraft while Stoney and Lee headed into the cockpit.

As Stoney was putting his flight case and over-night case in the cockpit closet, Steve came up the stairs and entered the cabin. "Did you talk to Stan and get all of the weather information he had for me?" Stoney asked.

"Yes, sir; sure did; boy, did he load me up."

"I want you to keep that information handy, and once we depart, keep a tab on the closest airfields along our course just in case that engine acts up. I'll want to know what our options are as soon as possible, and I don't want you to waste time hunting around for weather information."

"You sound like you are a little more than slightly concerned about that engine. Is there something you know that I don't?" asked Steve.

"No, I just don't like surprises when flying over hostile territory. As you know, this old bird will fly just fine on three engines; we lose a considerable bit of speed, but we can make London. But, should we lose one and something else happens, we could be in trouble."

Steve took off his coat and hat and stowed them away along with the other overnight bags and flight cases. Stoney left his coat and hat on since he always greeted the passengers as they boarded the aircraft. It was not standard practice among the APA captains; however, it was something Stoney had done since those charter days flying the Cessna-421 Golden Eagle, and he enjoyed doing it. "Steve, you and Lee, get settled while I greet the passengers, and I'll be back in a few minutes."

As Stoney headed down the stairs in the cool, early morning air, he looked toward the sky and saw Apollo's chariot beginning its daily race across the clear blue sky. He glanced toward the terminal building and saw the passengers start to head across the tarmac to the waiting aircraft.

Waiting to greet them at the foot of the boarding stairs, Stoney looked back at his aircraft as he had done a thousand times. Taking in the sight of that jet black Constellation with the silver accents and the APA logo never ceased to take his breath away. From the outside, the aircraft was a remarkable sight. APA painted the exterior black to make it more visible against the white ice of the polar area. This made the aircraft easier to spot should something go wrong and force it to land on the ice.

Stoney knew the aircraft designers had created an interior that was just as breathtaking as the outside. The deep pile carpet on the floor was a deep maroon color and the seats, which reclined completely flat and swiveled similar to a traditional 'Captain's Chair', were black leather with the northern constellations stitched into the back in silver accents.

31

The light green silk covering on the cabin walls provided a nice contrast to the other interior colors. Gold leaf accented many of the cabin features from the edge of the fold out tables to the reading lamps and even the bathroom fixtures. The rich walnut tables rivaled those found inside the infamous Rolls Royce luxury cars. APA wanted to simulate the casual atmosphere of a railroad club car or a lounge on the great steamers, therefore they arranged the passenger seats accordingly unlike the rigid rows and aisles of other commercial airliners.

This allowed the passengers to visit, play cards and socialize just as they would on a long train or steam ship journey. The only limitation was they could not take a stroll on the 'promenade deck' after dinner, and they could not smoke cigars with their after-dinner brandy.

The engineers used state-of-the-art soundproofing inside the cabin to minimize engine noise. The engines were barely audible so the passengers traveled in quiet, pressurized air-conditioned comfort. The amenities included a movie projector that could show the latest films, even the ones currently playing at the theaters. APA had an agreement with the film studios and there had even been first run premiers on some of the Northern Star flights.

The interior designers incorporated every creature comfort possible into an airliner. After all, the passengers were paying small fortunes to take the flight and to be able to say that they flew over the polar area. APA tried to time the flights so they flew over the polar area during daylight so the passengers could see the pole and surrounding area. The FO would make an announcement when they were near enough to the actual pole for the passengers to see it. Each passenger received a framed certificate signed by the flight crew indicating his or her flight near the pole. The certificate arrived at their home after completion of the flight.

Normally the captain of a commercial flight would not greet all of his passengers, he would be in the cockpit getting the aircraft ready for departure. However, this was not your ordinary flight, and Stoney was not an ordinary captain. Stoney had always enjoyed getting to know his passengers on those long charter flights in the Golden Eagle, and he had grown to miss that when flying the regular APA commercial routes. After transitioning to the Northern Star aircraft, he realized that he would be able to interact with his passengers once again.

"Good morning, Mr. and Mrs. Whiteman," said Stoney as a couple and their son walked up.

"Good morning, Captain Stone; how's the weather look?"

"It looks like a smooth flight the whole way. Welcome aboard."

That is how it was with the other seventeen passengers in turn. As they boarded, Stoney thought about the passenger makeup on this trip: There were seven married couples, two with kids, two single gentlemen, and two single ladies. Everyone but the Whitemans, Mrs. McQuinn and the McNeelys were from the U.S. Mrs. McQuinn and the McNeelys were from Scotland and the Whitemans were from England. After the last passenger headed up the ramp, Captain Stone took the passenger manifest from the gate agent and thanked him for his help and then headed up the stairs.

When Stoney reached the top, Virginia was there to meet him. He handed her the passenger manifest knowing she would re-verify that everyone had boarded, and it was okay to shut the door. Stoney heard the thump of the main entry door being closed and secured as he headed into the cockpit. He took off and stowed his hat and coat and then climbed into his seat. Just as he sat down he looked out his window and saw the tug pulling the stairs away.

Stoney heard Maria begin the standard cabin announcements as he asked Steve for the Pre-Engine-Start Checklist. Steve picked up the checklist and began to read off the items. Many of the items were for the flight engineer and Lee responded to those, and Stoney responded to the items meant for the captain.

Captain Stone started number one engine causing the floor to shudder as the big radial engine coughed its way to life. After several seconds the engine transitioned from a coughing, sputtering, vibrating beast to purring like a cat. Stoney repeated the sequence with the next engine. The engines on a multi-engine airplane are started in a specific sequence based on the manufacturer's requirements. Lockheed required that the inboard engines be started first, i.e. number one, number two then the outboard engines number three and number four were started. All of the extra sound-proofing in the cabin virtually eliminated the noise from the engines unlike a standard Lockheed Constellation that was quite noisy. The vibration from the Wright Super Charged Cyclone engines was the only way the pax knew the engines were running. While Captain Stone was starting the engines, Maria had come forward to close the cockpit door which locked automatically.

Once all of the engines were running smoothly, Steve called the ground controller on the radio and received instructions to taxi to the active runway. Upon reaching the end of the runway, Stoney called for the Pre-Take-Off Checklist which Steve pulled out and began to read the items. Both the Captain and the Flight Engineer completed their respective tasks making the aircraft ready for departure.

Picking up the interphone, Stoney told Virginia they were ready for departure at which time she replied the cabin was ready and secured. Swapping the interphone for the radio microphone, Stoney said, "Victoria Tower, this is APA Flight 28-Alpha ready to depart."

"28-Alpha line up and wait; there is a maintenance vehicle on the runway," came the reply from the tower.

Stoney taxied the aircraft onto the runway and waited for clearance to depart.

"Lee, make sure to keep an eye on number three for me during take-off. Let me know immediately if any engine parameter is abnormal."

"Yes, sir," the flight engineer replied.

"APA 28-Alpha you are now cleared for take-off, wind calm," said the tower controller over the radio.

"28-Alpha is now rolling," was Steve's reply. Steve put his hand on top of Stoney's which was already on the throttles. Stoney and Steve together advanced the throttles until they were at full power. Stoney released the brakes, and 28-Alpha began to roll down the runway.

"V1" called out Steve as they continued to accelerate down the runway.

"V2", and finally "V-Rotate" came the calls from the co-pilot who closely monitored the airspeed indicator and made those announcements to the captain.

When Steve announced "V-Rotate" Stoney pulled back on the control wheel and the big black Super Constellation began its climb toward the heavens.

I never tire of watching those APA black Constellations climb out. Those Lockheed engineers really gave her some great curves, thought the tower controller as he watched 28-Alpha lift-off and climb out.

When they reached 500 feet above the runway, Stoney called out, "Wheels up!" and Steve removed his hand from the throttles and reached over on the panel and moved the gear lever to the "up" position. All at once, the sounds of hydraulic pumps began, and a few seconds later, everyone on the aircraft felt the wheels "thump" into the wheel wells.

The aircraft continued to accelerate, and a short time later Stoney called for "Flaps up" and once again Steve moved a lever to its up-most position. As the flaps retracted the aircraft accelerated a little more.

"APA 28-Alpha turn left," instructed the voice on the radio.

Steve picked up the microphone and responded, "APA 28-Alpha turning left."

"28-Alpha frequency changed approved; have a safe flight."

"28-Alpha going to Polar Control frequency; have a good day," Steve responded into the microphone.

After he dialed in the correct frequency on the radio, Steve said, "Polar Control, this is APA Flight 28-Alpha."

"APA Flight 28-Alpha, this is Polar Control, Radar contact. I show you at 5,000 feet and climbing; proceed on course."

"Polar Control, 28-Alpha, confirm out of 5,000 feet, climbing to 25,000 feet, and turning right on course."

With Polar Control's blessing, Stoney turned the aircraft to the right and settled down on the course that would take them across the pole and into London's Heathrow airport.

Having set the engines for climb configuration, Stoney said, "Lee, you have engine control; maintain this configuration till we reach our cruising altitude then adjust them for cruise."

"Yes sir, and I'll lean the mixtures as we climb to maintain climb performance."

Climbing on top of a small deck of clouds, Stoney turned to Steve and said in a loud voice for all to hear, "Best view in the world!"

CHAPTER 4

Zooming across the frozen snow, Captain Anatoli Leshev verified his course using the compass built into the snowmobile's small information panel as his special operations team followed close behind.

Just an hour before, they had been warm inside the bowels of the Leon Trotsky, a Soviet nuclear submarine as it cruised under the polar icecap. Leshev and his Spetsnaz team had been guests aboard the Trotsky for several days while en route from the Soviet submarine base in Murmansk to this desolate section of the arctic. The whole ship had shuddered when it broke through the ice as it surfaced.

Aboard the submarine, Leshev had received a coded message from Moscow indicating the KGB agent in Victoria had successfully completed her part of the plan.

That message had set the timetable in motion causing the submarine to surface at a predetermined time whereupon the snowmobiles had been quickly unloaded. The entire Spetsnaz team had unloaded their gear and had set out across the snow just thirty minutes after the submarine had punched a hole in the ice to reach the surface. Now they were racing across this land of the polar bears looking for a small airport in the middle of nowhere.

Four months ago, Captain Leshev had been on military leave in the Crimea. At six-foot, four-inches with close cropped dark hair, dark green eyes and a body made hard through years of special operations training and covert missions, Leshev's confidence was high that he would find a young curvaceous student of Lenin to enjoy during his leave.

The night he arrived, he was at a club drinking vodka and scouting the women when *she* walked in. Her long black hair, full lips, long slender legs and ample bosom had mesmerized him from the moment she walked into the room. He jumped up and rushed over to buy her a drink and proceeded to wine and dine her for the next several days in the ways only the privileged few could do.

Leshev was lucky that he had a benefactor who made sure he had plenty of Rubles to spend pursuing his desires. Leshev and Katia had had a good time both in the bedroom and on the beach during those few warm blissful days of sun and vodka. Now Leshev wished he was lying in that big down-filled bed with her in his arms instead of racing across this frozen bit of hell in pursuit of a big black airplane.

Within just a week of arriving in the Crimea, Leshev had received the telegram ordering him to catch the next transport to Moscow as soon as possible. He had arrived in the early hours of the morning and had reported directly to Colonel Sikovski's office. Fortunately, the colonel had not yet arrived, so his secretary had taken Leshev down to the dining hall to get some breakfast and he still had time to shave and clean up before his meeting with the colonel.

When Sikovski entered the outer office, Leshev jumped to his feet and stood ramrod stiff as the colonel, dressed impeccably in his Spetznas uniform adorned by a chest full of medals, walked by and straight into his office shutting the door behind him. A veteran Spetsnaz officer, Leshev was not easily rattled, however since the telegram arrived with Sikovksi's name on it he had been on edge. He had never met Sikovski but his reputation as a hard master was well known within Spetsnaz. Leshev's first impression as the colonel whisked by cemented that reputation in his mind

Colonel Alexi Sikovski had served in WWII and had commanded the so-called "Ghost Command" during the German siege of Leningrad. His units had earned this name from the Germans since they had been very skilled at covert operations. These units had successfully killed several high ranking German officers without one Russian soldier being caught or killed. Leshev had heard that Sikovski was approximately sixty years old and had spent many years in the field. He was known throughout the Spetsnaz as a commander who didn't expect miracles, but severely punished mediocrity.

Leshev also knew that despite his hard reputation, he always took care of anyone that performed their job well and didn't try to hide a lackluster performance behind a cloak of lies and half truths.

Within about five minutes, the intercom buzzed, and the secretary jumped up with a "Right away, Comrade Colonel!"

"Leshev, you will enter as I take the colonel's morning tea to him," said the secretary as she hurriedly made a fresh pot of tea. Placing the tea service on the gleaming silver tray, the secretary asked Leshev to get the door, and they both filed into the office.

Leshev was surprised at how sparsely furnished it was compared to other such offices in the Kremlin. The only decorations consisted of several military awards and a picture of the Father of the Soviet Union, Vladimir Lenin, and another one of the current General Secretary of the Communist Party. Since he had never actually met the colonel, he was surprised at how fit he looked despite his age and graying hair. Snapping to attention in front of the colonel's desk, he waited to be acknowledged.

"Ah, Captain Anatoli Leshev; welcome to Moscow. I hope your leave was not cut too short, but we are on a timetable that has already started, and we are a little behind the power curve. Please sit down," Sikovski said.

The colonel opened a folder on his desk as the secretary poured his tea. Setting it on the desk she turned to Leshev and asked, "Would you like some tea?"

"No thank you, comrade."

Sikovski continued to look through the folder as he noisily slurped his tea. The seconds slowly ticked by and it wasn't until Leshev heard the office door quietly close that the colonel began to speak.

"Leshev, I have been keeping an eye on you as your career has progressed. You were hand chosen for this mission because of your record of results. Together, you and I will complete the last minute details, and you will hand pick your mission team. I have the utmost confidence that if anyone can pull this off, you can."

"Several months ago, the head of the Navy, Admiral of the Fleet Ninski, explained to me the Navy's frustration with the Americanski's Northern Star Polar Flight program. It seems the flights have been able to pinpoint our submarine fleet with annoying precision and the time had come for something to be done to stop it. So far, the KGB and the GRU have been unable to infiltrate the program either in the U.S. or in British Columbia. After long discussions, we decided that in order to stop the flights or at least to take action to reduce their accuracy we needed to capture one of the actual aircraft and study the electronics and sensors. That is where Spetsnaz and specifically you come into the picture. If we overtly attack or try to commandeer one of the aircraft, the U.S. Government as well as the U.N. would take that as an act of war and we would have a political nightmare on our hands since the aircraft carry verified civilian passengers. Our leadership does not have the fortitude even during these tense political times, to shoot down or force down a passenger plane. Admiral Ninski asked me to put together a plan using *covert action* to capture the sensor equipment from an aircraft.

"I have spent several weeks putting a plan together and now is the time to put it into action."

Continuing on, Sikovski described in detail the plan Leshev would execute.

Once he had finished, Sikovski asked if there were any questions. Leshev asked several and the colonel answered each to his satisfaction. At the conclusion of the meeting, Leshev stood and was just about to leave the office when he stopped in his tracks and turned to face the colonel once more.

"Sir, with your permission, I have one final question."

"Go ahead."

"Assuming that all goes well, and we have secured the emergency landing strip according to schedule, what will force the aircraft to land there? Will we have a hijacker on board?"

"Captain Leshev, that information is above your classification level, so I cannot directly answer you. But I can say that KGB has placed an agent at the Empress Hotel in Victoria, B.C., whose actions will ensure that the aircraft *will* be landing a short time after you secure the airfield. At that point, it is up to you to get the equipment and rendezvous back with the submarine."

Over the next several days, Leshev worked closely with Sikovski finalizing the planning of *Operation Dark Night*. They decided to commandeer one of APA's emergency airfields; specifically the one named 'Q' since it was located near the Arctic sea where a submarine could surface through the ice to drop off the team. They went to the Spetsnaz technical department and requested the modification of snowmobiles that could pull sleds to bring the commandeered equipment from the aircraft to the submarine. Additionally, they requested radar jammers as well as aircraft radio jammers.

Racing through the pre-dawn darkness, Leshev looked at the faintly glowing hands of the small clock on the instrument panel. *Based on the time we should be getting close,* he thought as he peered through his snow goggles into the darkness, searching for the lights of the airfield. Since the snowmobile was bouncing as it raced across the frozen ground, he couldn't really focus well enough to see the lights. He pressed the small switch on the left handle bar of the snowmobile that caused a small red light on the rear of the machine to flash; thus signaling his team to halt.

He came to a stop and his team dutifully stopped behind him. Using a specially designed pair of binoculars, he peered into the darkness, *Aha, there it is,* he thought as he saw a faint light in the distance. His experience told him they had about five kilometers to go.

Putting away the binoculars, he gunned the snowmobile's engine and it leaped forward in the darkness. He pressed a button on the handlebar, and a green light on the back of the snowmobile flashed; his comrades followed.

Leshev slowed the team down to a crawl as they approached the far side of the runway. He was grateful the KGB engineers were able to muffle the machine's engine noise so the only sound they made was the crunching of the snow. Leshev maneuvered the team behind a large snow bank and using arm signals told them to secure their snow machines. Crouching low they inched around the snow bank so they could see the runway.

Damn, we're going to have to plow the runway. I had hoped they would keep it plowed. It is too far to go around the runway so we'll have to cross it, thought Leshev as he surveyed the area across the runway looking for places to hide as well as looking for anyone walking around. Glancing down at his map, he realized he was looking at the maintenance building and the communications/control tower building.

That soft light between the buildings must be what I saw coming in. Everywhere else is dark—perfect conditions for a night raid. These fools won't know what hit them, he thought. Putting down his binoculars he motioned 'all clear' and sent them across one at a time. Each man darted across the runway as quickly as possible. Their white snow suits helped them blend into the snow, but they left a nice trail of footprints. Once across, they ducked into the shadows alongside the maintenance building. Crossing last, Leshev met up with the team.

Leshev's intelligence briefing said the airfield existed only for emergencies so the control tower was not normally manned except when either a supply aircraft or an emergency was in progress. The communications building upon which the control tower cab sat was dark. Continuing to use hand signals, Leshev told Sergeant Danshov to make sure the communications building was empty, as he sent Corporal Osinov to check the maintenance building. Within a few minutes, both returned. All was clear. At this early hour, everyone must still be in the main building which included the sleeping quarters. Soviet intelligence had said there was no evidence of a military presence at the airfield, but years of training told both Leshev and Danshov to be extra careful. More than once they had been surprised by something that intelligence had said didn't exist.

Corporal Osinov and Corporal Vavilov moved to flank the entrance to the main building. While they crouched in the darkness, Leshev and Danshov made a circuit around the building to check out any back doors and reverify there were no patrols.

They again reached the front entrance. All was clear.

Leshev chuckled to himself, *how dumb can these Americans be? No Soviet commander would leave his base unprotected against such a sneak attack!*

Again, using hand signals Leshev indicated the corporals should open the door and make sure that no one was waiting for them inside. Silently opening the doors the corporals looked inside and indicated 'all clear'. Leshev motioned for everyone to enter with their weapons at the ready. Sergeant Danshov entered last and silently closed the door behind them. Leshev again used hand signals to tell the group to move down the corridor with the corporals checking each room as they went. As they crept down the hall, a door opened, and a man stepped into the hallway looking right at them. He spun around and ran back inside the room shutting the door behind him.

"Vavilov, get that door open!" whispered Danshov as loud as he dared.

After grasping the door knob, "It's locked."

"Knock it in,—quietly."

Stepping back a couple of feet, Vavilov a rather muscular young man who would have been a welcome member of any American football team, lowered his shoulder and rushed at the door breaking it open with only the sound of splintering wood shattering the silence. As the door latch gave way, Vavilov fell to the ground so Osinov who had followed him could take out any assailant standing in the room. As Vavilov fell to the ground, Osinov scanned the room with his rifle at the ready.

Danshov stayed in the hallway covering their rear while Leshev followed Osinov into the room shutting what was left of the door in an attempt to minimize noise.

Pointing out the door in the back of what was obviously a bedroom to Leshev, Osinov said "We know you are in here, come out with your hands up," as he motioned for Vavilov to get up.

"If you come out voluntarily, you will not be harmed," said Leshev.

Several seconds ticked by.

"My corporal will break down the door and kill you unless you come out—now." Still no movement.

"Corporal Vavilov break down that door and shoot anyone inside," Leshev said in a louder voice.

There was a *click* and the door began to open slowly. "Don't shoot, I'm coming out," said the man as he continued to open the door wider.

Vavilov, standing in front of the door, had his Kalashnikov rifle pointed at the man as he emerged from the room—his hands in the air with a pistol in one of them.

"Drop the gun," said Vavilov. *Clank*, the gun hit the floor.

"Keep walking forward—Stop. Put your hands behind your back," said Vavilov as Osinov moved to tie the man's hands with plastic restraints. Osinov picked up the pistol and put it in his pocket.

"Who the hell are you people?" said the man.

Ignoring the question Leshev asked, "Where is the man in charge of this facility?"

"Well, it just so happens, that I am," replied the man.

"I am Captain Anatoli Leshev, and, as of this moment, this facility is under the control of the Soviet Spetsnaz. Who are you, and how many people are in this facility?"

"My name is Kent James. This is a civilian facility, and I demand to know why you are here."

"Mr. James, why we are here is not your concern; the fact that we are is. Now answer my question. How many personnel do you have here?"

James just stood there and glared at Leshev.

47

"I assume you do not want me to quietly round up your personnel and shoot them starting with you?"

"Even for a Russian that is a stupid question," James said.

The words had hardly left his mouth when Vavilov forcefully put his rifle butt into Kent James's stomach causing him to double over and fall to the ground.

"I would recommend that you cooperate a little better with us and answer the questions as asked or the next time my corporal will not be so lenient on you. Now, get up and answer the question. Do you want to cooperate, or have us round up your folks and shoot them?"

The man struggled to get on his feet, made harder by his bound hands behind his back. He stood at his full five-foot eight-inches and turning his head upward in a vain attempt to look Leshev in the eye struggled to catch his breath and said, "Fif-teen"

"Thank you, now do you have a public address system that I can use to get everyone to come out into the hall?"

"Yes, it's in my office three doors down on the left," said James having caught his breath.

"Let us go there—now," Leshev said, pointing his pistol at James.

Opening the door, Danshov signaled that all was still quiet as Leshev motioned for everyone to go into the hallway. Leshev had James lead him to his office while the rest of the team took up defensive positions in the hallway.

Reaching the office, James said, "Pickup the phone and dial one-zero-zero, wait for the click and that will connect you to the PA system. Everyone in the facility will be able to hear you."

Leshev picked up the phone and after dialing the number, he heard a click and began talking, "Attention all airfield 'Q' personnel. This is Captain Anatoli Leshev of the Soviet Union. Everyone will come out of their rooms and gather in a single line with your hands raised. Once in the hall you will kneel down facing the walls with your hands held high in the air. I have a pistol pointed at Mr. Kent James' chest and I will not hesitate to shoot him. I guarantee the first shot will not kill him but he will die very slowly and painfully. Line up in the hallway—now. We will thoroughly search everyone and the discovery of any weapons will be dealt with in the harshest manner. You have one minute to comply with my directions or I shoot Mr. James." Leshev hung up the phone.

"I hope your personnel do as they are told. For your sake there better be fifteen people in the hallway. Anyone found after this initial roll call will be shot."

"As I told you, there are only fifteen people here. We are all civilians and you realize invading American territory is an act of war," James said.

Once again ignoring James' outburst, Leshev said, "Let's go into the hall, and hope they all show up."

James headed for the door with Leshev behind him. As they stepped into the hallway they saw a group of people on their knees with their hands held high above their heads.

"Danshov, there should be fifteen people here. Count them, and, for their sakes, I hope there are."

Danshov counted heads—fifteen of them. One-by-one Vavilov had each person stand up with their hands in the air as he frisked their body—once complete he bound their hands using the plastic restraints at which time he kneed one of their knees causing them to fall to the floor. When he finished, he commanded that everyone stand up with their backs to the wall.

With everyone restrained, the two corporals proceeded to check every room in the building to ensure no one else was hiding. The rooms were empty.

"Mr. James, what room is big enough to hold everyone at once?" asked Leshev.

"The cafeteria, just down the hall."

"Everyone march in single file to the cafeteria, James you lead the way," Danshov ordered.

With everyone seated at the cafeteria tables and under Danshov's watchful eye, Leshev took the satellite communications radio from Vavilov and went outside to contact Moscow. Once he had the radio set up, he keyed the microphone and said, "Night is day, I repeat, night is day." Repacking the radio, Leshev knew that within minutes a phone would ring in Sikovski's office announcing the successful completion of phase one.

CHAPTER 5

With the call to Moscow complete, Leshev returned to the cafeteria to get down to business. He had a timetable to meet and the next deadline was rapidly approaching. Looking around the room, he analyzed his hostages and realized they would cause problems, given half a chance. He knew these 'civilians' were handpicked by CIA to man the emergency landing strip. Most of them were ex-military though some were pure civilian. James, the man in charge of Emergency Landing Site 'Q' was ex-military. Leshev could tell just by his manner.

Leshev was grateful that Sikovski's intelligence seemed very accurate, and it had paid off in a quiet invasion with no gun fire at all. *The less bloodshed the better*, he thought. *I just hope it stays that way.*

"James, it is about time for you to check in with your superiors. I will take you to the communications room to accomplish that. You will not resist, or Corporal Osinov will have to remove one of the fingers of the man to your left," Leshev said.

"There is no need for me to check in at this time."

"That is where you are mistaken. I know what your schedule is, and I also know your superiors will be notified if you don't check in, and they will air drop troops to see why. No, you will check in as required. Do not test me."

"Comrade Captain, there is no check-in requirement. I am telling you the truth. If I check in off schedule it will cause an alert at our headquarters."

Pointing at the man to James' left, Captain Leshev said "I have finished arguing with you. Corporal Osinov, kindly remove the small finger from that man's hand."

Osinov asked, "Comrade Captain, which hand would you prefer?"

"Your choice," replied Leshev.

"You, on the ground face down—now," Danshov said as he pointed his pistol at the man's head.

The man didn't move, instead he just sat there glaring at Danshov.

"You people don't seem to understand that I am in charge here," said Leshev as he walked over to the seated man and yanked him up by one of his bound arms. The man tried to head butt Leshev who gave him a karate knife chop with his hand to the back of the man's neck causing him to collapse in a heap on the floor.

Danshov grabbed the man by the shoulders and dragged him face down from between the rows of tables. Just as Danshov was cutting the man's bonds, he tried to jump up. Danshov immediately put one of his rather large boots in the middle of the man's back and pushed, flattening him back against the floor.

"Let's see how much fight you have with only nine fingers. Osinov, get over here and let's explain to these people the need to follow the captain's orders," said Danshov.

Even with a foot in the middle of his back, the man tried desperately to fight back, but Osinov overpowered him, grabbed his right arm and stretched it out from his body. Kneeling down beside the arm, he put one knee on the man's forearm near his wrist to restrain it. Holding the man's hand still with one hand and the bayonet in the other Osinov chopped off the man's small finger as he screamed, cursed and tried to thrash around. Afterward, Danshov yanked the man to his feet then shoved him into a vacant seat.

The man sat cradling his hand as he continued to glare at Danshov, the rage clearly visible on his face.

"Osinov, go into the kitchen and find something to wrap the hand in and throw that bloody finger into the trash. You people listen up, I have no problem killing or mutilating any or all of you, but I will get cooperation. James here will be the last to die. My patience is running out," said Leshev.

Osinov threw a towel at the nine-fingered man who used it to wrap his hand.

The whole room glared back at Leshev, but no one said a word.

"Fine," said Leshev as he grabbed the man closest to him and yanked him to his feet. Putting his pistol to the man's head he cocked the hammer.

The man's face radiated terror as he stood quite still.

The look on that man's face must have affected James since seconds later he said, "All right. I'll cooperate yes, I do have to check in with headquarters within the next ten minutes."

Leshev uncocked his pistol and pushed the man back into his chair saying, "That is more like it. Your commander has temporarily spared this man's life. If he continues to cooperate no one else will be harmed."

"Then let's go send that message. Sergeant Danshov, I want you to organize a party to clean the runway. We wouldn't want our prize to crash on landing, would we? Corporal Vavilov and Corporal Osinov will keep the other hostages here, and if they so much as breathe incorrectly, shoot them to hurt but not kill. We'll save that for later. Now, Mr. James, *move!*"

Pointing his pistol at James, Leshev motioned for him to start walking toward the door and into the hallway. Leaving the main building, James pulled up his collar as they left the warmth and stepped out into the early morning darkness and arctic cold. Leshev still had on his arctic suit so he just pulled the hood over his head. They walked to the communications building which had the control tower cab sitting on top of it. The compound only had three buildings: the communications building-control tower, the command building that they had just left and the combined maintenance and vehicle storage shed. The maintenance shed was located to the right of the aircraft parking ramp, and the communications building was located between the primary building and the parking ramp.

The communications building was a standard rectangular building with the octagonal glass-encased tower control cab sitting on the roof where the second story should have been.

James stopped at the door to the communications room and waited for Leshev to cut his plastic restraints.

Once cut, he entered the combination, heard an audible "click" as the lock opened and they entered the room. With Leshev closely watching his every move, he retrieved his authentication codes from a safe and sat down at a teletype writer that he used to send out the "All is well" message that was required every two hours.

"James let me see that code book," said Leshev.

Handing him the book, James said, "I doubt it will make much sense to you."

"Actually, you might be surprised."

Handing James the book back, he pointed to a specific code and said, "This is the one you would normally send, correct?"

"Yes, how did you know that?" asked James with a somewhat astonished look on his face.

"The KGB does have its uses."

Leshev had learned during the final planning stages of the operation about the 'check-in' messages each emergency airfield relayed to HQ during a Northern Star scheduled flight and he had been shown a copy of an old status message code sheet so he would know how to read it. Leshev had asked Sikovski how this information had been obtained, as a method of determining its reliability, but his question was answered as so many were with the colonel's standard answer, "You don't have a clearance high enough to know that."

Whatever the source, Leshev had left Moscow with a table of check-in times that were valid during the time he would be arriving and hopefully departing Airfield "Q". His table had told him a check-in time was rapidly approaching.

Once at the teletype console, James waited for the exact hour to occur and then he began to type in the code letters exactly as listed in the code book. Once he pressed the "send" key he waited for the confirmation to come back. This usually took several minutes since the teletype signal was slow during its transmission over a powerful HF transmitter located on the top of the command building. Within minutes the teletype suddenly came to life and printed out the required message received confirmation code as indicated in the daily code book.

"That is good, Mr. James. Thank you for cooperating. It would have been bad if you forced me to continue harming your personnel. Now, we will go up to the control cab and wait for our guests to arrive." He motioned for James to head out the communications door. They paused just long enough for Leshev to pull a roll of gray tape out of his coat pocket. Leshev tore a piece and covered the strike plate of the door latch to keep it from re-locking when it shut behind them.

James climbed the stairs to the control cab with Leshev right on his heels.

When they entered through the floor of the octagonal shaped glass encased control tower cab, Leshev told James to turn on the landing lights so they could check the status of the runway. As Leshev feared, the landing strip had too much snow on it. He pulled out his portable radio. "Sergeant Danshov, come in."

"Danshov."

"Why have you not started plowing the runway as I instructed?"

"Sir, we are on our way out now. We had to rough up some of the hostages to find out who could run the plow. We did not have to shoot anyone but there are some bloody noses and unfortunately it took longer than it should have."

"*Get a move on.* That aircraft will be here soon."

"Yes! Comrade Captain!"

"Now, James, fire up the aircraft radios, and the radar unit. Make sure to connect the radar to the real antenna, not the test device. I want to be able to see and hear 28-Alpha as soon as it is in range."

Reading the puzzled look on James' face Leshev said, "Yes, I know about the dummy antenna. And I know quite a lot about this base, and I am letting you in on that little secret hoping it will keep you from doing anything unwise."

Leshev was a little surprised that James did not react to that information; he just continued to keep turning on the equipment as instructed.

Leshev stood gazing out the windows of the tower cab admiring the orange and yellow hues against the blue sky born of early dawn in the frigid north and looking for the plow to start clearing the runway. Through the ambient light he saw the entire runway area for the first time. Leshev took the radio from his pocket, "Danshov, what is taking so long? Why is the plow not running?"

"Sorry, Comrade Captain, the equipment is not cooperating. We are having trouble starting it."

Glancing at his watch he responded with a gruff, "Get it going quickly! We are running out of time."

"Yes! Comrade Captain."

Aboard 28A, Brad was warming up his equipment. He could not turn it on until they reached at least 10,000 feet since the electronics needed the cold outside air to keep them within operating limits. Even though the aircraft was pressurized, there existed air scoops on the outside of the airframe to scoop in the cold air and there were outlet vents as well. As the equipment warmed up, Brad activated the antenna release switch.

A door opened at the base of each vertical stabilizer. As each door opened a small drag chute behind it began to flap in the surrounding airflow and after several seconds the drag chute popped out completely and opened to its full size. The air pressure caused by the aircraft's slipstream tugged on the chutes as a kite tugs on its tether pulling the attached antenna wire out of the back of the aircraft. The small chutes tugged mightily as they fell further and further behind the speeding aircraft until they were trailing three hundred meters behind. Once all of the wire from each reel was fully deployed behind the aircraft small micro switches attached to the reels activated causing three lights on Brad's equipment status panel to change from amber to green.

28-Alpha continued its journey northeastward with the three antennas trailing behind it, ready to search for Soviet submarines.

CHAPTER 6

As Stoney leveled out the aircraft at 25,000 feet Steve called the Polar Air Traffic Control Center to check in. With those duties completed, Stoney suggested that Steve go ahead and take an initial navigation reading to begin charting their position even though he knew that they were still visible on PATCC's radar based in Victoria.

The route of the Northern Stars had been chosen to cover as much of the arctic ice cap as feasible, so the only reliable method of navigation involved the use of a sextant and the associated tables and charts. Normally the aircrew used electronic signals emitted by special ground-based radio transmitters to determine their position in flight, but shifting arctic ice made that system useless.

Since the aircraft would fly out of the range of the available ground based radars, both the aircrew and the

PATCC's controllers would use these readings to track the flight's progress toward its destination. Rescuers would use this information if the Northern Star had to make an emergency landing away from any airport.

These celestial navigation readings, taken at periodic intervals, gave Stoney the information he needed to make decisions based on accurate time, distance, speed, and fuel burned calculations. Additionally, Brad and his equipment needed accurate position reports to map out any submarine signatures that he detected during the flight. It was one thing to detect a submarine; it was another to pinpoint its location. One of Steve's primary duties as First Officer was to take periodic readings with his sextant and then calculate their current position.

Once he had determined their position, Steve called Brad on the intercom and relayed the information.

"Captain Stone, Brad reports the antennas have been deployed and his equipment is just about ready to begin the sweeps." Steve announced after hanging up the intercom handset.

"Lee, call Brad and remind him about the data collection requirements from HQ," Stoney said.

"Yes, sir; I'll take care of that," said Lee,

After waiting for Lee to hang up the interphone, Stoney asked, "Lee, how does the board look?"

"I've kept a close eye on everything since takeoff and nothing has been out of the ordinary. Matter of fact, everything has been *very* normal. Brad reports that the power up and stabilization of the equipment went very well. All parameters are completely normal," Lee answered back.

"Since everything is stable and we have a while before the next position report, I am going to do the cabin run. Let me know if I need to hustle back," Stoney said.

Once the aircraft was on course, and everything looked good, Stoney always went to mingle with the passengers and make sure that all was well in the cabin. It also gave him a chance to talk to Virginia and make sure they weren't having any problems. Putting on his hat and uniform coat, Stoney unlocked the cockpit door and headed out. When the door closed, he heard the lock click and pulling on the handle he made sure it was secure.

APA had engineered many security measures into the aircraft to minimize the chance of a successful hijacking. The aircraft captain was the only person who knew about most of the security measures. The auto-locking cockpit door was just one example of APA's layered security approach. As the captain, Stoney had knowledge of certain other security measures which were unknown to other crew members. Other than the actual sensor equipment secrets, these security measures were the most closely guarded of all the secrets of the Northern Stars.

Upon leaving the cockpit, Stoney stepped into the forward galley area. To his right was the lavatory and to his left was the galley where Virginia was making cocktails, and Maria was preparing lunch.

"Hi, ladies."

"Hey, captain, hope all is well up front," Virginia said.

"Well, actually Steve was taking a nap, and Lee was reading a magazine when I left," he said.

"Very funny, sir," said Maria.

"How are the pax?"

"Seems like an ordinary group so far," Virginia said.

"What's for lunch today?" Stoney asked.

"Looks like you will have a choice of the beef brisket or the roast chicken," replied Maria.

"Well, since I'm back here, and Steve is napping, guess I get first dibs on the chicken."

"That means Steve gets the brisket and Lee gets the ham sandwich," said Virginia. "Oh, when you talk to Brad, find out which one he wants, please."

"Can do: will let you know on the way back through."

As Stoney left the galley area, he transitioned from the galley's stark functionality to extreme luxury. The contrast was so extreme that it was almost as if he had stepped from one aircraft into another. It never ceased to amaze him how the interior designers had transformed these old airliners into the epitome of flying luxury. From a pilot's standpoint, the amazement was not so much the interior appointments, but how the designers accomplished it while simultaneously not making the plane so over weight that it couldn't get off the ground. He started walking down the aisle and noticed Mike Whiteman and Lillian McNeely locked in conversation, both verbally and visually. Stoney thought that they made a nice couple and wouldn't be surprised if there was a wedding in their future. Seated at the club table were the Goosemans and the Deems playing Bridge. Several passengers were taking naps, and the rest were sipping drinks and talking among themselves. As he passed each group, Stoney stopped and said hello. He stopped at the bridge table where the players were engaged in a political discussion as they played.

"You know Gooseman, old boy, this Johnson guy and his cronies are really mucking things up. They are trying to run this war from the White House instead of letting the commanders on the ground make the decisions," stated Robert Deems as he laid down a trump thus winning the trick.

"The Democrats are simply trying to keep communism at bay and keep the North Vietnamese from over running the south," Harold Gooseman shot back.

"That is exactly what they want you to believe. In reality, there are deep pockets who want to keep Johnson in office after the next election, so they can keep the war going and make handsome profits from selling war material to the government. They sure don't want to see this end."

"Now, now, boys," said Ida-Mae Gooseman, "I am sure Captain Stone does not want to hear you talk politics during this great trip across the pole; am I right?"

"Absolutely, I couldn't have said it better myself, Mrs. Gooseman," Stoney said. "What with two beautiful ladies to play cards with, a couple of drinks, and the beautiful scenery outside, how in the world could you spend time talking about politics? It will still be there when we land in London. It unfortunately makes the world go around, and no matter where you go you cannot escape it."

"Good call, captain," said Harold, "My thoughts exactly. By the way, how are the winds up here? Are we going to make London on time?"

"That we are, sir; I am happy to report. We have great winds and weather the whole way across. The visibility is great so you should be able to see the pole, that is if it looked different from the surrounding landscape; unfortunately it does not. There isn't a flag or even a big red 'X' to mark the spot," Stoney said.

"Will you announce when we get close to the pole?" inquired Lola Deems.

"Yes, you will hear an announcement when we're near it. Since we are so far north and compasses can have issues here, we use celestial navigation to accurately plot our course to London. We have to be very careful since it would be easy to cross over into Soviet airspace if we don't stay on course."

"We don't actually get that close, do we?" inquired Ida-Mae.

"We would have to get *way* off course for that to happen, but with the winds that can blow up here, it theoretically could happen however one of my primary jobs is to make sure that it doesn't happen. Now, if you will excuse me."

"Of course captain, thanks for stopping by," said Robert.

Once Stoney started down the aisle to the back of the aircraft, he heard the bridge players talking politics again. *It is always the same*, Stoney thought. *Politics or sports are generally the two subjects that most folks use to start a conversation. For young guys it is generally sports and the older ones jump right into politics.*

When he arrived at the rear of the plane, he pulled a curtain across the aisle to block any view of what happened next. He stepped forward a couple of feet to another curtain disguised as a decorative covering on the rear bulkhead of the aircraft. That covering had a hidden slit in it that nicely covered a locked door. Next to the door and recessed into the bulkhead was a keypad and a fingerprint reader with a small display. Stoney pressed his left thumb against the finger print reader pad and with his right hand entered a personal ten-digit number. The display turned green and flashed, 'Accepted' and the door clicked open.

"Hey, Brad," Stoney said as he stepped through the door. "How are things going back here?" Looking around, Stoney saw the system's panels full of dials, switches, lights and other indicators, and he heard the sound of a small teletype machine clicking in the background.

I am really glad I don't have to know how to operate all of this stuff. It looks like something out of an Apollo spaceship. I'll bet even the president has never seen this stuff. All he sees is the intelligence product that the NSA data gurus produce from all the data this thing collects. I'll bet there probably aren't more than a handful of people that even know it exists, much less laid eyes on it.

"Hey, sir, things are A-Okay. I have the antennas out, and the equipment has just reached operating temperature, so the sensors will be up and running by the time we cross the start line," Brad said.

"Good, glad to hear it. So the new equipment hasn't been causing problems?"

"No sir, I was on the test team when it was under development and saw how well it performed in testing. I've been anxious to see how well it performs in the field and so far so good, but until we cross the 'start line' I won't know for sure."

"We should be there in about twenty minutes. Lee should let you know. By the way, how long did it take you to learn how to operate all of this?" said Stoney.

"The primary school lasts for six months and then we spend another month on the simulator. For me those were the easy parts, the hard part was agreeing to be on PRP."

"Wow, I would have thought it took longer. To a pilot like me, it looks like something out of science fiction. I know what you mean about the PRP. When I was hired and they told me about the 'no anesthesia' clause and the constant surveillance, I almost turned down the job. However, I realized the job we are doing might just be keeping the U.S. safe at night so here I am, Personnel Reliability Program and all.

"I know how you feel. When I first went on PRP, they told me a story about a guy whose foot slid under his lawnmower. He let the ambulance take him to the hospital, but he had to lie on a table in severe pain for almost an hour until his PRP minder arrived. When they got ready to take him to surgery, the minder had to get the hospital administrator's authorization to go into the O.R. per PRP regulations so he could hear everything the patient said under anesthesia. I had friends who wanted to get into the program, but when they read the details on PRP they said 'No Way'," said Brad.

"Good thing I didn't hear that story before I signed, I might have gone to work for TWA. On the flip side, I do love flying these birds and it's a lot more fun than being a glorified bus driver. Back to business; make sure you let Lee know of any anomalies once you really get going. I am concerned about that number three engine acting up."

"If anything were to happen, I tend to think it will be once I start the sensors at full power. Did you know that Dr. Kauffman has amplified their power to increase their range and sensitivity?"

"Yes, I know about the modifications; all us captains were briefed a couple of months ago when the equipment was being installed. We are the first operational flight and supposedly, they ran a lot of tests to make sure no aircraft systems were affected, but after that last flight and the issue with number three, I don't want any surprises."

"We'll know shortly when we start using the sensors. If number three acts up then, I'll shut down everything back here and advise you up front," Brad said.

"Go ahead and let me know when you get up to full power once we cross the start line." The start line was the point of reference given to each aircraft when it left Victoria, B.C., so that they would have a starting reference for their sensor sweeps. The start line changed with each flight based on the current intelligence that NSA/CIA had received from earlier flights and intercepted communications from the submarines.

"I am going to head on back up front," Stoney said. "Oh, Virginia wanted me to ask you if you wanted the beef brisket or the chicken for lunch."

"The beef will be great. Thanks for asking. I remember one flight when the caterers messed up the order, and all I got was a stale peanut butter sandwich. Anything is better than that."

Picking up the interphone, Stoney entered the code for the galley.

After a short pause, Virginia said, "galley."

"Virginia, this is the captain, I am ready to leave the radio room."

"Yes sir, one minute please."

Hanging up the interphone, Stoney said, "Brad, let me know when the curtain is pulled."

Seconds later, he said, "All clear sir," and entered the door unlock command into his console. After the *click* Stoney pressed on the door and it opened. "See you in London," Stoney said as he stepped through the door shutting it behind him. After the second *click* of the door lock, he nodded at Virginia who opened the curtain.

"Captain, what did Brad want for lunch?" Virginia asked as she secured the curtain.

"He wants the beef brisket, so hold the stale peanut butter sandwich."

"Just what we need to make a trip interesting, a crew full of comedians," Virginia said as she headed back to the galley.

What a way to make a living; I get to fly and command this wonderful airplane and work with great people. Stoney thought as he walked up the aisle. Feeling the vibration of the four powerful engines in his feet filled him with pride as the quiet din of conversation and the clank of ice filled glasses filled the otherwise quiet cabin. As he made his way toward the front, Sarah-Ann Smith, who was sitting next to John Lilliman, stopped him.

"Captain Stone, this is my first flight this far north. When the stewardess gave the safety briefing, she did not mention any arctic survival gear being on board. I had a distant relative that died during the sinking of the Titanic, so I tend to notice little things like that."

"Miss Smith, let me assure you that we do indeed have the necessary safety equipment on board. Not only that, we can fly this aircraft on three engines and in a pinch, we could do it on two. APA has a perfect safety record on these flights, and we do take safety very seriously. Additionally, we have landing agreements with many of the foreign airfields that would be within range of our flight path even on only two engines. Not only that, but APA maintains small emergency airfields located along our flight path. At worst case, we could land at one of those and contact APA who would send a plane to get everyone," Stoney said.

Putting down his drink, John Lilliman jumped in. "Captain Stone, aren't these airplanes fairly old, and as such more likely to have problems?"

"No, Mr. Lilliman, each one of the APA Northern Star Constellations was rebuilt and modified to meet strict APA requirements from the ground up once the company buys them. Unfortunately, Lockheed Aircraft Works doesn't make them any more since all of the other airlines have transitioned to the Boeing 707 and the McDonald Douglas DC-8 jet aircraft; however, APA bought all of the tooling necessary to make any part that might be needed for these planes. Matter of fact, APA could even start manufacturing them, if there was a demand large enough."

"That is very reassuring, captain. Thanks so much for stopping by," said Sarah-Ann.

"Captain, I didn't know that APA was in that kind of position with regard to these Constellations," John said.

"That information is not widely publicized however, it is not a company secret. The FAA and the International Civil Aviation Organization required APA to meet strict safety guidelines before approving these flights. Those alternate airfields I mentioned earlier are just one example of those extra requirements. Now, if you'll excuse me I need to get back to the cockpit. I hope you enjoy the rest of the flight and please let Maria or Virginia know if you need anything."

Stoney continued his trek back to the cockpit. *Seems that the questions never change as well as the political or sports discussions. You would think that if people thought these old birds weren't safe, they wouldn't pay the price for the tickets,* Stoney thought.

Passing the bridge players, he noticed that the women had changed the conversation from politics to shopping in London. Further up the aisle, the Whiteman kid was still under the young Miss McNeely's spell. As he knocked on the cockpit door, he thought to himself, *The names and faces change, but the passengers never do.*

Chapter 7

Entering the cockpit, Stoney said, "Where are we, Steve, and how are things here?"

"Sir, by my calculations we have just crossed the start line, and I was just about ready to call Brad to give him the heads up," Steve said.

"Go ahead and call him. Lee, keep a close watch on that board as the sensors come up to full power," Stoney said.

After stowing his hat and coat in the closet, Stoney climbed back into his seat and re-adjusted it. Glancing over the instrument panel while waiting for Steve to finish his conversation with Brad on the interphone he said, "Lee, how's everything going?"

"Just fine sir, she's purring like a kitten. All OK in the back?" said Lee.

"I tell you, I have to take my hat off to Brad, there he is sitting in a windowless room in the back of an airplane knowing that if someone tries to break into that room he could be blown to bits. Personally, I'll take the view up here any day."

"Yes sir, I hear the bonus pay more than makes up for that possibility. Also, they have a special life insurance policy that pays double should that happen, but like you I wouldn't want that job."

Continuing to look out the front window at the endless sea of white in front of him, Stoney thought to himself that this is probably one of the most beautiful places on Earth. Yes, it could be deadly, but treated with the respect it deserved, its beauty couldn't be beat.

While Stoney gazed out the front windows, Steve monitored their position and Lee watched the aircraft's systems. The four Wright Super Cyclone engines throbbed as they propelled the big black Constellation through the frigid arctic air and across the endless sea of white.

Almost in a daydream Stoney thought about the secret work going on in the back while the passengers drank and played cards not knowing about the three long antennas trailing out the rear. Those antennas provided the electronic eyes that peered through the thick arctic ice searching for those elusive submarines bearing the red hammer and sickle of the Soviet Union on their thick black conning towers. The sailors and officers of those submarines silently waiting for the coded message that would send them crashing through the meters of ice above them to launch their compliment of ballistic missiles bringing Armageddon to North America.

All of those nuclear missile drills that the kids did in school would be useless, and the underground shelters that FEMA had built and loaded with food would be worthless as well. There wouldn't be enough time between the announcements from the government for the people to get into the shelters before the missiles hit. At present only these big black airplanes with their complement of unsuspecting passengers kept that hellish day at bay, at least for now.

I wish I could bring Becky on one of these flights. She would really enjoy it, but there's that darn company rule against relatives and significant others flying with a crewmember, he thought.

I am going to have to counsel Steve and Virginia about their romantic behavior last night. They know it is against company policy for crewmembers to sleep with one another. According to the security policy, breaking that rule can get you fired. Both are good crewmembers and any other captain would turn them in, but I think APA is better served by bringing it to their attention and telling them to cut it out. I'll handle it in London, Stoney decided.

Looking over the instruments, Stoney noted that 'Ole George,' the common name given to aircraft autopilots, was keeping them on course, and all systems looked great. He also noted, there was no adverse weather showing on the weather radar and there were no clouds above them, only scattered ones below. So far, no indications of the low that Stan had talked about during the weather brief.

A beeper sounded, and a light on the instrument panel began to blink. *Time to check in with Polar Control,* Stoney thought.

"Hey Steve, I'll need a current position report, time to check in with Polar."

Steve handed Stoney a slip of paper with their current position on it as Stoney picked up the radio microphone.

"Polar Air Traffic Control, this is APA flight 28-Alpha calling."

There was no response.

"Polar Air Traffic Control, this is APA flight 28-Alpha calling on frequency 118.95."

Again, no response.

"Steve, verify the frequency for this region."

Checking his aeronautical chart Steve replied, "Sir, according to the chart, 118.95 is the correct frequency. I'll check for an alternate." Steve looked at the alternate frequency printed on the chart. "Here it is, try 125.82."

Stoney dialed in the new frequency on the stand-by radio, thereby leaving the original frequency for reference in the primary radio. He picked up the mike. "Polar Air Traffic Control, this is APA flight 28-Alpha calling on frequency 125.82." Static was the only reply. "Polar Air Traffic Control, this is APA flight 28-Alpha calling on frequency 125.82, do you read us?"

In the background noise both pilots could just hear "APA flight 28-Alpha this is Polar Control. We are experiencing radio difficulty in your sector. Please contact us again when you get farther down your track."

"Polar Control, this is 28-Alpha; message understood. We will call again in sixty, that is six-zero minutes from now," Stoney said.

"Steve, set a timer for sixty minutes. This is peculiar; in all of my flights I have never had trouble reaching Polar Control at any location on the track. Go ahead and shoot our position again and predict our position sixty minutes from now. I want to start listening on that frequency."

Steve pushed back his chair so he could climb out to take the sun shot. He retrieved his sextant from its case mounted on the bulkhead, and then grabbed the aircraft navigation clock mounted next to the sextant so that he would have an accurate time of the reading. He climbed up on his stool so that his head fit into a special bubble in the roof of the aircraft where he had a 360-degree view of the sky. He fit his sextant to his eye and began to adjust it.

Five minutes and several calculations later, he announced their position. He then keyed it into the system that would send it back to Brad. Using that information, he calculated where they should be when the timer went off. Picking up the aeronautical chart, he found frequency 119.45. He dialed it into the primary radio and set the audio panel so they could hear both radios over the speaker system.

Lee looked at his panel of gauges and noted supercharger temperature, engine cylinder head temperature, oil temperature, cabin pressure, engine speed, manifold pressures, voltages on the generators and total current flow within the electrical bus system. He also noted the outside air temperature and the atmospheric pressure. The only item that seemed a little out of sorts was the RPM versus manifold pressure on number three engine. He made a note of that and immediately called Brad.

"Brad, what kind of current flow and voltages are you seeing on your inverters?"

"They seem very normal, at least normal for the amount of current the new equipment requires. It is almost double what the old system needed. Do you see something wrong up there?"

"The RPM on number three is a little lower than it should be in relationship to the manifold pressure. In order to balance it out, I am going to have to increase the throttle setting on number three to get the RPM up. I have tried adjusting the prop control, but I could not get the RPM up where it should be," said Lee.

"It is possible the additional load on the generators and the high current flow are loading down that particular engine. One of the changes that Kauffman made was to change the frequency of the voltage that feeds into the regulators and the inverters. It is one of the methods he used to keep the current flow down to a level the wiring in the aircraft could handle without burning the insulation off. That may be causing small ignition problems in the engine hence the lower than expected manifold pressure and RPM for a given throttle setting," said Brad.

"I increased the throttle setting and the manifold pressure rose as expected. I have readjusted the RPM back to normal. Keep an eye on the voltages and current flow back there and I'll keep a closer eye on number three," said Lee.

"Captain Stone, looks like we are having a minor anomaly with number three engine again. I have had to increase the throttle setting to bring up the manifold pressure in order to get the RPM to the correct setting," Lee said.

"Lee, why didn't you just change the propeller setting to increase the RPM without increasing the manifold pressure?" Stoney asked.

"I did that and there was no change. I adjusted the propeller control, and there was no change. I could decrease the RPM, but I could not increase it to the same level as the other engines. I had to increase the manifold pressure to get the RPM back up. Brad seems to think there may be a relationship between how the engine is running and the amount of load his equipment is putting on the whole electrical system. Our theory is there may be interference with the ignition system in the engine. I don't know why we are not seeing it in the other engines. I would think that it would affect all of them. Numbers one, two, and four are all running just as they always do."

There was a knock at the cockpit door. Lee got up and looked out the peeper and saw that it was Virginia with lunch. He opened the door and she stepped in carrying three trays.

"Lunch is served, gentlemen," she announced as she entered.

"Captain Stone, I believe you ordered the chicken. Steve gets the beef and by regulations, that means Lee gets the ham sandwich." APA regulations stated that all three cockpit crew members must have different food to eat. No two crewmembers could eat the same thing. This was just in case of an accidental food poisoning or perhaps a purposeful one. This significantly reduced the probability of more than one person getting sick from bad food. Most captains would take a turn eating the "random" food, in this case, a ham sandwich, during at least one leg of the trip. Stoney was no exception, he had decided to take the random food for dinner.

"Thanks, Virginia please keep mine covered and put it on the shelf behind me. I'm going to let Steve eat first. By the way, how are the passengers doing?" Stoney asked.

"Well, they are all eating lunch. I have to make a note to the caterer that they need to put more chicken dinners on the plane and less of the beef brisket. Everyone wanted the chicken for some reason. They also need to increase our stockpile of gin; everyone seems to be drinking Martinis."

"Sounds like a normal trip to me," Stoney replied. "How 'bout a cup of coffee to go with this?"

"Coming right up; Maria is making a last round for drinks, then she'll bring up the coffee pot. We are percolating one now. It is that good Columbian coffee."

"Great. Tell her, thanks. I don't know about you other guys, but I am looking forward to that first pint at the pub on the corner from the hotel," Stoney said.

"Don't you know it!" replied both Lee and Steve.

"You fellas need anything else? I need to get back to work."

"Thanks, Virginia, you ladies take great care of us," Steve said. With that, Virginia turned and left the cockpit.

"Thanks for keeping an eye on things; I am starving," said Steve as he dug into his lunch.

"No problem, just remember that when dinner comes around," said Stoney.

—BANG—BANG—BANG

"Lee, what the hell is that?" yelled Stoney as the loud gunshot type noises of a radial engine backfiring filled the cockpit causing the whole aircraft to shake.

CHAPTER 8

"Captain, the RPM and manifold pressures for number three engine are all over the place. I set the mixture full *rich* and it hasn't made any difference. Checking the ignition system now," said Lee as he switched between the two independent ignition systems on the number three engine.

"Nothing is making a difference, recommend we shut down the engine," said Lee.

"Agreed, shut it down *now*!" said Stoney.

Steve, who had quickly moved his food tray out of the way said, "Captain, I have the Emergency Shutdown checklist ready."

With Stoney's order to shutdown the engine, Lee had shut off the fuel and moved the mixture to *idle-cutoff* and closed the throttle. Immediately, the loud bangs and shaking ceased.

I hope that shaking didn't cause major structural damage to that wing. If it did, this could be a real short flight! Thought Stoney as they went through the checklist.

"Autopilot *off*," said Steve.

"Check" replied Stoney.

"Ignition *off*," Steve said.

"Check," Lee replied.

"Engine controls to *idle-cut-off*," Steve said.

"Checked and verified," Stoney said.

"Propeller control *full feather*" said Steve

"Check" said Stoney.

"Engine secured with no fire indication," Lee said.

"Increase RPM and manifold pressure on the remaining engines," Steve said.

"Check," Lee replied.

"Lee, contact Brad and tell him to shut down the equipment and secure the trailing antennas," Stoney said.

"Steve, get out your charts and start looking for alternate airfields within seventy-five miles of our position. Look behind us as well."

"Polar Control, this is APA flight 28-Alpha declaring an emergency. Do you read us?" Stoney said into the microphone.

The interphone rang at the flight engineer's console. Lee answered. "Sir, the equipment is in its cool down cycle, and the antennas are being retracted."

"Thanks, Lee. Polar Control, this is APA flight 28-Alpha calling on frequency 125.82—do you read us?" Static was his only reply. Stoney looked at the airspeed and altimeter instruments noting they had lost twenty knots of airspeed but had managed to maintain altitude. The interphone rang again.

"Sir, Virginia is on the line, what should I tell her?" Lee asked.

"Tell her to collect all of the service items and to limit the alcohol distribution. I will make a cabin-wide announcement in a few minutes.

"Steve, where are you on that emergency field information?" said Stoney.

"Looks like there is a field fifty miles behind us and the next one is not for another one hundred and seventy-five miles ahead of us," Steve replied.

"What's the plan, Captain?"

"We should be able to maintain our altitude and airspeed so we'll continue on to London. We'll be late, but we won't have to land at one of the emergency fields. Keep an eye on our position and the nearest airfields that are in front of us, just in-case. Steve, take the aircraft while I make the announcement."

"I have the aircraft," Steve said.

"You have the aircraft," Stoney replied.

Stoney picked up the microphone. "Ladies and gentleman, this is Captain Stone. Please remain calm. We have had an engine malfunction but there is no need for concern, this aircraft will fly just fine on three engines. If you look out the window you will see one of the propellers not moving. It is set that way to minimize its effect on the aircraft. On three engines we lose a little airspeed, but we can maintain altitude and continue on our flight to London. I have asked the stewardesses to suspend the lunch service and all alcohol service for the time being. I am also asking everyone to remain seated with their seatbelts securely fastened. I will turn off the *Fasten Seatbelt* signs as soon as I can. Just remember to remain calm and we'll make it to London just fine. Thank you."

Stoney tried calling Polar Control once more.

Still there was no answer. "Steve, how long has it been since we had last contact with Polar Control?"

"Only thirty minutes, sir."

"Guess we'll have to wait another thirty minutes before we can get through to them. Steve, I'll take the aircraft back so you and Lee can go ahead and eat since we seem to be stable and the sunny side is still up," joked Stoney.

Stoney reached down and once again set the microphone for the cabin PA system. "Ladies and gentlemen, this is Captain Stone again, since everything has stabilized, the stewardesses can continue with the lunch service. However, I am requesting that the alcohol service remain suspended for the rest of the flight. I hate to do that, but in the interest of safety I believe it is necessary. I am going to turn off the *Fasten Seatbelt* sign, but please remain in your seat as much as possible with your seatbelt on. Thank you for your attention."

While Stoney flew on, Lee and Steve ate lunch.

The interphone rang, "Captain Stone here."

"Sir, Brad here. I have retracted the antennas and the equipment is cooling down."

Putting the aircraft on autopilot, Stoney continued the conversation.

"Did your instruments show any anomalies whatsoever before or after that engine went haywire?"

"Well, sir, there was a major spike in the inverter voltage and frequency just as the engine started to act up."

"How long will the cool down take?"

"About fifteen minutes," said Brad.

"Call Lee as soon as the cool down cycle is complete and the equipment is fully powered down."

"Yes sir, will do."

Stoney hung up the interphone and turned in his seat to look at his flight engineer.

"Do you think it is safe to try and fire up the engine since Brad's equipment is shut down?" asked Stoney.

"The only problem I can see is if the electronic ignition control system on that engine was damaged when the voltage spiked. It could have destroyed the unit. If the controller is dead, that engine won't fire up at all, and if it is working then my instruments will tell us if the engine is running well enough to continue," Lee said.

"Okay, that is the plan. We'll finish lunch, wait for Brad's call and then see about firing up that engine." Picking up the interphone again, Stoney dialed the galley.

"Virginia here, sir," said the voice on the interphone.

"Virginia, we are going to try and restart number three here in a few minutes. I will make a general announcement, but I wanted to let you girls know first. Make sure everyone is strapped down."

"Yes, sir."

So much for a routine flight. Even if that engine doesn't fire up, we'll be fine as long as nothing else goes wrong. Fortunately, everything else seems to be fine, thought Stoney as he monitored the instruments and manually flew the aircraft since he turned off the autopilot. *There's the interphone ringing, hopefully that is Brad telling us the equipment is completely shut down.*

"Captain that was Brad, his equipment is fully shut down," Lee said.

Glancing over at Steve, Stoney said, "We'll try the restart before I eat, so when you're finished well go for it."

"Sir, let's do it," Steve said as he handed Lee his tray to stow out of the way.

"Lee are you ready?"

"Yes sir."

"I'll make the announcement. Steve, pull out the checklist," said Stoney.

"Ladies and gentlemen, this is Captain Stone again. After assessing the situation, I have decided to try and restart number three engine. If you're looking out the window you will see it begin to turn. You may see a short flame come out of the exhaust during the start sequence which is perfectly normal. Please return to your seats and fasten your seatbelt securely. Thank you."

After turning on the *Fasten Seatbelt* sign, Stoney turned to Steve and called for the In-flight Engine-start checklist.

"Fuel—on," Steve said as he started the checklist.

"Fuel—on," Lee replied.

"Ignition—on," Steve continued.

"Ignition—on," Lee replied.

This continued until it was time to press the starter button. Tension was high in the cockpit as everyone anticipated the traditional cough and sputter of a radial engine starting up.

Figuratively crossing his fingers Stoney thought, *Well, time to see if I've used up my allotment of good luck. If it doesn't start and we have another major problem, I'll have no choice but to put her down at one of the alternate airfields. Please Lord, let this engine start!*

Taking a deep hopeful breath Stoney called out, "Starter engage." Lee pressed the starter button on his control panel. Looking out the window, Steve started counting blades as the starter motor turned the engine.

"One, two, three, four."

"Damn, four blades and no start!" Steve said out loud.

"Lee, are you showing good engine readings?" Stoney asked.

"Yes, sir, that engine should have fired. Fuel flow is good; mixture is set correctly. It should have started."

"Try leaning the mixture just a little more, the checklist setting may be too rich at this altitude."

"Yes, sir," Lee replied as he moved the mixture control.

Stoney called for the start button again.

Lee pressed the button and again Steve counted the propeller blades as they turned. "One, two, three, four, five, six, seven, eight."

"Sorry sir, doesn't look like the engine is going to restart," Lee called out.

"I didn't even see it trying to fire," Steve said.

"No flame, no ignition," Stoney said. "I am afraid we're stuck on three engines until we get to London. Secure the engine."

Steve started calling out the checklist items to secure the engine as Lee responded.

"Engine secured, sir," Steve said when the checklist was complete.

Stoney picked up the microphone and switched to the cabin PA once again. "Ladies and gentlemen, this is Captain Stone. We tried to restart the number three engine but to no avail. We will continue the trip on three engines. As I mentioned earlier, we can make it to London with no problems; however with our slower airspeed we will be late getting there. There are no reasons to be worried, these airplanes fly just fine on three engines. I am going to turn off the *Fasten Seatbelt* sign so feel free to move about the cabin as you wish. Thank you."

Hanging up the microphone and turning the switch to connect the mike to the radio,

"Steve, call Virginia and tell her to continue cabin service as normal except for the alcohol. When you finish that, take a navigation reading. I want to be able to update our ETA with Polar Control," Stoney said.

"Yes sir," Steve replied as he picked up the interphone.

After hanging up the interphone, Steve got up from his seat, retrieved his sextant and clock then he climbed up into the bubble to take his reading.

Several minutes later, he announced their ground speed was forty knots slower that it had been and with that revised speed, London was still five plus hours away. Looking at the stop watch that he had started when they last contacted Polar Control he told Stoney that forty-five minutes had elapsed and that they should be able to contact them soon. Stoney realized they would have to add additional time to that original sixty-minute estimate due to their slower groundspeed; however, he decided to give them a call anyway.

"Polar Control this is APA flight 28-Alpha calling on frequency 125.82, come in please," Stoney called on the radio.

Static was the answer he received.

"Polar Control, this is APA flight 28-Alpha calling on frequency 125.82, come in please."

Still no response, just static and a somewhat strange and unfamiliar sound filled the cockpit speaker.

CHAPTER 9

A clear blue northern sky greeted Leshev and James as they stood in the glass-walled control tower cab. The reflection of the sun off the snow made the light in the tower that much brighter.

Leshev looked at the freshly plowed runway and had a warm sense of satisfaction that all was going according to plan. All would be ready when his prize—the Super Constellation known as Northern Star Flight 28A—arrived into his waiting arms.

"Good, all is ready for our *guests* to arrive. I want to thank you for your cooperation and the cooperation of your staff."

"Captain Leshev, it is very difficult to argue with the point of a gun," James said.

"It is unfortunate we had to hurt one of your comrades, but it seemed the only way to secure your cooperation."

"How is it that you plan to cause 28-Alpha to land here at all? There would have to be a major emergency on board for them to even *think* of landing here. We are here strictly for emergencies," James asked.

"Ah yes, that is a very good question. I understand your curiosity, but alas, I am not at liberty to explain that to you. Just rest assured that it *will* be landing here. There is no question of that," Leshev said.

Meanwhile down in the cafeteria, Mike Hudson, the deputy airfield commander was watching the young Russian corporals very carefully. *They may be young, but so far they are following the book on guarding prisoners. Damn, they'll have to make a mistake sometime and I'm going to be ready to take action. We need to get hold of a weapon—of some kind!* He thought as he sat with all of the other airfield personnel.

The door opened and the plow operator who had been with the Russian sergeant came in, surprisingly enough, without the sergeant. Seeing the man pull off his gloves and rub his hands together as he sat down immediately gave Hudson an idea.

"Corporal, how 'bout letting me make some coffee to help warm up everyone?" Hudson said loudly.

"Who said that?" asked Corporal Vavilov.

Standing up, Mike Hudson said, "I did."

As Hudson stood up, the movement caused Vavilov to aim his rifle in that same direction.

Holding up his hands, Hudson just stood there thinking, *Good he might take the bait.*

Pointing at Hudson, Corporal Vavilov said, "You go and get the things to make coffee. Bring the pot and the supplies and put them on this table so all can see. Corporal Osinov will go with you. Don't do anything foolish or someone will get hurt."

"Agreed, coffee, nothing else," said Hudson as he started moving toward the door to the kitchen.

Entering the kitchen he found a percolator and filled it full of water. He opened and closed several cabinets as if looking for the coffee items. *There,* he said to himself, *a knife laying on the counter partially covered with a towel.* Glancing toward Osinov who had positioned himself just inside the kitchen door Hudson thought, *if I do this right, he'll never see me scoop up the knife with the towel.*

Gathering up the percolator coffee basket, the coffee and the percolator full of water he walked past Osinov and set them on the table closest to an electrical outlet. He filled the basket with coffee and taking the lid off of the percolator he pushed it down inside causing the water to overflow soaking the electrical connections on the outside of the pot.

"Darn it, what a mess," Hudson said before he quickly walked back towards the kitchen. Moving as fast as he dared without causing suspicion he went through the door and scooped up the knife inside the towel and turned around to find Osinov standing in the doorway intently watching him. *This won't be pretty if he saw me take the knife.* Not waiting to see if he had been caught, Hudson hurried back toward the door. Just as he passed Osinov, who had moved out of the doorway, Hudson spun around behind the startled Russian and put his arm around Osinov's neck in a choke hold as he held the knife in the opposite hand. His arm around Osinov's neck, Hudson poked his hostage's back with the knife point and said, "Drop the gun!"

Looking past Osinov to gauge Vavilov's reaction Hudson saw his inexperience surface as Vavilov stood there almost paralyzed. A split second later, the door to the cafeteria opened and the Russian sergeant appeared. Osinov still had his gun in his hand though he was quite still.

"What the hell is going on here?" said Danshov as he quickly assessed the situation.

"I am going to kill this man if you don't put down your weapons—now!" Hudson shouted.

"Comrade, if you kill him, then I will kill you and three other hostages; no one will win. Now let my corporal go and hand over your weapon," said Danshov calmly.

Hudson held Osinov firmly and pushed the knife a little harder into his back hoping he would plead with the sergeant. *I don't want to kill him, but he should be saying something.* Osinov remained silent.

"I will kill him!" said Hudson.

Danshov said something in Russian to Vavilov who immediately grabbed the closest hostage and yanked him out of his chair and forced him to the floor on his knees and put his rifle to the man's head.

"He will die first, then those three," said Danshov as he motioned to the three people closest to him.

The tension in the room was electric as the seconds slowly ticked by.

Damn, I can't be responsible for three innocent deaths.

"All right you win," said Hudson as he let go of Osinov's neck and dropped the knife to the floor.

Osinov quickly took several steps to widen the gap between them and whirled around to level his weapon at Hudson.

"Pick up the knife with two fingers, by the blade, and give it to me handle first," said Osinov who had recovered from his initial shock.

Hudson squatted down to retrieve the knife and as he looked down to pick it up Osinov kicked him in the face knocking Hudson sprawling backward blood running from his nose.

Danshov said something else in Russian and Vavilov walked around in front of the kneeling man and kicked him in the face sending him sprawling and then as the man lay on the ground Vavilov shot him in the leg.

When Hudson heard the gunshot he yelled, "NO" and got up as quickly as he could. With Osinov's weapon pointed at him, Hudson rushed over to see to the man on the ground as blood ran down his fingers holding his nose.

Reaching the moaning man on the ground Hudson said, "You Russian bastards, he didn't do anything to you—I did!" Putting his hand on the man's wound, hoping the pressure would stop the bleeding, Hudson continued, "Somebody throw me that towel."

Vavilov dropped the towel and Hudson used it to put pressure on the wound.

Loudly Danshov said, "Let this be a warning, the man only has a flesh wound but next time we will shoot to kill. Do not try any more heroics or we will just shoot everyone and be done with it."

"Please let me go get a first-aid kit!" someone yelled.

"*Neyt!*" was the emphatic reply. "He will serve as a reminder to everyone to cooperate!"

"Activate your radar, Mr. James. I want to see if they are getting close," Leshev said.

James reached down and pressed the radar start button. On top of the control tower cab, the radar antenna began to turn in a circular pattern, searching for any aircraft within the range of its electronic eyes.

Both men stared at the circular green screen watching a green line sweep around the blank screen in a circle, looking for a little green blip indicating a contact. The rotating green line had a mesmerizing effect as nothing but the radio's static noise broke the silence.

Back aboard flight 28A, life had returned to an almost normal routine.

In the cockpit, Stoney and Steve were busy monitoring the aircraft systems. Lee was keeping a very close eye on the remaining three engines and their instruments. In the rear of the aircraft, Brad was looking at that Play Boy magazine he had purchased in Victoria. Since all of his equipment had been shutdown he really did not have a job to do, so he read his magazine.

Steve continued to periodically pull out his sextant and clock then he climbed up on the stool to put his head in the dome to ascertain their current position. After he performed his calculations he announced that they were still forty knots slow, but were right on course to London.

As he was putting his equipment away, he stopped and started to carefully sniff the air.

What is that smell? He thought to himself. *Wait, there it is again.*

"Hey, does anyone else smell anything peculiar; almost an electrical smell?" Steve asked.

"I don't smell anything," said Stoney.

"I don't either," said Lee.

"It must be my imagination," said Steve. *I am sure I smelt something, must be getting jumpy,* he thought as he climbed back into his seat.

✪

All at once there was no doubt; everyone smelled the distinct odor of burning wires in the cockpit. Stoney immediately told Lee to start looking for fire as the cockpit began to fill with smoke.

"Everyone go on oxygen masks!" Stoney yelled as the smoke became as thick as an arctic snowstorm. The acrid smell of burning wire was very evident in the air and everyone was having trouble seeing as the smoke burned their eyes. The oxygen masks didn't help their vision since they only covered the mouth and nose.

"Steve, call Virginia and have them strap everyone down. We are going to have to do an emergency descent so we can clear the smoke out of here! Lee, have you found anything burning? What is the source of the smoke?" Stoney yelled through his mask.

"I can't find anything, Captain. All indications are normal. I can't explain the smoke. I can't find a fire anywhere!" Lee shouted back.

Stoney turned off the autopilot and began a rapid descent to a lower altitude where they could open the small windows in the cockpit and suck out the smoke. He knew he took a chance doing this as the suction and the introduction of fresh oxygen could make the fire worse. He took an educated gamble since they couldn't find any visible evidence of fire. Once they had descended below 10,000 feet, he had Lee de-pressurize the cabin. Once the cabin was at atmospheric pressure, he opened his window and told Steve to do the same.

"Steve, based on your last position, find me one of those emergency fields. With this smoke and only three engines, we need to put her on the ground!"

Virginia was in the galley cleaning up after lunch when the interphone rang.

"Galley, this is Virginia."

"This is Steve, we have an emergency up here, need everyone strapped down ASAP!"

"Yes sir," said Virginia as she pressed the button for the cabin PA.

"Everyone sit down in a seat and fasten your seat belts—now!" Virginia said as she hung up the interphone and rushed into the cabin to make sure everyone took a seat. Just as she was hurrying down the aisle, the aircraft suddenly fell out from beneath her feet as she grabbed a seat back and hung on for dear life. She felt her stomach rise up into her throat as her instincts said, *Oh God, we're diving!*

Virginia saw Maria in the back of the cabin and heard her yell, "For God's sake get into a seat!" Maria had grabbed onto a seatback to prevent her from rolling head first down the downward sloping aisle.

"Maria, sit down and strap in!" yelled Virginia as she fell into the seat she was holding onto and tightened her seat belt as the aircraft continued its downward plunge.

Virginia could hear passengers crying as she fought back her own tears. Crash! She heard several glass items fall to the floor in the galley. *Oh God, what if we're crashing?* her consciousness yelled at her, *Gotta get everyone in crash position!*

With as much authority as she could muster she yelled to everyone, "Lean forward and put your heads in your laps and remove your glasses. Cover your head with your arms and if you have a pillow cover your face with it!"

With the entire cabin in crash position they waited for the impact, each second that ticked by seemed to take an entire lifetime as everyone waited for the violent jolt and the screeching of metal being torn apart as the aircraft disintegrated in the crash everyone was sure awaited them.

After what seemed like the passing of years to everyone in the cabin but was really only about five minutes, the aircraft leveled out and continued to fly like nothing out of the ordinary had happened. The unmistakable sounds of humans in distress were the only abnormal sounds in the cabin. Relief was beginning to spread when everyone's ears suddenly popped in response to a large change in cabin pressure.

Lee continued to look for the source of the smoke. Since opening the windows had cleared the cockpit and the outside air was breathable, everyone took off their oxygen masks. The acrid smell was still very evident in the cockpit, but it seemed to have subsided, and no more smoke appeared. Still, Stoney was not going to take any more chances.

Steve had discovered that Emergency Airfield 'Q' was about fifty miles away and at their current speed, they would make it in about fifteen minutes.

"Steve, look up the approach frequency for 'Q' and dial it into number one radio," Stoney said.

"Frequency is dialed in and ready to go."

"Call the tower and see if you can raise them, but before you do that give me an approximate heading to get there."

"Turn thirty degrees right of present course."

"I need the approach plate for that airfield as well. Lee, pull it out while Steve contacts the tower."

"Quebec tower, this is APA Flight 28-Alpha calling on tower frequency. Please respond," Steve said.

"Sir, here is the approach plate for the airfield," Lee said as he handed the plate to Stoney.

Stoney attached it to his control yoke and began to study it.

Runway length—check
Runway orientation—check
Obstacles—none

"Quebec tower, this is APA Flight 28-Alpha calling on tower frequency, do you hear us?" Steve repeated.

From out of the static came the reply "APA Flight 28-Alpha, this is Quebec tower. How do you copy?"

"We read you loud and clear. We are declaring an emergency. We have shut down one engine and have had smoke in the cockpit. We need to land at your facility. Do you see us on radar?"

"APA flight, radar contact; turn to a heading of 110 degrees for vectors to runway one-eight. Do you require any emergency medical assistance?"

"No, we have no injuries; just need a good mechanic to find out what is up with our bird," Steve replied.

Inside the control tower cab at Quebec, Leshev told James to get that aircraft on the ground immediately and to be very careful what he said on the radio as one false word would get him killed instantly.

Stepping to the other side of the tower cab, Leshev called Danshov on the radio. He made sure to keep his voice and the radio volume down so James' microphone wouldn't pickup his conversation.

"Danshov, the aircraft is in-bound. Secure all of your hostages in a locked room and prepare for our guests. Have Osinov take the plow operator and position the plow at the edge of the runway and use it to make sure there is no escape for the aircraft."

"Yes, comrade captain. I will take care of it. We have had one problem. We had a small uprising and Vavilov shot a man in the leg." Danshov said.

"I don't care about that now as long as everyone is under control. Get out to that plow *now*!" Leshev commanded.

Meanwhile, James continued to issue guidance instructions to the Northern Star flight.

On board the Northern Star, Stoney had Steve make an announcement to the cabin.

"Ladies and Gentlemen, this is First Officer Valdochi. We have decided to land at one of the alternate airfields that APA maintains for emergency situations. We have contacted the tower, and they are expecting us. We should arrive in about ten minutes. As a precaution, I want the stewardesses to prepare the cabin for an emergency landing. However I expect this to be a landing like any other. Please follow the stewardess' instructions. This will be the last announcement from the flight deck until the aircraft is on the ground. Everyone please remain calm, and thank you for your cooperation."

"Let's hope nothing vital was damaged in that fire. Steve, pull out the Pre-Landing checklist and everyone cross your fingers," Stoney said.

"Fingers crossed, boss, here goes," said Steve as he began reading off the items.

Good everything seems OK so far, but we haven't gotten to the gear and flaps. If the gear doesn't respond we'll have to crank it down manually, Stoney thought.

"Flaps down," said Steve.

Well here's the first test, thought Stoney as he moved the flap lever to the *down* position.

Stoney could feel the aircraft's nose pitch up slightly as the flaps extended.

One down, one to go, thought Stoney as he responded, "Flaps down."

"Gear down," said Steve

Stoney reached the landing gear extension lever and moved it to the *down* position.

The aircraft shuddered slightly as the hydraulic motors opened the gear doors and began moving the gear into the down position.

"Captain, I'm getting a gear malfunction light on my panel," said Lee.

"I show one green light and two yellow 'in transit' lights here," said Steve.

"I'm going to raise the gear and then try it again. Steve call Quebec tower and tell them we are going to circle to the left while we work this gear issue. Lee reset breakers for the gear hydraulics once the gear is back up," said Stoney as he moved the landing gear control to the *up* position.

As the gear was moving to its *up* position, Stoney banked the aircraft to the left entering a circular flight path.

"Sir, I have reset the circuit breakers for the hydraulics," said Lee.

"Let's try it again," said Stoney as he moved the landing gear control to the *down* position.

Once again everyone felt the aircraft shudder as the landing gear untucked itself and began moving to the *down* position.

Several seconds later, "I have three green lights, indicating the gear is down and locked," said Lee.

"I confirm, three green. Steve, tell Quebec we're now in-bound," said Stoney as he leveled the aircraft and once again headed for Quebec's runway.

After relaying the information to the control tower, Steve said, "Captain, the checklist is complete."

"Let's put her on the ground." Stoney said.

Stoney made one more turn to line up the aircraft for his final approach.

"APA check wheels down, and you are cleared to land on runway one-eight. Winds are light and variable. Be advised that the runway was just plowed so it may still be somewhat slicker than you are used to," said the voice on the radio.

"Roger, Quebec tower, wheels are down and locked. We are three miles out on a straight-in for one-eight," Stoney replied.

Leshev picked up his radio. "Danshov, the aircraft is on final approach. Are you in position?"

"Yes, comrade captain. We will block any attempt they make at escaping," came the reply.

"Corporal Vavilov and Corporal Osinov, have you secured the hostages?"

"Yes, comrade captain; we have them locked in a supply room with no way out. They will be fine until we need them again."

"Meet me on the airfield but stay *out of sight* until the aircraft has stopped and the engines are shut down. *Remain hidden* until I arrive!"

"Yes, comrade captain."

"Mr. James, please sit down and put both hands behind your back."

James sat in the chair whose back was up against a pipe that ran from the ceiling down through the floor. He put his hands behind him, and Leshev bound them so the pipe was locked between his arms preventing him from scooting the chair across the floor.

Reaching into a pocket in his snow suit, Leshev pulled out a small roll of American Duct tape. Pulling off two long strips, Leshev said, "This is one of the best things to come from America and its capitalist society, duct tape! We use it for everything."

As Leshev squatted down to tape James' ankles to the legs of the chair, James thought, *I would love to kick that Russian bastard in the nuts! But I can do more for the folks here if I am alive.*

"So, *comrade* what is the other thing we capitalists do right?" James asked.

"Why, rock and roll of course! I love the Beach Boys."

When he finished Leshev stood up and taking his automatic rifle from his shoulder he pointed it at the controller's console and said, "I am afraid your *duct tape* won't fix this!" and he opened fire on the console. Glass, bits of metal and electrical sparks flew everywhere, leaving the panel nothing but a hunk of twisted metal and broken glass.

"I have destroyed the radios and airfield lighting controls just in case you manage to get free, but there is no way you can warn the aircraft or call for help. You will be as comfortable as possible for the time being. I will send someone up to get you later." Leshev turned and bolted down the stairs running out to the runway pausing just long enough to grab an interphone headset hanging on the wall by the door.

He met up with the two corporals, and they all hid in the shadow of a building as they watched the large black aircraft touchdown on the runway and using reverse pitch on the engines slow itself down to a crawl. It then exited the runway and taxied to the ramp. Once there, the engines began to shutdown.

"Ladies and gentlemen, this is Captain Stone we have landed at airfield Quebec. Please remain seated until the stewardesses instruct you to exit the aircraft. We will be using the normal stairs as our situation does not require the emergency evacuation slides. Be sure to put on your warmest coat, though you will not be outside any longer than necessary."

"Lee, call Brad and make sure he has everything locked up and tell him to come out ASAP."

"It is damned peculiar that there was no one to guide us to the ramp," Steve said.

"Agreed. Also, no one has come forward to bring the stairs. Try calling the tower on the radio," Stoney replied.

"Tower, this is APA flight, where are the stairs?" Steve asked over the radio.

"Steve, this is damn peculiar. I know we're the first Northern Star to use one of these airfields, but something just doesn't feel right."

"Aye sir, do you see that plow over there?" Steve asked pointing out the window.

The plow was coming straight at them with the bucket raised in a menacing fashion. As it neared the aircraft it did not veer off, but came right at them and stopped just a few yards from the nose wheel.

"Ok, guys what the hell is going on? I am starting to get a really bad feeling about all of this," Stoney said.

As the scene outside unfolded, Steve tried the radio again—still nothing but static.

Lee stood just behind the two pilot's seats also watching the scene outside.

"Who the hell are they?" asked Lee as he saw three figures emerge from the shadow of a nearby building.

Each was wearing a snow suit and as they walked toward the aircraft they pointed weapons directly at the cockpit.

All three crewmembers looked in the direction Lee pointed as the silence of uncertainty and dread permeated the cockpit.

CHAPTER 10

"Oh Shit!" came out of all three mouths as the snow suit clad figures with guns continued in their direction. There was nothing Stoney could do. Even though there was nothing wrong with his radios, he could not call for help since they had very limited range on the ground.

All at once, the door of the snow plow opened and two figures emerged, one had a weapon and was dressed the same as the other three and the other was holding his hands up and appeared to be a hostage. The hostage knelt on the ground with his hands behind his head facing the cockpit so the aircrew could see him. As he knelt in the snow, the snow suit clad figure who had emerged from the snow plow took his rifle and pointed it at the man's head.

One of the other figures pointed to his ears and held up a headset with a long cord attached. Recognizing the signal, Stoney reached down and turned the cockpit speaker selector switch to "Nose Wheel Interphone."

Meanwhile, the figure with the headset disappeared from view presumably to connect his headset at the nose strut interphone connection. With the headset on, he walked back into view of the cockpit crew and they heard, "Airplane Commander please pick-up on the interphone." The heavily Russian accented English voice broke the silence in the cockpit as it boomed over the cabin speaker.

Picking up the microphone, Stoney replied, in as calm a voice as he could muster, "This is Captain Stone, to whom do I have the pleasure of speaking?"

"I am Captain Leshev of the Soviet Spetsnaz Command. I am in control of this airfield and as of right now I am in control of this aircraft. Do you see the man kneeling on the ramp?"

"Yes, we do."

"Good, then you will do as I say, or I will have my sergeant shoot him. Do we understand each other?"

"Yes, what do you want us to do?" Stoney asked.

"We will bring up the stairs. You will have all of your passengers come out one at a time with their hands on their heads. We will shoot anyone not following instructions, *exactly* . . . I give you ten minutes to get everyone ready. When the stairs arrive at the aircraft you will immediately open the door. Failure to do so will result in the death of the man on his knees. By the way, all aircrew members will stay on the aircraft after all passengers have left. When I enter the cabin, they will be seated separately with their hands on their heads. Do you understand?"

"Yes, we do captain. We will follow your instructions," Stoney replied.

"Good! You now have nine minutes in which to ready everyone."

Stoney jumped out of his seat and grabbed his coat. He flung open the cockpit door and once again was standing in the luxurious cabin. Only this time, instead of relaxed passengers on a holiday he now had a group of terrified hostages.

"Everyone listen up. A group of Soviet Special Forces soldiers have taken control of the airfield and now threaten to kill a hostage if we do not follow their instructions. Each passenger will walk down the stairway with their hands on their head. MAKE SURE that you do this exactly. The Soviet Captain said he will personally shoot anyone on the spot who doesn't do as instructed. Everyone, please get your hats and coats on now. We have about two minutes before the stairs arrive. The crew was told to remain on the aircraft for now."

All at once, the cabin exploded in loud voices, shouting questions and concerns. Holding up his hands for silence, Stoney said "Ladies and gentlemen, at this point I do not know any more than what I have told you. There is a man on the ramp with a rifle pointed at his head, if we do not get moving, they will shoot him. Please remain calm and cooperate with these soldiers and I will do everything I can to make sure we all get through this alive. The key is for everyone to do as they're told. We don't need any dead heroes. All aircrew have been told to remain on board."

To Stoney's surprise, everyone got out of their seat and put on hats and coats in a relatively quiet and orderly fashion. The women were crying, and the men had snarls

105

on their faces, but no one spoke. Several people quietly asked how this could happen. That was the one question Stoney could not answer.

Stoney heard the stairs lightly tap the side of the fuselage, and he hurried over to open the door. As the door opened he was greeted by a cold blast of arctic air and a rifle pointed directly at him. The snow suit clad figure said in Russian accented English, "I am Sergeant Danshov. Do as you were told, and no one will be harmed. Disobey and there will be consequences." To emphasize his point Danshov put the end of his rifle against Stoney's forehead.

"Everyone get ready to walk down the stairs." Stoney commanded as he slowly backed away from Danshov's rifle, his hands in the air.

The first passenger went to the door and Sergeant Danshov told him to go down the stairs and he motioned for the rest to follow one at a time.

Stoney heard Mike Whiteman trying to comfort Lillian McNeely, but she continued to sob louder when it came her turn to go down the stairs.

"Stop crying and hurry up!" Danshov yelled at her. That only made her cries louder as she slowly made her way to the door and down the stairs.

One by one they continued down the stairs. From his vantage point, Stoney could just see the passengers, down on the tarmac, as the Russians formed them into a double column where they stood with their hands on their heads. He also noticed the figure, who had been kneeling on the ramp with the rifle at his head, standing in the passenger line. When the last passenger headed down the stairs, Danshov told the remaining aircrew to sit at least one seat apart with their hands on their heads. He stood there ram-rod stiff with his automatic rifle at the ready. Since the door was still open, the cabin was starting to get colder and colder by the minute. As they sat there, the aircrew's teeth started chattering as they began to shiver.

"Can we please get coats for everyone? My crew did not have a chance to get their coats while getting the passengers ready," Stoney said.

"*Neyt!*" was the reply.

"Can we at least get blankets from the overhead bins?" Stoney said trying again.

"Da, but any wrong move, and I shoot this lady. The other lady will get blankets," was the response as he pointed his weapon at Maria's head.

Virginia slowly got out of her seat and carefully opened the overhead bins and handed a blanket to each crewmember. Finishing her task, she sat back down and put her hands on her head. As she handed out the blankets, one at a time, the hostages wrapped themselves up and then returned their hands to their heads.

Down on the tarmac, Leshev had dropped his headset on the ground and walked around to the side of the aircraft to supervise the passengers as they descended the stairs. In Russian, he directed the corporals to form them up into two lines and to watch them.

All was quiet in the lines when one lady began to cry uncontrollably and a man got out of line to try to comfort her. Vavilov ran over and hit the man in the stomach with the butt of his rifle causing the man to double over in pain. He gruffly grabbed the man by the arm and forced him back in line. Vavilov returned to his previous guard position.

Seeing this, Leshev, in a loud voice said, "There will be no movement or talking in the line. Next time my corporals won't be so nice."

Leshev was grateful the passengers were standing quietly, each one appeared lost in their thoughts and emotions. They were quietly stomping their feet to keep the blood flowing. This continued for fifteen long cold minutes. *At least they are cooperating*, he thought as he stood there and watched the helpless group. He did not really want to shoot any of them as they were just pawns in this game and not responsible for their situation.

Looking up at the top of the stairs, Danshov waved, indicating that all of the passengers were down on the tarmac. Walking to the head of the two lines, Leshev addressed the hostages. "Ladies and gentlemen, you are now guests of the Soviet Union. I have no interest in you or your belongings. I am, however, very interested in your aircraft. As such, if you cooperate with us we will not harm you and eventually you will be returned to the United States. I must emphasize that cooperation is essential to survival. Do not try anything or my men will not hesitate to shoot you, or they may shoot someone else to atone for your mistake. I don't think that anyone here wants to be responsible for someone else's death. At this time, Corporal Osinov will take you to the cafeteria where you can drink coffee and warm up. Follow his orders, and everyone will be fine. Corporal Osinov, take the prisoners to the cafeteria. Contact Sergeant Danshov each fifteen minutes. If he does not hear from you each fifteen minutes, then he will come to the cafeteria and randomly pick a passenger to shoot. I believe he prefers to start with a shot to the knee and work his way up."

"Yes, comrade captain. Sergeant Danshov does like to shoot people in the knees!"

Corporal Osinov commanded everyone to face the opposite direction, and with Corporal Vavilov watching the rear they marched the hostages to the cafeteria.

★

After all of the passengers had descended the stairs, the large bald Russian told Stoney to take a seat. Sitting there in silence Stoney racked his brain to try and figure a way out of this situation, but nothing in his security training had prepared him for a ground hijacking. Resigned to the reality of not being able to do anything at that moment, he resolved to let this play out and seize upon any opportunities that presented themselves.

He began to hear someone coming up the stairs and within seconds a large man with an automatic rifle walked into the cabin. He pulled back the hood of his parka, and Stoney could see that he was a relatively young man with a very hard looking face. The man took several seconds to look around. "Who is in charge here?"

"I am," Stoney said.

"And who are you?"

"I am Captain Victor Stone. I am in command of this flight."

"I am Captain Anatoli Leshev of the Russian Spetsnaz Command. I am now in command of this aircraft."

"What do you want with us?" Stoney asked.

"You, your crew, and passengers, are nothing to me! We want this aircraft and its secrets."

"This is a standard Lockheed L-1649A Super Constellation passenger liner. I am sure that the aviation design bureaus in Russia build far better aircraft than this one. Not only that, Aeroflot could buy one easily on the used market. Why go to the time and effort of causing an international incident by hijacking this one?"

"Yes, we could buy one on the open market and you are VERY correct that the Russian Aviation Design bureaus could build one much better than this one; however, it would not have the 'special' modifications that this one has, eh?"

"I have no idea what 'special' modifications you are talking about," Stoney replied.

Stoney and the crew noticed a distinct antagonism in Leshev's reply "Oh, don't play stupid with me, captain. You know very well what I am talking about. Unless you agree to show them to me NOW, I will shoot this pretty blond stewardess." Pointing his weapon at Virginia, he continued, "I am tired of talking and am on a tight schedule!"

"You have no right to do that!! I have no idea what special modifications you are talking about," Stoney cried.

Leshev grabbed Virginia by the arm, as Sergeant Danshov pointed his rifle at the other crew members to keep them seated. Virginia screamed and Maria pleaded as Leshev dragged her to the open cabin door.

"Captain Leshev, STOP, please don't harm her!" Stoney pleaded as he jumped up to go after her.

"STOP WHERE YOU ARE!" Danshov yelled, "OR I WILL SHOOT YOU NOW!"

Stoney froze in his tracks and stood helpless as Leshev told Virginia to stand in the doorway facing out. He raised his weapon and pointed it at the back of her head and once again turned to Stoney.

"Captain Stone, this is your final chance to save the pretty lady. Show me what I want to see, and I will spare her. I will count to three and then you will be less one crew member."

"One . . ."

Stoney stood still as Maria continued to sob.

"Two . . ."

"ALL RIGHT! I will show you the room!" Stoney yelled.

"Go and sit down, before I change my mind!" Leshev told Virginia as he pulled her back inside the cabin and shoved her toward a seat.

Virginia stumbled as she hurried to get in a seat and was visibly shaking both from the cold and from fright. Maria was still sobbing while she tried to comfort Virginia as Lee took off his blanket and handed it to her to help with the cold.

"All right, now SHOW ME!" demanded Leshev as he waved his weapon motioning Stoney to move.

"It's in the back; follow me."

Stoney turned and slowly walked, with his hands up, to the back of the aircraft where he moved both the curtains revealing the door leading into the sensor area.

"Here it is, but you cannot enter that room without blowing the entire aircraft to smithereens! Once secured, only two people in the world have the correct thumb print and access code to open the door and enter that room. Neither one of them are here. That door is made of a special titanium alloy. You cannot cut through it, and you cannot blow it with explosives. It has heat and other sensors that will blow this aircraft to bits If anyone tries to open or tamper with it," Stoney said.

"I will shoot every passenger and crewmember if you do not open that door now!" screamed Leshev.

"You can shoot them or do anything else you please, but no one on this airfield can open that door. Here, I will show you," Stoney explained once again.

Stoney put his thumb against the reader and after it beeped he typed in his ten digit personal pin number. When he entered the last digit a red sign on the reader flashed, 'Room Sealed, Entry Not Permitted."

"See captain, I cannot open that door," Stoney said again.

"Sergeant Danshov, take the other girl out and tie her to the nose wheel strut. No blanket. No coat!" commanded Leshev.

"She will die of exposure!" yelled Stoney.

"Da! I think you will open that door for me before that happens."

"I told you that no one can open that door."

"Then . . . she dies . . . ," Leshev replied as he shrugged his shoulders.

Danshov grabbed Maria by the arm as Stoney and the rest of the crew watched helplessly as he dragged her kicking and screaming out the door and down the stairs.

As Stoney continued to plead with Leshev to let him save Maria, Leshev just stood there and glared at him. Stoney could hear Virginia still sobbing up front, and he knew Lee, Steve, and Brad were wishing they could help Maria.

Since Stoney was facing the forward cabin while Leshev had his back to the aircrew sitting up front, Stoney saw Lee jump up out of his seat and turn to run down the aisle when Danshov suddenly appeared in the doorway.

"Kapitan, povyernitye vokroogu syeychas" yelled Danshov.

Leshev whirled around weapon at the ready. At the same time Danshov brought his weapon up and taking three quick giant steps he came up behind Lee and hit him on the back of the head with the butt of his rifle. Lee went down in a heap on the floor. Danshov brought up his weapon to shoot him.

"NEYT!" shouted Leshev.

Stoney pushed by Leshev and ran down the aisle, to where Lee lay sprawled out on the floor of the cabin. Leshev ran after him and motioned to Danshov, who was swinging his aim between Stoney and Lee. Leshev kept his weapon pointed at Stoney but did not shoot.

Stoney noticed Lee's head was bleeding where Danshov had hit him, so Stoney took out his handkerchief and applied it as a makeshift dressing. Stoney shook Lee to try and wake him up. Slowly, Lee came around, and Stoney helped him into a seat. Lee appeared woozy but muttered that he was OK.

"Let that be a lesson. The next time we will shoot to maim, not kill. I assure you it will be much worse," said Leshev.

"Captain, you can't open that door, I can't open that door. Please let me go get Maria before she freezes to death," Stoney pleaded.

"Open that door and all will be well," was all that Leshev said.

"You can kill every crewmember, all the passengers and all of the airfield support staff, but I am telling you that NO ONE here can open that door. If you try to cut it, blow it up or cut into the fuselage to get to It from outside, this aircraft and everything in it will self-destruct. There is nothing you, me, or anyone else can do!" Stoney explained again.

Looks like a big wrench has been thrown into his plans. I'll bet he thought he'd waltz in here and take whatever he wanted and then would slip away to where ever he came from. I would blow up this plane myself to keep the equipment out of his hands! Only thing is, he might be more dangerous now since his plan seems to be falling apart. Stoney thought as Leshev just stood and stared at him.

After what seemed like hours to Stoney, Leshev broke the silence and said, "Sergeant Danshov, take these people to the same area as the passengers. Release the lady tied to the nose wheel. I am going to the control tower to talk to Moscow."

"All right, you heard the comrade captain; form a line with your hands on your head and go down the stairs. You, airplane captain, you may go first and free the lady. NO funny business!" commanded Sergeant Danshov.

Stoney ran out the door and down the stairs in a desperate attempt to save Maria. About five steps from the bottom he grabbed the right hand rail and vaulted over it and ran toward the nose strut. His heart sank when he saw Maria's lifeless head and arms hanging down pulling at the ropes. Quickly he untied her and her body fell into his arms.

"Maria, Maria" he said repeatedly as he tried to wake her up. When she didn't respond he felt for a pulse and put his ear near her nose and mouth to see if she was breathing.

Nothing. No response at all.

The tears welled up in his eyes as he stood up with her in his arms and joined the rest of the crew waiting at the foot of the stairs.

"Captain, is she . . ." asked Virginia the tears starting to run down her face.

With a slight nod of his head, he walked to the front of the group and headed in the direction indicated by the large Russian sergeant.

I will get you Russian bastards for killing her, some how, some way, thought Stoney.

When they reached the warmth of the cafeteria, Stoney carefully laid Maria on one of the tables along the side of the room and covered her with his coat. Everyone in the cafeteria stood up to pay their respects and Stoney could hear several people quietly weeping. Sergeant Danshov did not bother them for several minutes then he began to bark out orders again.

"Everyone sit down at the tables." Then pointing at Virginia, he said "You make coffee for all," and he motioned her with his rifle to the coffee pot still sitting on the table. Doing her best to keep her composure, Virginia began making a fresh pot of coffee.

When everyone had left the plane, Leshev used his hand held radio to tell Vavilov to meet him at the control tower. He would need the secure radio to contact Moscow for instructions.

When he arrived, Vavilov was there to meet him with the secure radio. He took the radio and told Vavilov to go back to the cafeteria and wait there.

Leshev went out on the control tower balcony to get a clear view of the sky. *Sikovski will not be happy that I am calling him. Only use it in extreme emergency the colonel had warned. Originally, he didn't want me to take the radio at all, but this is just the type of situation that I was planning for when I insisted on bringing it,* thought Leshev as he unpacked his secure radio, setting up the antenna and pointing it in approximately the right direction. When all was ready he picked up the microphone.

"Moscow, this is Dark Night team leader, please come in."

"Dark Night team leader, this is Moscow," said the voice in the speaker.

"I need to speak with Colonel Sikovski on a matter of supreme importance."

"Stand by," replied the voice from the radio.

After what seemed a long time, Leshev heard Sikovski's voice emit from the radio.

"Comrade Captain, what is the problem?"

"We have run into a problem, and I need your decision on how to proceed. The mission has been very successful thus far. The aircraft landed without a problem, and we removed all of the passengers and secured them. We tried to force the crew to open the sensor area as you commanded. However, the airplane captain said in very convincing terms that if we try to open the door the aircraft will self-destruct."

"Captain Leshev, why should you believe him? He is a CIA operative. Of course he will tell you anything he can to protect the equipment, but why do you need me to tell you that?"

"Comrade Colonel, I have killed one of the stewardesses, and the captain did not flinch. He said I could kill everyone, and he could not open the door. His argument is very convincing, and I don't think he would throw away the lives of everyone here by lying to me."

"Stand by, I want to consult with Admiral Ninski."

"Yes, comrade colonel."

★

"Get me Admiral Ninski on the phone immediately!" exclaimed Colonel Sikovski to his aide.

Within a couple of minutes, the light on the secure phone at the desk began to flash.

"Comrade admiral, this is Colonel Sikovski."

"Yes, comrade, how is our operation going?" inquired the admiral.

"We have run into a bit of a problem. Seems the door to the sensor room is booby trapped, and if our team tries to open it then it will destroy the aircraft. While waiting on this call, I took a quick look at the plans we had acquired, and I do believe Captain Leshev is correct and the aircraft will self-destruct if they try to force their way in. The security information on the diagram is encoded but knowing it is booby trapped explains some of the items we were confused about in our original assessment. There were items and extra wiring we couldn't explain before. It is unlike the Americans to put innocents in such danger therefore it did not occur to us they would actually rig the aircraft to explode."

"Then it seems, comrade colonel, that in order to get the knowledge of the sensors, we will have to bring the aircraft to the Motherland. Do you not agree?"

"Yes, admiral, I reached the same conclusion. I do need to ask about the political implications of that action. We have already hijacked a supposed commercial airliner and detained her passengers. If we commandeer the aircraft and the crew to fly her out then the American government will make sure that the whole world knows what we have done. If you will forgive me, I don't think the Politburo will look too kindly on that amount of publicity."

"You are correct. The only way to make this work is to take the aircraft and make it appear that it was lost en route somewhere in the Arctic. Fly it to one of our bases in Siberia and work to get into the sensor equipment without blowing it up. Therefore, you will need to force the crew to fly the aircraft to Siberia, and our job will be to make the world think that it crashed into the Arctic and sank to the bottom of the Arctic Ocean."

"Comrade admiral, you do realize that we will have to kill all of the passengers and dispose of their bodies, yes?"

"No, everyone knows that the aircraft was forced to make an emergency landing. You will have the airfield commander along with the aircraft captain send a joint message to their headquarters saying the passengers remained at the airfield while the crew flew the aircraft to another location for repairs. Since the success of such a flight is not very good, the captain decided not to take anyone but the flight crew. Once it is in flight, Leshev will force the aircrew to make an emergency distress call on the radio giving a false location, then we will continue to jam all of the frequencies, and Leshev will direct the captain to fly to Siberia. Once they arrive and spend time with the KGB in Lubyanka prison, they will disappear. Leshev will keep all the passengers and the airfield crew in the dark about their exact destination and time of departure. Once the airfield crew fails to make their scheduled reports, the Americans will send in a rescue team. By that time the aircraft will be safely in Siberia. Since the aircraft will vanish, the American's will think it did in fact crash and will not be able to prove we have it. If Leshev needs anyone's help before departure, then he will make sure they have an unfortunate accident before he leaves; especially the airfield commander."

"A brilliant plan, comrade admiral; success will be ours!" exclaimed Sikovski.

Returning to the secure radio connection, Sikovski relayed the admiral's plan to Leshev.

Back in the cafeteria, there was a slight murmur around the room as the hostages talked quietly among themselves. Stone, leaning over to talk to Brad, Steve and Lee quietly said, "We have to figure a way out of this. I will bet your bottom dollar that they will want us to fly her out of here and back to Russia. I don't think Leshev is stupid enough to try and open the room here. Their only option is to make us fly it out."

"Afraid you are right, captain. I don't see any other way either," Steve agreed. Just then Stoney saw Captain Leshev walk into the room.

The room fell silent as Leshev began barking out orders in Russian.

"You and you," pointing at Virginia and Brad, "come with me," said Danshov.

They rose from their seats and Virginia gave Stoney a long look for comfort. Brad took her arm as Danshov and his rifle ushered them out.

Captain Leshev turned to his hostages and said, "You, airplane captain and your crew will fly the airplane to a point of our designation where we will release you to your embassy. You will do this since I will have my men plant explosives around the room containing the hostages. The explosives will have a radio controlled detonator on them. Should you not cooperate I will be able to kill them all just by pushing a button. Don't get any ideas since it will

119

work in flight as well as on the ground. I will leave written instructions so that when your army arrives, they will be able to free them from the explosives. So, you see, we Russians are not so heartless after all."

"Our airplane is damaged, that is why we landed here to begin with. We have a damaged engine and we had smoke in the cockpit," Stoney said.

"Yes, I know about the smoke, and that is all that it was—just smoke. A clever little device created by the KGB that proved most effective."

"Even if you take out the 'fire' issue, we still have a damaged engine."

"We will have the mechanics look at it. They will let us know whether we will be flying on three engines or four. To me it does not matter, we are flying out of here in two hours time," responded Leshev.

Once again, Leshev took his radio from its pouch and fired off orders in Russian. Turning to Stoney he added, "You will not say a word about us flying the airplane out of here! If you do, I will tie the other stewardess and two males to stakes in their underwear and let them freeze to death, and it will be your fault! When Vavilov brings the mechanics, we will go and look at the aircraft."

Several minutes later Vavilov arrived with the mechanics and Captain Leshev instructed the aircrew to explain to them the nature of the engine problem. Leshev agreed to let Stone and the mechanics go out to the aircraft to work on it under Vavilov's watchful eye.

"Vavilov, if anyone tries to do anything but work on the aircraft shoot them dead!" Leshev commanded.

"Yes! Comrade captain," responded Vavilov who, using his rifle, motioned for Stoney and the mechanics to get moving.

Stoney, the mechanics and Vavilov walked out to the aircraft. During the walk, Stoney explained to the mechanics that while in flight the number three engine had started to act up and they had to keep increasing the throttle to keep the engine running at the same RPM and eventually it became necessary to shut down the engine after violent shaking and misfiring. When they reached the aircraft the mechanics split up and one went into the cockpit with Stoney and the other went down to the engine. Vavilov entered the aircraft where he could keep an eye on the cockpit crew as well as the mechanic outside.

"Sir, try to start number three engine. I will help with the checklists," said the mechanic. As he said that he slipped into the copilot seat and made a circular motion with his index finger in the window to tell the other mechanic they were going to try starting the engine. He received thumbs up from the guy on the ground and he picked up the Start Engine Checklist and began to read off the items. When they reached the step to press the starter button the blades turned as before and the engine coughed and sputtered but refused to start.

They went through the sequence several times, but the engine refused to start. Everything seemed normal, but the engine still refused to start. After checking the magnetos, left and right, the mechanic instructed Stoney to shut down the electrical system, and he opened the window and yelled down to the other mechanic that they needed to pull the cowling on the engine.

Turning to Vavilov he said, "We need to take the cowling off of the engine so we can get in and see what is wrong. I will need to get equipment and tools from the tool shed."

"Go ahead and get what you need, but make it quick," said Vavilov.

Stoney said that there was nothing more for him to do here and he requested permission to join the others inside. Vavilov talked on his radio, then said, "Go back to the cafeteria."

As Stoney headed back to the main building he saw the mechanics starting to erect the scaffolding they would need to reach the engine.

Once they erected the scaffolding, the mechanics removed the cowling from the engine. It was slow going for the men since they wore insulated overalls and had large gloves on their hands to keep their fingers from freezing.

Once into the inner guts of the engine, they immediately noticed the black smoke/soot around the large ignition module.

"Damn, looks like this thing is not only fried but incinerated," said Justin, the head mechanic in his thick Louisiana Bayou accent.

"They are lucky those fuel hoses didn't start to melt or they would've had a catastrophic fire in here," replied Mark.

"I know we have one of those in our parts kits. Go ahead and start the removal while I get the part," said Justin as he climbed down the ladder and went into the maintenance shelter to look through his parts supply.

Stoney quickly walked back to the main building. As he walked, his brain was going a mile-a-minute as he tried to think of a way out of this mess.

I am a bloody airplane pilot, not a CIA operative—Damn it! I need a squad of Marines to get us out of this. But since he knew there wasn't going to be a rescue any time soon and certainly not before he was forced to fly to Russia, he got down to business trying to come up with a plan. He hadn't gotten very far when he reached the door of the building. Once inside, he made his way to the door guarded by Corporal Osinov, which happened to be the cafeteria.

Osinov kept his rifle leveled at Stoney as he opened the door and walked in. Osinov shut the door behind him.

Entering the room, he saw the passengers and some other people he did not know sitting at tables conversing among themselves. Though he had been here before, he hadn't really noticed the room since he was blinded by the emotion of Maria's senseless death.

The room's walls were a light brown color, similar to the color in the hallway. There were several long tables with chairs and a typical cafeteria style serving line along the back wall. The door to the kitchen was at one end of the line. *I wonder what they did with Maria's body?* he thought as he scanned the room.

"Hey captain, welcome back. Can you tell us what's going on?" said Mike Whiteman who happened to be sitting nearest the door.

"Hi Mike, if everyone will quiet down I'll fill you in," said Stoney and immediately the room became silent.

"Before I get started, is that a pot of coffee over there?"

"Yes, sir though it's kind of old," said a man Stoney didn't recognize.

"It smells good to me, I'm freezing, these uniform coats are not the warmest things in town," said Stoney as he walked over to the pot. Grabbing a cup and pouring the hot liquid into it he wrapped his hands around it to warm them up.

"Captain, here's a blanket if it will help," said John Lilliman.

"Thanks much" said Stoney as he set down the cup and wrapped the blanket around himself. After taking a few sips of the coffee, he said, "You're right this stuff has been cooking quite a while, but it is warm. OK, right now the mechanics are working on the number three engine to find out why it quit. We tried to start it again, but no luck so they are tearing into it right now. I don't know what our hosts have in store for us but . . ."

"Everyone must get up and form two lines!" yelled Danshov from across the room. Stoney stopped in mid-sentence and walked over to him as everyone else got up from their seats and started to form two lines.

"Why can't we stay here?" Stoney asked.

"I have orders to move everyone to a secure room."

By now Osinov had entered the room and both he and Danshov marched the group down the hall to another room. Once everyone was inside, Danshov shut the door and Stoney heard the lock click.

The room erupted with people talking all at once.

Climbing onto a chair Stoney said, "Everyone quiet down, we may only have a few minutes without them hearing us. Who is in charge of the airfield crew?"

A tall man whose face looked like he had just finished a heavy weight boxing match walked over holding out his hand.

"I am Mike Hudson the assistant commander. Kent James is our commander but Leshev took him to the control tower before you arrived and we haven't seen him since."

"Nice to meet you, I am Victor Stone, but please call me Stoney. If you don't mind me asking, what happened to you?"

"I had an accident with one of the Russian's boots after I put a choke hold on one of them and pushed the point of a knife into his back—he didn't take too kindly to it."

"Thanks for trying, I'm just glad they didn't shoot you. What can you tell me about this room?"

"They did shoot one of my men in the leg. Fortunately, the bullet passed straight through the fleshy part. I am sure it hurt like hell, but no permanent damage. This is our main storage room. There is only one way in and one way out," said Hudson.

"Do you have any weapons on the airfield at all?"

"No, the big bosses in Washington decided that it would not be a good idea."

"Is there anything on the base that we can use as weapons?"

"No, sir, do you know what their plans are for us?"

"Yes, they are going to keep you locked up here and make us fly the airplane to Russia. They are going to booby trap the room so that no one can get out. They said they would leave an instruction sheet for the rescue team that is sure to come when you don't make your regular communication times. Everyone listen. DO NOT let on that you know their plans as Leshev said he would take out reprisals on everyone. Mike, what is over this room? Is there anyway to get out through the ceiling?"

"There's a dead space above this room, but above that is the roof. It's metal, and there's no way through it."

125

"What about the other side of these walls?"

"There are more storage areas and some of the sleeping quarters. These are standard walls with nothing but Sheetrock and wall studs supporting them."

"That will be your way out. Surely, the Russians don't expect us to tear down the walls to get out of here."

The door opened and Captain Leshev came in with a man Stoney did not recognize leading the way. As quickly as he came in, Captain Leshev departed and locked the door behind him.

"Kent, where have you been, and what is going on out there? But first let me introduce you to Captain Stone," said Mike Hudson.

Stoney stuck out his hand and said, "Glad to meet you Kent, please call me Stoney."

James shook Stoney's hand as he replied, "Nice to meet you Stoney, wish it was under different circumstances." Looking at Hudson, he added, "What the hell happened to you?"

"I tried to take out one of the guards after you left. I lost! They shot Jack in the leg to punish me. He is OK; it was just a flesh wound."

"Where is Jack and how is he doing?"

"I'm here sir, the leg hurts like hell, but eventually they did let us get a first-aide kit to clean and dress it. I won't be running any marathons any time soon, but I'll be all right," said Jack.

"I am glad it wasn't any more serious then that. I want to take these guys out as much as anyone here, but we don't need any dead heroes. Anyway, after I guided 28-Alpha to a landing, Leshev tied me to a pipe and left me there. About fifteen minutes ago he came back and took me to the radio room to make the periodic communication to

126

Washington and after that he brought me here. I made sure to make the check-in message slightly late in timing the transmission. Not late enough to cause Leshev's alarm bells to go off, but later than usual. I am hoping the communications officer will notice that it was late and will realize something is amiss since I am normally very punctual. Maybe it will cause enough concern for them to do a little checking. Since no one is manning the radios, they will get no answer if they try to check in with us. That should cause them to be more concerned, at least I hope so."

"That was a good idea on the almost late check-in. Before we had smoke in the cockpit, we had had trouble contacting Polar Control. Obviously we have not checked in and the time they were expecting us has long since passed. That, along with your 'late' communication, could indeed set off alarm bells," said Stoney.

"HQ is particular about regular communications, and I would bet they are making phone calls right now to ascertain if there is a problem. What with abnormally late communications from here, and no communication from the plane with Polar Control, all that put together should get someone's attention. Do you have any thoughts on getting us out of this mess?"

"Right now, I was concentrating on getting us out of this room. Mike, here, says the ceiling is not a good idea but based on what he told me, seems the walls may be a way out," replied Stoney.

"Stoney, what about the explosives that Leshev mentioned?" asked Steve who was standing nearby.

"We will need to try and break out before they get them in place. Their well oiled plan has already developed several kinks. Let's see if we can continue to provide obstacles—that is until help arrives."

CHAPTER 11

In the bowels of the NSA, Tom Train was sitting in his spacious executive office, working on routine correspondence with Congress regarding funding issues for the Northern Star program. Several members of the Senate Armed Services Committee had recently begun to question the ethics of intelligence gathering using civilian airliners and fare-paying passengers as cover.

They understood that the Northern Star program had produced reams of valuable intelligence, but they were beginning to feel that the ethical aspects of the program were starting to outweigh the intelligence gathered. They concluded that the new generation of satellites could provide the required intelligence without the need to put passengers in harm's way.

Train's task was to continue to provide justification to keep the program alive. He felt, as did his CIA counterpart, that the intelligence was indeed valuable and with the funds already put into the program to develop the sensor equipment, it justified the continuance of the program. He did, however, realize that they had been lucky, so far, that the aircraft had performed flawlessly.

In the five years of the program, no accidents, incidents or emergencies had occurred. Additionally, Kauffman's equipment had been performing flawlessly and the quality of the intelligence would become much better thanks to the newly installed upgrades. Overall, Train felt the taxpayer's money was well spent since the quality of the intelligence had kept the Soviets from doing anything adventurous or politically unwise, so far.

Ring, ring . . . ring, ring . . . Train picked up his secure phone.

"This is Smith, down in communications. It appears we may have a situation. Flight 28-Alpha departed Victoria on schedule, and they checked in with air traffic control. However, as the flight proceeded, 28-Alpha attempted to check in with Polar Control during a routine position report, but there was enough interference that they could not really communicate. Polar Control told the flight to proceed to the next check-in point where another communications outlet is located. So far they have not checked in. Additionally, Emergency Airfield 'Q' has made one communications check-in on time, however their most recent one was later than normal, but not late enough where it would be considered actually late. However, the late flight and the lateness of the last airfield check in are beginning to cause concern. I wanted to let you know what was up and see what you thought."

"Thanks for calling. I'll come down to the comm room. Please call Mr. Burton at CIA and ask him to get here ASAP."

Hanging up the phone, Train grabbed his suit coat and headed down the hallway to the elevator; next stop, the communications area. When he reached the elevator, he inserted his coded ID card which let the elevator know which floors he could access. He pressed the B1 button for the communications area located in the basement of the building. Noiselessly, the elevator started down the shaft. His ID card also told the elevator that he was a priority passenger so it automatically bypassed all other floors and ignored all other elevator calls.

Several seconds later, the doors opened to a long hallway illuminated by recessed florescent light. The scene almost reminded him of the long white corridors common to hospitals of the day. However the U.S. Marine security guard who was pointing his machine gun directly at him brought him back to reality. In response, Train held out his ID card which the guard inspected and then checked the name against a list of personnel with access to the area.

"Good morning, Mr. Train. Have a nice day," the guard said as he lowered his weapon and handed the ID card back. The protocol for getting off the elevator and showing ID to the guard was scripted and failure to follow it resulted in the offender immediately being handcuffed and detained.

"Thanks, George, Mr. Burton should be here in a few minutes. Please ask him to come down to room B45," Train said.

"Can do, sir."

Train headed down the hall to B45 and as he walked, he thought about all of the things that could have gone wrong with 28-Alpha. Kauffman had not gotten back to him on his testing results and this had begun to bother him. He walked up to room B45, took his ID card and pressed it to the door plate. The red light turned green and the door slid noiselessly open and Train stepped through.

"Good morning, Mr. Train," Smith said. "I wish I had better news for you."

"Good morning, Smith; why don't you fill me in."

"Other than what I told you over the phone, there has been no further communication from the aircraft. Their transponder code has not shown up on radar. You know we have somewhat spotty radar coverage along the route anyway, that is why the co-pilots use celestial navigation and then they manually transmit those coordinates to Polar Control during their regular check-ins. Over here we have a plot of those check-ins correlated with our somewhat spotty radar data and I have plotted their course on this wall map."

Train followed Smith over to the wall where the map was hanging.

"Let me fill you in on all of the information I have at this time. The red line is 28-Alpha's documented course prior to communications failure. This first black 'X' is approximately where Polar Control reported they heard from 28-Alpha but were unable to pass any information. Polar Control did manage to tell them to wait until they got closer to the next radio communications outlet before attempting communications again."

"Isn't it unusual for Polar Control to lose radio contact during these flights?" said Train.

"Yes sir, it is very unusual. As you know, we have standing agreements with Polar Control regarding communications and these flights. They contacted me right after their failure to communicate with 28-Alpha."

"OK, please continue."

"28-Alpha acknowledged that message, and they estimated that it would be about sixty minutes later in the flight before they would try again. To reiterate, that is the first 'X' on the map. The aircraft never checked in again with Polar Control. Using all available information we have drawn a projected course line, depicted in blue, showing where they should be. The 'X' along that line is their projected location sixty minutes down their track where they should have been able to contact Polar Control. Additionally, we have drawn a circle around the first 'X' using their projected fuel reserves which shows where they could have gone if they deviated from their course. We have no indication that there was a mechanical failure causing them to go down off airport."

"Have we received any distress calls or emergency locator beacons in that area?" asked Train.

"No sir and standard procedure at Polar Control is to monitor the locator beacon frequencies at all times. If one had gone off, they would know about it."

"OK, so we're pretty sure they didn't go down, but we don't know their status either?" said Train.

"That is correct, however as you will notice, there are several emergency airfields along their path and within range. Based on my calculations and approximate positions, airfield 'Q' is the most likely place for them to put down. This is where things get interesting. As you know, there are regularly scheduled communications check-ins to ensure that all is well with each emergency airfield during a scheduled Northern Star flight."

Just then, Train heard the door open and looking in that direction saw Glen Burton walk into the communications room.

"Good morning Glen, sorry to ask you to hurry over here, but it appears we may have a situation with flight 28-Alpha," said Train.

"Good morning Tom. I got here as quickly as I could," said Burton.

"Smith, here, was just giving me an overview of the situation. Bottom line is, flight 28-Alpha has not checked in with Polar Control, and there are no transponder codes or returns showing on radar at Polar Control. Smith, go ahead and pick up there."

"Good morning Mr. Burton; as I was saying, alternate airfield 'Q' made their regularly scheduled check-in this morning. However, their subsequent check-in was so late that we were just about to consider it as missed. I personally know the airfield manager, Kent James, and for him to check in late is cause for concern. Knowing him, he would try to make us aware of a problem via the unsecure communications network if there was something that would prevent his normal check-in, say an equipment malfunction. He would maintain COMSEC, but he would let us know and then he would check in as soon as possible. He did not do that. As I mentioned, he did check in, but he just barely made the cut-off time. Given what I said previously, a late check-in would not be that much of a concern, however, combined with the peculiar circumstances surrounding 28-Alpha, it elevates both anomalies to worrisome. Given that 'Q' appears to be the best alternative airfield based on position reports and my projections, and the low probability of simultaneous communications failures at 'Q' and 28-Alpha, I pushed the panic button."

"I think I can speak for both of us, I am glad that you did. These are most peculiar circumstances, and until we definitively know about the status of 28-Alpha, we have to assume they are on the ground somewhere. The problem is finding out where. Glen, do we have any indications from the Soviets that they may be planning to get their hands on one of our birds or any other abnormal radio or communications traffic that could hint they may be up to something?" Train asked.

"There has been scuttlebutt for years that they wanted to get their hands on the sensor technology. However, having a plane full of civilians on it has always kept them at bay. The political pressure of taking them hostage or even hijacking the flight has been too much for the General Secretary to agree to. Their political stance in the world is not very healthy, and this new General Secretary has made it his goal to improve their standing with the world bodies. That said, however, there are elements within the military and KGB that would gladly sacrifice world political capital to acquire our technology, even against the General Secretary's wishes. The KGB chief is powerful enough with friends on the Politburo that even the General Secretary wouldn't dare smack him down. Bottom line is, yes, I do believe they would do anything to get one of those Constellations."

"We will need to proceed cautiously since this could easily escalate to the White House. Glen, I need you to inform your higher ups that we believe the Soviets may have hijacked or somehow taken control of flight 28-Alpha. I will do the same. I would like to propose that we send a squad of Arctic Marines to alternate airfield 'Q' to have a look around."

"Smith, I presume that you have attempted non-secure communications with 'Q'?" inquired Burton.

"Yes, and as of this time we have had no response to our attempts. There is one more piece of information that I need to pass along as well. According to Polar Control, when 28-Alpha initially tried to contact them, there was a lot of interference on that particular frequency. Standard procedure is for them to try the alternate frequency, and it seems that, too, had a lot of interference on it. It is most unusual to have interference of that magnitude on VHF frequencies, and for the alternate to have issues as well is quite concerning. I am of the opinion that a radio jammer of some sort could be involved," said Smith.

"Then it is settled. We will handle this as a hijacking with the Soviets as suspect number one. Glen, please get the ball rolling with the CIA, and I will do the same with NSA. I think we need to bring the Director of Intelligence and the National Security Advisor in on this as well. I will ask my Deputy Director of Operations to initiate those calls once I have briefed him. Smith, you need to continue to try and make contact with both 28-Alpha and 'Q' by any means at your disposal including contacting Polar Control. Tell them to notify you immediately with any status change regarding 28-Alpha, but also tell them we will handle any rescue attempt should it be necessary; I do not want International Rescue teams alerted. Also tell the Polar Control Manager that he is *not* to respond to any media requests or information requests from anyone but you. Keep me informed as to any change in status. When is the next regular check-in due from 'Q'?" Train said.

"They are not due to check in for at least four hours," replied Smith.

"We cannot wait that long. I will brief the Deputy Director of Operations for CIA and ask him to add his blessing for a reconnaissance mission to 'Q'," said Burton.

"I am headed back to my office to make those calls. Glen, we'll use my office as a command post until we get this problem solved. Come on up. I'll have the secretary put on a new pot of coffee. I have a feeling this is going to be a long day," and with that Train headed out the door and back to the elevator.

When he arrived at his office Train instructed his secretary to put on a fresh pot of coffee and to call the Deputy Director of Operations (DDO) and arrange a quick meeting.

A couple of minutes later, the secretary buzzed him on the intercom and announced that the DDO was in and could see him. Train got up from his desk and after adjusting his tie in the mirror, headed out the door.

"Hold all calls except from Smith down in the communications room. If he calls, forward it to the DDO's office immediately, Sarah," Train said as he walked out the door.

Besides being a very striking blond with long slender legs, Sarah was a very efficient secretary. She kept his office running like a well oiled machine. He did take notice that most of the men on his floor would go out of their way to walk by his office just to get a glimpse of those shapely legs. He had heard a rumor that every single guy on the floor had asked her out on a least one occasion; he didn't doubt that it was true. Heck, even his wife had given him grief about her when he first hired Sarah.

After they had mingled at a few office parties, his wife learned that she was all business and under no circumstances would she date or be involved with someone at the office. Hence the reason that the guys kept asking and she kept saying "No."

"Yes, sir," Sarah replied.

Hurrying down the hallway he formulated his quick brief to the DDO. Normally the DDO liked to see overhead charts and graphs when being briefed, but there was no time to put that together this morning. Unlike the previous people to hold that position, this DDO was easy to get along with, and he handled emergencies in a very logical manner. He did not jump to conclusions, and he usually went along with subordinate's advice. Train hoped that would be the case this morning.

Taking the elevator to the top floor, Train stepped out into an office suite that would make any corporate executive envious. He walked over to the DDO's secretary who said, "Go on in, Mr. Train, the DDO is expecting you."

"Good morning, sir," Train said as he walked into the spacious office.

"Good morning, Tom, I understand there is an issue with one of your Northern Star flights?"

"Unfortunately sir, there are several signs pointing in that direction."

"Sit down and fill me in."

Train sat down in the overstuffed leather chair and explained the situation to the DDO.

"What course of action do you recommend?"

"Sir, if you recall, the Northern Star program provides funds for a platoon of Arctic Marines based out of Elmendorf Air Force Base. I think we should send a C-130 from Elmendorf with a squad of those Marines to airfield Quebec. They would check out the airfield and see if they can determine what's going on up there, and if necessary, protect our personnel and the Northern Star aircraft, if it is there. I wouldn't be surprised to find the Soviets are somehow behind the current events."

"Go ahead and call the commander at Elmendorf and fill him in on our situation. Since the Air Force and the Marines will be involved, I will call the Secretary of Defense and then give the secretaries of the Air Force and Navy a call to let them know their folks may be headed for trouble. Keep me informed of any changes at 'Q' or if you hear from 28-Alpha."

"Will do sir, thanks for the support, and we'll let you know of any changes in the situation." The meeting concluded, Train got up and walked out the door. On his way past, he heard the DDO buzz his secretary to get the Secretary of Defense on the line.

CHAPTER 12

"**C**orporal, can I use your radio to talk to Captain Leshev?" asked the head mechanic.

Pulling the radio out of his pocket, Vavilov said, "Comrade captain, the mechanic needs to talk to you."

"Yes Vavilov, what is it?" replied Leshev's voice.

Vavilov handed the radio to the mechanic who said, "Captain, we have replaced the burned out module, however, there is a lot of heat damage to surrounding wiring harnesses. I cannot guarantee the engine will run correctly without replacing them. You could be faced with another in flight failure."

"How long will it take?" said Leshev.

"About three more hours."

The radio's speaker erupted in a torrent of Russian at which point the mechanic quickly handed it back to Vavilov as if it were a hot rock burning his hand.

Several exchanges later, Vavilov said, "Go ahead but make it quick!"

"I will make it as *quick* as I can," replied the mechanic hoping Vavilov hadn't caught the sarcasm in his voice.

You bet your Russian ass I'll make it quick—about as quick as a salmon swimming up stream! thought the mechanic as he went to get the needed parts from the maintenance shed.

★

"Danshov, since we have about three more hours before departure, I want you to go and look in James' office to see if there is any useful information there. We might as well bring back all that we can. I am going to the communications room and look in there," said Leshev.

"Yes sir. I will meet up with you in the communications room."

Walking toward the office, Danshov passed the sleeping quarters and realized he needed to go to the bathroom. He walked into the closest one, found the bathroom and started relieving himself.

What the devil is that strange noise? If I were in my tenement in Moscow I would call the building kommissar and complain about the rats again.

Zipping up his fly, he suddenly realized what the noise could in fact be. He yanked his radio out of his pocket and said, "Comrade captain, meet me at the hostage room—and hurry!"

Stuffing the radio back in his pocket he ran to the locked storage room. Osinov was standing guard at the door and Danshov held his finger to his lips to keep him quiet.

They waited at the door and Leshev came running up a few seconds later. Danshov held his finger up to his lips telling Leshev they should be quiet, Danshov whispered, "I think the rats are trying to escape. I heard noises when I was in the crew quarters."

Leshev nodded in understanding and indicated they should go in. Osinov slowly turned the key in the lock and all at once they burst into the room.

Danshov saw everyone's back as the door opened and just as suddenly they all turned around to face him and the captain.

"What the hell is going on in here?" thundered Leshev.

"Everyone move away from the back wall," added Danshov as he and Osinov brought up their weapons in a menacing fashion.

The sea of hostages parted and plain as day were the fresh holes in the Sheetrock. Danshov saw white powder on the hands and pants of several of the men, including Stone.

Leshev pointed to one of the white powdered men and said, "You come here!"

The man walked up and as soon as he was close enough, Danshov, who had made a fist behind his back, drove a right upper cut into the unsuspecting man's jaw with the lightening speed of a cat. The man fell backwards to the floor. Danshov took several steps forward and aimed his rifle at the man's head.

"Leshev don't shoot him; this was my idea; take it out on me!" said Stone as he rushed forward through the crowd.

"What is your name?" Danshov asked the man on the floor.

"BBB.r..a..d," replied the man slowly as blood ran down the corner of his mouth from his busted lip.

"Well Stone, say good bye to Brad," said Leshev.

"WAIT! Don't shoot him, it was my plan!" said Stone.

"Why not, I need you but I don't need him,"

"Don't shoot him and I give you my word that no one will try to escape again."

After several long seconds, Leshev said, "Fine, but if *anyone* breaks your word, then I will shoot three random people. You, pointing to the man on the ground get up and bring me that rope lying on the shelf over there."

Stone reached out a hand and helped Brad stagger to his feet.

"Osinov take the rope and cut it into pieces to tie everyone up with. Stone you will tie up each person and Danshov will check to make sure they are secure," said Leshev.

Osinov pulled out his knife and cut the rope Brad had retrieved. As he cut each piece he handed them to Stone who had each person, in turn, put their hands behind them and he tied them as loosely secured as he could. He didn't want to cut off circulation, but he didn't want Danshov to complain either.

Danshov checked each one, with everyone tied up, Leshev instructed them to sit on the floor facing the walls. He told Stoney to follow him, and they went out the door. Danshov locked the door after it closed behind them.

Turning to Corporal Osinov, Leshev erupted in a torrent of Russian and Stoney could see the young Corporal quaking in his boots. *Leshev is reaming him for our escape attempt. Oh, well,* thought Stoney.

When Leshev finished with Osinov, he paused and then he addressed Stoney.

"Captain Stone, your mechanics are almost through with the repair work. We will start all of the engines to make sure that everything is set for our flight. How much fuel do you have left?"

"Where do you want to fly?" asked Stoney.

"That is not your concern just now. How many kilometers will she fly with the fuel on board?"

"I don't know. We will need to check the gauges and calculate a range."

"Well then, Captain Stone, let's get started," said Leshev as he indicated that Stoney should lead the way to the aircraft.

Once they arrived, they walked over to the scaffolding to see how the repairs were coming.

"Well sir, we have replaced the ignition control module, and are about a third of the way through replacing wiring harnesses that were damaged by the excessive heat in the engine cowling," replied the head mechanic.

"Good job fellas, wish we could have her in a nice warm hanger for you. Keep up the good work, and let us know as soon as she's ready," said Stoney.

Turning toward the stairs, Stoney led Leshev up into the aircraft. The door was stiff as Stoney tried to open it—*the cold*—he thought as he struggled to get it open. They walked into the aircraft and had to wrestle the door shut behind them. Walking into the cockpit, Stoney sat down at the engineer's panel and began to look at the fuel gauges. He wrote down some figures on a scratch pad. He then picked up Lee's Flight Computer and performed some calculations. After several minutes, he looked up at Leshev and said they had a seven hundred kilometer range before empty tanks. "Where did you say we were going?" he asked.

"I did not say, and will not say until we are airborne. Just suffice it to say that we need to fuel the aircraft before departure," said Leshev.

"You realize that the engines must also be warmed before we can even try to start them," commented Stoney.

"How long will that take?"

"At least an hour," replied Stoney.

"The fueling process must be started now. How many men do you need?"

"I don't know how this airfield operates. I don't even know where the fuel is stored or how it is stored. We need Kent James to set that up."

"Then we will go and ask him. Lead the way." Stoney headed to the door with Leshev right behind him. He wasn't brandishing his pistol, but Stoney was smart enough to not try anything.

Once again, they forced the door open and started down the stairs, carefully closing the door behind them. After climbing down the stairs they headed for the holding area. Opening the door to the building, Stoney thought about the mechanics that had been working out in the cold. He made a mental note to ensure HQ rewarded them when this was all over. He entered the building and walking down the corridor they came to the locked room. Danshov and Osinov were standing outside keeping an eye on things. When Stoney and Leshev approached, they jumped to attention and Osinov proceeded to unlock the door. Leshev and Danshov entered the room leaving Stoney and Osinov in the hallway.

When James came stumbling out the door, Stoney grabbed him by the upper arm to help him keep from falling.

"Kent, how is everyone?"

"As well as can be expected."

"Captain Leshev, is there any way you could see fit to allow our medical man to give morphine shots to the man that was shot as well as the one who lost the finger? Their dressings need to be changed as well."

Through the open doorway, Leshev barked out something in Russian and then he shut the door leaving Danshov inside the room.

"They will be tended to," said Leshev.

"Kent, we need to have the aircraft fueled and the engines pre-heated in preparation for take-off. I do not want to involve any more of your personnel than is absolutely necessary. Can you and I and the mechanics handle the refueling and engine heating tasks?" inquired Stoney.

"Yes, we can. However the pre-heating will take at least half an hour to setup and at least an hour to adequately warm the engines. The fueling will take no less than an hour since we have to fill the tanks from fifty gallon drums of fuel. Fortunately we don't have to hand pump the fuel, the truck has an engine powered one. All in all, we're looking at no less than two and a half hours from now before you can leave."

"Turn around," commanded Leshev.

Kent James turned around and Captain Leshev cut his bonds with one quick stroke of his knife. When Leshev pulled out his knife, Stoney was wishing he could get his hands on it. He needed to figure a way out of this mess. The last thing he wanted to do was fly the Constellation to

145

where ever Leshev had in mind, and Stoney was willing to bet that was Mother Russia.

He knew that he and the crew would never make it out alive. The whole world or at least the American Government would think that they had perished in an aircraft accident. No one would come looking for them, and they would simply vanish. He knew that he needed to keep stalling as long as possible. The longer he could keep that airplane on the ground the better for all involved. That was the strategy that he had worked out with James the last time they had had a minute alone.

"Mr. James, I will give you an hour and a half to get that aircraft ready for flight. I intend to be airborne as soon as possible from when the maintenance work is completed. Do not try to stall me. I wouldn't want to stake a few hostages out in the weather for you to watch die while you fuel and warm the aircraft," Leshev said icily.

James threw Stoney a glance of understanding and then said "Captain Leshev, it is possible that rushing around with fuel and pre-heating the engines could result in an accident which might cause your prize to go up in flames. Assuming you don't want that to happen, I would suggest you withdraw your threat and let us do our job!"

"Mr. James, do not presume to tell me what I can or cannot do! I want that aircraft ready to go as soon as possible, and I will do what is necessary to make that happen! I will shoot everyone in that room if I have to! DO WE UNDERSTAND EACH OTHER?" thundered Leshev, his face turning redder by the second.

"Shall we get started, or is it more productive for you two to stand there and scream at each other?" asked Stoney.

"Yes, we shall proceed. Let's go and see how the mechanics are doing. The two of you will refuel the aircraft while they are working," Leshev said, his face starting to return to a normal color. With that, he motioned for the two hostages to lead the way back to the aircraft.

"Kent, are there any extra gloves and a heavy coat I could borrow?" inquired Stoney.

"If the good captain will allow us to stop by the clothing supply room, I believe I can help you."

"Da," was all Leshev said in response to the request.

By now, Sergeant Danshov had left the hostage room and was standing near Leshev. "Danshov, I want you to come with us to help me watch them. Osinov keep an eye on the hostages and call Vavilov to join you."

"Yes, comrade captain, I will call him now," said Osinov as he pulled out his radio and began speaking in Russian.

Captain Leshev, satisfied his orders would be carried out, motioned for Stoney and James to start moving. James led them down another corridor to the clothing supply room. Opening the door, they turned on the light and Stoney went over to the rack of parkas and selected one that would fit. He also picked up a pair of warm gloves and put them on as well. Once outfitted, James led the group back outside to the aircraft.

Once outside, Stoney walked up to the aircraft and asked the mechanics how things were going.

"We have the new ignition module installed and will finish up with the last wiring harness in about ten minutes."

"We are going to start the refueling process. We'll take the help when you get that buttoned back up," said James.

"Yes, sir." came the reply.

James and Stoney headed to the supply shed to get the fuel drums. Since this was only an emergency field, the fuel was stored in drums since it was easier and cheaper than building a tank area. The only drawback was they had to bring out the drums using a forklift and a small flatbed truck which had a built-in fuel pump powered by the engine. They had to attach the fuel hose to each drum, in sequence, and then utilizing the pump, had to pump fuel into the wing and tip tanks. When a drum was empty, they had to turn off the pump, move the hoses and begin the sequence again. Since the tanks were fairly empty, it would take almost the entire fuel dump to fill them. Once they got started, it was obvious that James had been correct on the fueling time. He didn't need to fudge on the time as it was going to take all of the hour and then some to get the drums to the airplane and emptied into the tanks.

Standing where he could see the entire operation, Leshev was sorry he had not paid more attention to the work the ground crews did to prepare the aircraft he flew on during the winter. He was sure that James was trying to slow down his departure. *In a vain hope the Americans would rescue them.* Leshev thought quietly to himself.

He did not know if Stone and James were telling him the truth about this engine warming process. He did know that if he didn't allow it, and the cold damaged the engines causing the aircraft to crash, he would have a long cold train ride to that gulag in Siberia.

Assuming they survived the crash long enough to be rescued.

Personally, he would rather take the time to heat the engines and fly this aircraft to Siberia where his superiors would hail him for a job well done. He had already decided that if the Americans did not cooperate he would shoot them all and wait for Moscow to fly in an aircrew to bring the aircraft back to Russia. He knew that Moscow would back him on that decision whether he asked permission or not.

CHAPTER 13

Train was sitting at his desk trying to put a plan together when the intercom buzzed, "Sir, I have the DDO on the phone for you," said his secretary.

"Sir, what news do you have?" asked Train.

"Tom, we have the go-ahead from the SECDEF. He is putting out an emergency message to the Elmendorf Base Commander as well as the Arctic Marine Contingent Commander, and he is putting them at our disposal. I need you to set up a secure teleconference with them and fill them in on all details of the situation. Make sure that I am back-briefed so I can fill in the SECDEF. Remember, we cannot afford any civilian casualties. Also, do not let any of this leak to the press, the last thing we need is for it be tomorrow's headline in the *Washington Post*!"

"We will keep all information as tight as possible. There should be no reason for the press to be involved. We will have to debrief the passengers once we get them home. However, in the mean time, we'll get hold of Elmendorf and get the Marines on their way. Thank you for the help, sir."

"Keep me informed, Tom. I am sure we will be informing the White House, and we'll need all of the information current."

"Yes, sir," was the reply as Train hung up the phone. He got up from his desk and entered the outer office.

"Sarah, I am heading back down to the communications room. Please set up a secure teleconference with the Elmendorf Air Force Base Commander and the Commander of the Arctic Marine contingent. Have it piped into the communications room as soon as you get it set up. I should be there in a few minutes." For the second time that morning, Train headed to the elevator that would take him down to the communications room.

Entering the communications area, he saw Glen Burton on the phone. Tom walked over to Smith and asked if there was any additional information.

"No, sir still no communication from the aircraft. We are not scheduled to hear from 'Q' for at least two hours."

"My secretary is setting up a secure teleconference with Elmendorf Air Force Base, which phone can I use?"

"I will set you and Mr. Burton up in my office. I have a secure speaker-phone there," Smith said.

Turning to Burton who had hung up the phone, Smith asked them to follow him to his office. With Train and Burton in tow, Smith headed to the opposite end of the room where the glass enclosed office he called home was located. Entering the office, both Train and Burton immediately noticed all of Smith's civil service awards decorating the wall. Obviously, Smith had been around for quite a while, and he was good at his job.

There was a medium-sized conference table in the middle of the office. Train and Burton both took chairs around it and sat down. Smith sat at the end closest to the secure phone, so he could answer the call when it came through.

While they were waiting, Train told Burton about his earlier conversation with the Deputy Director of Operations. Just as he was getting to the end, the phone rang, and Smith pressed the "Speaker" button.

The phone made some strange noises as it tried to establish a secure connection with the phone at the other end. After ten to fifteen seconds of these strange noises, a rather tinny sounding voice on the other end said, "This is Colonel Tomlinson's office; to whom am I speaking?"

"This is Tom Train, NSA and Mr. Glen Burton, CIA along with Mr. Smith, NSA Communications Chief," replied Train.

"Please standby for Colonel Tomlinson and Colonel Miller," said the tinny-sounding voice.

"Roger," replied Smith.

"Mr. Train, Mr. Burton, and Mr. Smith, this is Colonel Tomlinson and beside me is Colonel Miller. Can you please fill us in on the events surrounding our current situation? The SECDEF has requested that we provide you assistance in some sort of search and rescue operation."

"Colonel Tomlinson and Colonel Miller, we are grateful for your cooperation. Mr. Burton and I are the co-program managers for the Northern Star Program. Have you been briefed on that program?" asked Tom.

"Yes, Mr. Train, we have both pulled up a synopsis of the program and are relatively familiar with it."

"Well, sirs then I won't waste your time with those details. If during my briefing I use a term or say something that is unfamiliar please stop me. About zero-nine-hundred, Victoria B.C. time, Northern Star Flight 28-Alpha departed Victoria Airport en route to London . . ." Tom took the next fifteen minutes and filled the colonels in on the events leading up to the conference call.

"Thank you Mr. Train, if you will standby I am going to mute the phone and discuss this with Colonel Miller," said Tomlinson.

"No problem sir, please take your time."

There was a dull click, and the phone went quiet. Turning to Tom, Glen said he felt the brief went well, and there should be no problems getting their support. About that time, the dull click sounded again and Colonel Tomlinson began to speak.

"Colonel Miller and I have discussed your request. I have a fueled C-130 sitting on the ramp and Colonel Miller said he has a squad of Arctic Marines ready and available to launch within a thirty-minute window. If you give the word now, we can have it airborne within that window and headed to airfield 'Q'. Once airborne, we anticipate about two and a half hours en route time. Can you have your folks fax over the airfield diagram with appropriate frequencies?"

"Yes sir, we feel this is the only way to ascertain the current condition and location of 28-Alpha, her crew and passengers. Please remember that we do not positively know that the aircraft is on the ground, however all factors point to it being at 'Q'. Additionally, this will allow us to positively ascertain the condition of airfield 'Q'. Please have your operations folks send a telex to the NSA communications room when the assets are airborne. I would make sure they are prepared for potential hostilities with Russian troops, specifically Spetsnaz Special Forces. I will have the information you requested sent as soon as we've concluded this conference."

"Mr. Train, we are already two steps ahead of you on that one. We will send a telex when they are airborne. Unless you object, I think this ends the conference, and we'll get to work."

"Yes sir, thanks again, and we will be looking for that telex." Smith pressed a button on the phone to cut the connection.

Turning to Glen, Train said "That went well. Now all we can do is sit back and wait. Smith, do you mind if we camp out here?"

"No sir, my office is your office as long as you need it."

Picking up the phone, Train called Sarah and asked her to have the operations folks send the information that Colonel Tomlinson had asked for.

While the two program managers continued to discuss the situation and the potential impact on the program as a whole, Smith got up and emptied the old pot of coffee that had been "cooking" all morning. Minutes later the smell of fresh coffee made both Train and Burton realize that lunch had come and gone. They called up to the cafeteria and had some sandwiches sent down to the communications area. Both men knew that it was going to be a long afternoon and night.

Much sooner than they expected, the teletype machine started to make a racket out in the main communications area. Train got up and rushed out to see if it was the airborne confirmation from Elmendorf. When the communications specialist ripped the paper from the machine and handed it to him, he gave a thumbs-up sign to Burton through the window. It was indeed the airborne confirmation message.

Twenty minutes, not bad at all. Hopefully the rest of the mission will go as smoothly. He said to himself as he walked back to the glass walled office.

CHAPTER 14

By the time they finished refueling the aircraft, Stoney's hands were numb, and he was sure those of the mechanics and Kent James felt the same as his. The whole time, Leshev had been standing there watching the entire process. Danshov had kept a very close eye on them in the supply shed when they had to go and pick up additional drums of fuel. There was no way they could slow roll the process to give time to a potential rescue. A couple of times, Danshov had thought they were not moving fast enough, and he had prodded them with his automatic rifle. The mechanics had finished up on the engine repair and had replaced the cowling. Once they moved the scaffolding back to the maintenance shed, they jumped up on the refueling truck to help Stoney and James.

"Since you've almost finished with the refueling, I want the mechanics to start the heating process on the engines on the other side. When you finish this side, then they can get these started as well," instructed Leshev.

The mechanics jumped down from the refueling truck and headed into the supply shed to retrieve the large covers that would go around the front of the engine to keep the heat in as they were heated. Since Danshov was watching Stoney and James, Leshev followed the mechanics to keep an eye on them.

With refueling finished, Stoney and James jumped down and drove the truck back into the supply shed. They then assisted the mechanics in rolling out the large heaters. There were two, one for each side of the aircraft. Along with the heaters, they also needed the long yellow flexible tubing that would guide the hot air into the engines. Each heater was almost the size of a small car. It was on four wheels and had a large fan and radiator that functioned as a heat exchanger. The large fan would suck in outside air, then using a heater similar to a home furnace it would quickly heat that air and blow it through a large tube up to the engine where it would heat the inside of the cowling and thus the engine. Each engine had a tube on either side. One was an air supply tube from the heater and the other would suck the air back out of the engine area to re-warm it and return it to the engine. Depending on the temperature of the outside air, both air tubes could supply air to the engine, or in cases where it was really cold, one would supply air to the engine and one would return it to the heater. Continuously recycling the air from within the cowling resulted in a higher temperature than using fresh outside air.

Both James and Stoney were hoping that Leshev would not know that much about aircraft pre-heaters, so they set up the heaters to suck in the cold outside air instead of recirculating the air from within the engine. Both men knew this would add a significant amount of time to the heating process thus keeping the aircraft on the ground that much longer. Additionally, daylight was running out fast. It would be dark within a couple of hours, and the temperature would really drop then.

Once the heaters were in place and running, Stoney told Leshev there was nothing else to do until the engines and oil were up to temperature as shown on the flight engineer's gauges. There was no need to stand here and watch the heaters, but they needed to periodically check them. Leshev agreed, and he and Danshov marched the mechanics, Stoney and James back to the hostage holding area.

When they entered the building, everyone was relieved to be away from the loud noise of the engine heaters.

"Captain, any chance we could feed everyone? It has been hours since they ate on the aircraft and personally, I am starving," Stoney asked.

"Da, I think that will be OK while the aircraft engines are being warmed."

While talking on his radio, Leshev motioned for James to lead the way, and the small group headed to the cafeteria as he followed behind.

They only had to wait a couple of minutes before the hostages arrived. Danshov, Vavilov, and Osinov were herding them like cattle into the cafeteria. Once everyone was there, Leshev asked who normally did the cooking for the airfield crew. One man said he did and Danshov removed his bonds and told him to go to the kitchen and get started. Leshev ordered Vavilov to stand guard while the man cooked.

"Captain, can we take the restraints off of everyone while they are cooking? I believe I can speak for James' personnel as well as the passengers that no one will attempt any more heroics," asked Stoney.

"Agreed," said James.

"Da. Corporal Osinov, keep an eye on everyone while Danshov unties the bonds. Do not cut them, since we'll need them again after everyone has eaten. Stone and James, I remind you that if anyone tries anything, I will shoot them and three others. This time there is no reprieve," said Leshev.

"We understand," said James.

With their hands free, everyone rubbed their arms to increase blood circulation as they found a place and sat down. Osinov kept a watchful eye on everyone while Vavilov had his hands full keeping up with the chef's frantic pace as he worked to quickly get something cooked.

Though everyone was in quiet conversation with each other, Stoney had positioned himself so he could keep an eye on Leshev and Danshov without their noticing him. He was quietly talking to James and Hudson when he saw Leshev and Danshov quietly slip out the door.

". . . with everyone tied up there's no way we can break through the Sheetrock into the next room," Hudson said.

"That plan will have to be aborted," agreed James.

"I noticed that Leshev and Danshov quietly slipped out the door while you were talking. I wonder what they are up to. I am sure this caper is not going as planned. I, for one, intend to put as many kinks in it as possible between now and when they make us fly out of here," said Stoney.

"As lightly as they seem to keep us guarded, I would think we could jump at least one of them and get a weapon," suggested Hudson.

"Bad idea, enough people have been hurt and mutilated already. They may be small in number, but from what we've seen so far, there isn't much they won't do to keep us in line. I do not want to take the risk of additional people getting hurt," said Stoney.

Just then the door opened and Stoney saw Leshev and Danshov return to the room. Leshev walked over and sat down next to Stoney and the group while Danshov continued to wander around brandishing his weapon.

"What kind of problems are you hatching for me?"

"Why captain, why would we want to cause you difficulty?" inquired James with a sly smile on his face.

"For the same reason, that if I was in your shoes right now that is exactly what I would be doing. People are people, no matter their nationality and when they are being held against their will, they will do anything to overthrow their captors," said Leshev.

"I don't know about any conspiracies being hatched, but I do know that whatever is being cooked in the kitchen has made my stomach start to growl," said Stoney.

"I agree," added both James and Hudson.

It had been many hours since that last interrupted meal on the plane and Stoney supposed the 'Q' personnel weren't any better off. Leshev just sat there as if he was studying his captives.

"Dinner is served," announced the chef from the kitchen doorway.

"I want the women to help with the serving. All men will stay seated," instructed Danshov. About that same time, Leshev got up and walked over to where Danshov was standing.

Obediently, all of the women got up and went into the kitchen to retrieve plates of hot food that they carried to each person. Stoney was not surprised when his plate came with only a spoon to eat with.

He asked the person who had served him and she stated the "kitchen minder" would only let them bring out spoons for everyone to eat with. Additionally, the women served large mugs of hot coffee. Immediately, all conversation ceased as everyone began to eat in earnest. It wasn't much, just some corned beef hash and a large bowl of chicken noodle soup. It was not the gourmet food the passengers had enjoyed on the flight, but it was warm and filling.

Stoney did not realize he was so famished. He and the cockpit crew hadn't been able to hardly eat at all when all the emergencies had started. The corned beef hash tasted wonderful and the soup helped to warm him up.

Stoney still kept an indiscreet eye on Leshev and Danshov while he ate. He noticed that after the cook emerged from the kitchen to sit and eat, that Leshev and Danshov both sat down away from everyone else. Vavilov emerged from the kitchen carrying plates of food and set them down in front of his captain and sergeant. The two corporals then wondered around the cafeteria keeping a wary eye on everyone.

Stoney and his table mates continued to eat as he kept an eye on his captors. He was sure James and Hudson were watching as well.

Once they had finished, Leshev and Danshov stood guard while the corporals ate. Stoney heard Leshev tell Virginia it was OK to bring out additional food. So she started bringing out seconds while the other women were eating. Slowly as the clanking of silverware against the plates and bowls began to diminish, the low din of conversation began to take its place.

When the meal was finished and all of the plates, cups and utensils were accounted for, each person dutifully put their hands behind their backs and let Danshov tie them up again. Just as Danshov was going to tie Mrs. Gooseman's hands, she went hysterical. She started screaming and shouting at the Russian while crying at the same time.

"I cannot take this any longer!" she said between sobs. Stoney didn't make a move until Danshov held up his hand to strike her across the face at which point he jumped out of his seat and took the few steps needed to get between Danshov and Mrs. Gooseman. Stoney was surprised that he caught Danshov off guard, but that feeling didn't last long as Danshov immediately put his rifle at the ready.

"If you want to hit someone, hit me. Leave this poor woman alone!" Stoney shouted at Danshov.

From across the room, Leshev yelled as he waved his pistol in the air "Enough! I will not tolerate any more outbursts. My patience is running thin and I am about ready to shoot someone!"

Danshov lowered his weapon and pushed Stoney aside. He then grabbed Mrs. Gooseman by the shoulders and forcefully turned her around. He grabbed her wrists to tie them together as she continued to sob, though much quieter.

"It's OK Mrs. Gooseman, they won't hurt you as long as you do what they say. This isn't easy on any of us, but we have to cooperate to get out alive," said Stoney as he tried to calm her down.

Between sobs she managed to say, "Thank you captain."

"Thanks," whispered Mr. Gooseman.

Stoney returned to his seat.

Mr. Gooseman tried to calm down his wife after Danshov had finished tying her up.

With everyone's hands tied up, Danshov and the corporals marched them back to the holding room. Only Stoney, James, Hudson, and Leshev remained. Leshev had his pistol out and told them to dress for outside since he wanted to check on the status of the engine heating.

Stoney and the group grabbed their coats and they headed out to the aircraft with Leshev bringing up the rear. Each one had a feeling of despair since there was nowhere to run and Leshev maintained enough distance behind them that any attempt to overpower him would be fatal. Opening the door, they walked out into the waning daylight and the blistering cold wind.

Reaching the aircraft, they ascended the staircase and entered the cabin. The cabin temperature was low enough to cause their breath to form smoke as they exhaled. Entering the cockpit, Stoney turned on the electrical system to check the engine temperatures. It had been nearly two hours since the heating process had begun. Turning to Leshev he announced that the temperatures were high enough to attempt to start the engines.

"What do you mean *attempt* to start the engines?" asked Leshev.

"Just because the engine is warm enough for the oil to flow, does not mean that the batteries have enough power to actually start one," explained Stoney.

Picking up his radio, Leshev barked out more orders in Russian. Turning to James and Hudson he told them to get the snow plow out of the way and to remove the heater equipment from the aircraft.

"Start with the left side," hollered Stoney as Leshev waved his pistol to motivate James and Hudson who hurried down the stairs to get started. Turning to Stoney, he told him to get in the left seat and get ready to start the engines.

Watching through the cockpit windows, Stoney saw James and Hudson shutdown the heater equipment and carefully remove the covers, ducting and ladders. As they finished clearing the area near the engines on the left wing, Danshov and the corporals arrived with the flight crew, minus Virginia and Brad, that is. Danshov stood outside as the corporals and the flight crew climbed up the stairs and entered the cabin. Once the equipment was out of the way of the left engines, Leshev told Stoney to begin the startup sequence.

Just then Steve jumped into his co-pilot's seat and Lee settled down at his engineer's console.

"Glad you guys could make it," Stoney said to Lee and Steve. He then called for the Pre-Start Engine Checklist. Lee started reading the items as Stoney and Steve called out their status. With all checks complete, Stoney called for the Start-Engine Checklist. This time, Steve called out the items and Stoney and Lee replied.

When the checklist was complete, Stoney turned his head to look at Leshev standing behind him and said, "We need to move the stairs before we start the engine."

Stoney saw Leshev glance out the door and when he turned back around he replied, "There is enough clearance, start the engine."

"You realize the stairs could be sucked into the propeller blades thereby grounding the airplane!" Stoney retorted.

"Yes, there is enough clearance, START THE ENGINE!" Leshev replied in that *DO IT NOW* tone Stoney had come to know.

Stoney turned back around and reached for the starter switch. Stoney called "CLEAR" out of his window to make sure that there wasn't anyone near the propeller blades as he attempted to start the first engine. Pressing the button he could hear the starter whine as it slowly spun up and then at the right time the propeller blades began to slowly spin. He counted four blades and then advanced the throttle to see if it would start. The engine coughed and sputtered but refused to start. Trying the sequence again, the starter took much longer to spin up before engaging the engine and Stoney could tell that the batteries were dying quickly. As before, he counted four blades and then advanced the throttle. Again, the engine sputtered, coughed and refused to start. Turning to Leshev, he said that there might be enough power for one more attempt, but if the engine did not start this time they would have to charge up the batteries before they could attempt to start it again.

"Well then, captain, you better hope that it starts this time. If it doesn't then there will be consequences which you will not like!" growled Leshev.

About this time, Steve announced that James and Hudson had moved all of the heating apparatus away from the right side of the aircraft. As Stoney waited for the batteries to recover, after the last failed engine start, he heard boots thundering up the stairs. The whole cockpit crew heard Danshov's voice as he yelled at the men on the ground to move the stairway away from the aircraft.

Watching the scene from his window, Stoney saw James and Hudson grab the stairs and pull them away from the aircraft. Just as they cleared the wing, two rifle shots rang out in the cold and Stoney saw James and Hudson fall to the ground. Deep red blood started slowly flowing out onto the once white snow where they fell.

CHAPTER 15

Flying high above the arctic snow and ice was a lone C-130, racing to find out what was causing the strange events concerning APA Flight 28-Alpha. The cold blue sky at 25,000 feet had four white contrails arched across it marking the progress of the aircraft. The winds at that altitude were strong enough that the contrails quickly lost their characteristic thin line shape and became wide spread as the winds blew them apart. Shortly after the passing of the aircraft, the contrails merged into one large area of thin white cloud. The aircraft, commanded by Captain Marcus, was making best speed to airfield 'Q'.

Captain Marcus looked down at the readout on the inertial navigation system (INS) to verify his ground speed and time to the programmed destination. They were doing well with a ground speed of almost 320 knots, mostly due to the winds at their altitude. Realizing that the trip home would take longer, Marcus hoped that there would be good news on board and not a load of filled body bags.

Marcus was also glad that they had assigned this trip to a later model C-130 that had been equipped with the INS system. Most of the earlier birds did not have such fancy equipment so the pilots had to navigate the old way which was very accurate, just labor intensive. He could still navigate that way and so could his co-pilot Lieutenant Bryan, but with a hastily arranged mission like this he was grateful to have the INS.

"Hey, L.T. isn't it time to check in with Polar Control?" asked Marcus.

"Yes, sir it is. I was just getting the frequency from the chart. Ah, here it is, 132.89." Reaching for the communications radio, the L.T. entered the frequency into the radio.

"Go ahead sir."

"Polar Control, this is Snowbird 24 checking in at flight level two-five-zero," Marcus said into the microphone.

The only reply he got was static and a strange noise in the background, almost buried in the static.

With no reply, Marcus again repeated his call, "Polar Control, Polar Control, this is Snowbird 24 calling on frequency 132.89. Respond please." Not receiving a reply, he said "L.T., change radios to number two and let's try again."

Reaching the radio console, the L.T. entered the frequency into the number two radio and told the captain to try again.

"Polar Control, Polar Control, this is Snowbird 24 calling on frequency 132.89. Respond please." Again, the same static with the same strange noise in the background was the only sound made by the radio.

"L.T., this is damned strange. I should be able to get Polar Control at this point in the flight. We'll continue on to the next check-in point which is just west of our destination. Keep monitoring the Guard frequency as well as the sector frequency for Polar Control. Let me know if you hear anything at all on either frequency."

Guard frequency was the frequency that military aircraft use to communicate with each other in flight as well as monitor for emergency beacons should a crash occur. Marcus knew that if Polar Control wanted to contact them and couldn't do so on the standard frequency they would try on Guard as well. They also might try using other aircraft to relay information for them.

Re-checking the INS, Marcus realized they had forty-five minutes before reaching airfield 'Q'. Switching his microphone to the PA system, he announced that they were forty-five minutes from their destination.

Marcus' passengers were sitting on seats made of red nylon straps fashioned into webbing strung down both sides of the C-130's cargo hold. These U.S. Marines specialized in military operations in the frigid conditions of the arctic. As they sat sleeping or talking amongst themselves each was silently wondering what was waiting for them on the ground. TSgt Smythe, the C-130's load master was in a discussion with Gunnery Sergeant McFlynn, commonly called just 'Gunny'. Captain Jones and Lieutenant Davies were discussing whether to land the C-130 or parachute into the airfield. They brought the right equipment for both contingencies.

Parachuting into the airfield would allow them time to assess the situation without putting the C-130 in danger. Additionally, since the C-130 would arrive just after nightfall, landing without lights on an unfamiliar runway carried its own set of potential perils. The C-130 crew routinely practiced landing on unimproved runways after dark however Jones had to weigh those risks against the risks associated with jumping.

After careful consideration, Jones made the decision to jump into the airfield and have the C-130 take up a holding pattern forty miles to the east. This would allow a silent arrival at the field and would protect the 130 from any potential harm. Getting up from his seat he addressed the group of Marines. The noise was loud in the cargo hold, but not loud enough to muffle the commands of a U.S. Marine Captain.

"Gentlemen, after careful consideration, I have decided this will be a night jump into airfield 'Q'. We have about forty-five minutes to get everything ready. Everybody up and get your chutes on and checked. Let's move!"

Jones was busy getting his equipment ready when someone tapped him on the shoulder. Turning around he saw it was the Load Master.

"Sir, Captain Marcus wants to talk to you on the interphone. Please follow me," Smythe yelled to Jones over the noise of the aircraft. Jones gave him a thumbs-up and followed.

When they reached the Load Master console, Smythe picked up the handset and connected it to the cockpit then handed it to Jones.

"Captain Jones here."

"Captain, I understand you have decided to jump into the field. Do you still want to use the same jump points we discussed on the ground?" asked Marcus.

"Yep, sure do. I think those will get us onto the airfield in the shortest time."

"We'll get you there. Have a safe jump and call us on the radio when you want us to come and pick you up. Remember that we will only have about an hour and a half of fuel to burn waiting on you. That will allow us to get on the ground, take-off and return to the base with a bare minimum of reserve. It will be a long, cold walk if we run short!"

"Aye captain, I'll keep that in mind. I know you Air Force boys don't like to walk that far unless you're chasing a golf ball and then only with a golf cart."

"Yeah, Yeah Yeah! See you on the ground!" said Marcus.

Returning the phone to its cradle, Jones turned to the Load Master and told him to keep the coffee hot. "The thought of that hot coffee will get us back to the aircraft ASAP."

"Will do sir,"

"Marines, we jump in a few minutes, check each other's straps and make sure your radios are setup correctly," said Marcus.

Since they wanted to arrive at the airfield with minimal noise, this would be a relatively high altitude low opening or HALO jump. Jumping from a high altitude would minimize the 130's engine noise which could alert whatever hostiles might be on the ground. Each Marine had on a thick arctic suit that allowed freedom of movement while keeping the occupant warm. Additionally, each Marine had a tank and mask that would supply them oxygen until they reached the ground. Their weapons all had silencers to assist in their stealth attack.

Jones was hoping there would be no surprises when they hit the ground and that this would just be a routine jump and all of the concern in Washington was the result of a communications outage.

Jones happened to look toward the Load Master's console and he saw Smythe holding up the interphone and motioning to him. Jones made his way forward once again.

"Jones, just to let you know, we have not been able to contact Polar Control since we left Elmendorf. We have tried multiple frequencies and have been listening on the Guard Channel as well. We have not received any communications other than static on the radios. I am beginning to suspect we are being jammed," said Marcus.

"Thanks man that is just the information we need. I was hoping this would be a routine jump but I am beginning to think that something funny is going on. Thanks for the heads up."

"Tell your folks to get ready. You jump in ten," said Marcus.

"Roger."

Jones hung up the interphone and rejoining the men he said, "Everyone get ready; we jump in ten minutes. Use the buddy system and check each other's equipment and line up for evac." Turning to Davies he said, "L.T. turn around and let me check your equipment. Straps tight—check; Oxygen on—check; Weapon attached and secured—check; Ammunition secured—check; portable radio on and working—check. You're good to go. By the way, how many halos is this for you?" said Jones who knew a nervous man when he saw one. His experience showed levity usually worked to calm them down.

"This is my third operational, sir," said Davies as he checked his captain's equipment. "After twenty-five or thirty, it is just like another day at the office," Jones said casually as he slapped Davies on the back then strapped on his oxygen mask.

"Thanks sir," said Davies as he strapped on his mask.

Once finished they headed over to join up with the men anxiously waiting at the large cargo door.

Just as Jones and Davies joined them, the Load Master worked his way to the cargo door controls. He was wearing a portable oxygen system and a large coat. He flashed a thumbs-up and in turn everyone replied with thumbs-up. He briefly spoke into the interphone ostensibly to tell the co-pilot is was OK to depressurize the cabin prior to opening the cargo door. Seconds later, everyone's ears popped as the cabin was depressurized and when the green light illuminated on the control panel, the Load Master dimmed the interior lights, and pressed a button causing the large cargo door to begin its journey to the open position. Within a short span of time after the door opened the large green "JUMP NOW" light illuminated indicating they were over the jump zone. Each Marine in turn ran down the cargo ramp and leaped into the black void that had no beginning and no end.

As each man cleared the aircraft he immediately went into a streamlined tucked body position in order to increase his speed. They needed to get down quickly and that was the best way to do It. Each person kept an eye on his portable altimeter and when it indicated 5,000 feet he would spread out his limbs in an effort to slow down as much as possible. At 3,000 feet each man's chute would open automatically and using special *riser* lines attached to the chute he would steer himself to the landing zone. As they reached the chute opening height, no one could make out any of the airfield lights. Darkness covered the airfield although the full moon provided just enough illumination to allow Jones to scan the area around the airfield.

3,000 feet, the chute opened and Jones looked around to see if the rest of the team was near. In the moonlight, he had to strain to make out the outline of the other chutes floating to the ground. He was relieved to see five other chutes all steering toward what appeared to be the parking apron of Alternate Airfield 'Q'. His level of concern increased when he saw the Super Constellation known as Northern Star Flight 28-Alpha was nowhere in sight.

Touch down was uneventful as each Marine used his canopy risers to virtually hover inches above the ground before dropping lightly into the snow. As each Marine landed he collapsed his canopy and wadded it up into a ball and began to disconnect the harness and the portable oxygen system. Their pure white outer garments helped them blend in with the snow. Finally free of their unneeded equipment each Marine took up a defensive position against the side of the communications building that had the glass encased Control Tower Cab on top. They quickly and quietly gathered there keeping strict radio silence.

As each person made their way to the side of the communications building they could not help but notice the portable aircraft stairs and the two bodies lying near it. The snow had turned red where the blood had flowed and from the frost covering their faces it was obvious the pair were dead.

Using standard military hand jesters, Captain Jones indicated to Lieutenant Davies that he and Corporal Dane should enter the building and check it for hostiles.

174

Minutes later, one word came over Jones' radio headset—"Clear".

The door to the building opened and the L.T. and the corporal stepped out. Motioning for the team to follow him, Jones began to carefully lead his team to the main building.

As quietly as possible they entered the main building. Jones had his men spread out to search the entire area. They entered the cafeteria and other than a few dishes on the tables and a burnt pot of coffee there was no sign of life or struggle other than a small blood stain on the floor. Satisfied there was no one about, the Marines continued to check the rooms in the building.

Room by room they searched the deathly quiet building. Eventually, they came to a room where they heard some noise coming from inside.

The Marines took up a defensive posture outside the door and once in position Maxwell kicked open the door. Inside they found a large group of people seated on the floor with gags in their mouths and their hands tied behind them all staring at the Marines.

The Marines checked the room for hostiles, then helped each person to their feet and cut their bonds. With their hands now free, each person removed their gag and began asking who had helped them.

"Who are you guys?" asked James Dumont.

"We are United States Marines and we're here to rescue you, I am Captain Jones. Who can tell me what the devil is going on here?"

"Captain Jones, I am Tyler Noland the Chief of Personnel here at airfield 'Q'."

"Good to meet you Tyler. Who are all these people?" asked Jones.

"They are the passengers from APA Flight 28-Alpha and what remain of airfield 'Q' personnel. We don't know what happened to Kent James and Mike Hudson our commander and his second. About two hours ago, the Russians tied us up and left with some of the flight crew and that was the last we saw of them. Is the Constellation still on the tarmac?"

"No, but we did find two bodies and I think it would be safe to assume it is your Mr. James and Mr. Hudson. Do you know how long the aircraft has been gone?"

"No, the Russians let us eat then they tied us up in here and they took the flight crew. I have no idea how long the aircraft has been gone but by my watch we've been sitting here for about two hours. We don't know when the aircraft actually departed, it could be five minutes or two hours."

"Why don't you go and check your communications gear. Corporal Maxwell will go with you; maybe he can help if there is damage. We need to know if we have long range communications or not. Maxwell, make sure you check in with Gunny when you reach the comm room. He will need a SitRep. L.T., you and Sergeant Daniels see to these folks and continue to search the remaining buildings. Gunny, Dane, and I are going to check the airfield and if it looks OK, we'll bring in the C-130," said Jones.

"Captain, did you bring an airplane to get us out of here?" asked Harold Gooseman.

"Sir, we parachuted into here, but there is an Air Force C-130 transport orbiting about forty miles from here that will land as soon as we can inspect the airfield."

"How soon do you think it will be before we can leave?" asked Finley McQuinn.

"Well, ma'am I don't really know. We have to figure out what's going on here, secure the area and then make preparations to leave."

"How long will that take?" asked Gooseman.

"I don't know, but rest assured we will get everyone out of here as soon as possible. Now if you all will hold your questions till later I need to get that 130 on the ground," said Jones.

Corporal Maxwell and Tyler Noland took off for the communications area while Captain Jones, Gunny and Corporal Dane went back out to the airfield.

When Jones and his Marines reached the flight line, they immediately checked out the maintenance shed for any hidden Russians. Finding none, they picked up the bodies of the two slain men, laid them on top of a work table then covered them with tarps. Once that was complete, they headed out to the tarmac and moved the portable stairs out of the way so the C-130 could park in the same place it appeared the Constellation once sat.

Jones' radio came to life as they began a quick inspection of the runway.

"Captain Jones, this is Corporal Maxwell. We have surveyed the communications equipment and we found the High Frequency Radio still functional. We have tried to contact Elmendorf but have had no luck. No hostiles in sight."

"Keep trying the radio. Check in with Gunny every half an hour with a status," replied Jones.

"Snowbird 24, this is Mongoose calling, how do you copy us?" Jones said into his radio. He had preset it to the frequency he and Marcus had agreed to.

With a lot of static in the background as well as a peculiar noise, Captain Jones could just barely make out the reply from the C-130.

"Mongoose, this is . . . . what is . . . situation . . . over."

"Snowbird, very hard to read your transmission. All OK here, Romeo-Tango my location, over," replied Jones. Romeo-Tango was the phrase they had agreed upon to indicate the C-130 should return to the base and land.

"Mong . . . Copy . . . . ETA twenty minutes," came the reply.

With the C-130 in-bound, Jones realized they needed to light up the airfield. He sent Sergeant Daniels up to the Control Tower Cab to see if the runway lights were functional. Meanwhile he called Davies on the radio and asked him to inquire if there was a supply of flares on the airfield.

Once again Jones' radio sparked to life, "Captain Jones, Sergeant Daniels here. The airfield lighting controls have been smashed, no way to get them functional prior to Snowbird return."

"Thanks Daniels, come on back down here."

"Captain Jones, one of the mechanics said there are flares in an orange box inside the maintenance shed," said Davies over the radio.

"Thanks L.T."

Entering the maintenance shed, Jones quickly found the orange box that contained the flares. He also found a vehicle, known as a half-track, which was a cross between a jeep and a tank. It had the front wheels and body like a jeep and in the rear there were tank treads that would allow the vehicle to be maneuverable across most types of terrain. He found the ignition and the engine turned over but it refused to start. Just then, Daniels reappeared from his foray into the Control Tower Cab. Daniels was the mechanic of the group. Many years earlier the Marine Corps had learned that small combat teams needed to be comprised of Marines of different skills. Every Marine was a combat trained killer who also had a secondary skill. Maxwell was the electronics expert and Daniels was the mechanic.

"Daniels, there you are. Can you get this contraption running? It turns over but it won't start," said Jones.

"Sir, if it has an engine, I'll make it run," said Daniels.

Walking over to the strange machine, Daniels popped open the hood checked a few items and then he climbed into the driver's position and after adjusting a few levers he tried the starter and the contraption fired right up.

"Sir, with the arctic climates, you have to adjust the mixture and the choke to get them started in the winter," explained Daniels.

"Daniels, you and Dane take these flares and set them off to outline the runway. We have about ten minutes before the 130 gets here," instructed Jones.

Corporal Dane jumped into the half-track and Jones handed him the box of flares. Daniels turned the half-track around and headed for the door. Gunny ran ahead to open the large barn doors so the half-track could leave the building. Once through Daniels gunned the engine and roared off into the darkness.

Jones and Gunny hurried to close the doors and then headed outside to watch their progress.

Making the half-track go as fast as possible, Daniels and Dane managed to get the last flare in position as the C-130 roared overhead getting ready to make its approach. The aircraft flew over the field at a ninety degree angle to the runway and then made a downwind turn left to parallel the runway.

When it reached the end of the runway it continued out for about thirty seconds before making a left hand

James A. Jack

base leg turn. The C-130 continued in the turn until lined up for its final approach. With its landing lights blazing it looked like a much larger aircraft coming in to land. As soon as the wheels touched the runway the pilot applied full reverse thrust to slow the aircraft as quickly as possible. With the propellers pushing air in front of the aircraft they stirred up a lot of snow and actually created blizzard conditions just in front of the aircraft.

Once the aircraft slowed sufficiently, the pilot cancelled the reverse thrust and the aircraft taxied to the tarmac where Jones was using two flares he had kept. Moving them in universally recognized arm signals he directed the aircraft to an area to park on the tarmac. Once he signaled engine shutdown by crossing his arms over his head, the mighty turbo-prop engines became silent and the only sound was the swish-swish as the propellers slowly came to a halt.

CHAPTER 16

As 28-Alpha climbed through the cloud layer at 10,000 feet on its way to 25,000 feet, Stoney felt somewhat relieved that they were still in one piece. After Sergeant Danshov had killed James and Hudson, he had closed the cabin door and entered the cockpit telling Captain Leshev all was ready.

Leshev immediately pulled out his pistol, pointed it at Stoney's head and demanded that he get the engines started or he would shoot him. Fortunately, that first engine had decided to cooperate just as the batteries were dying. Once started it supplied enough electrical power to get all of the rest of the engines started. Stoney had sweated bullets during the whole process, but down in his heart he knew the danger was just beginning.

They used the Constellation's landing lights to find their way to the end of the runway. As he began the take-off roll Stoney had to really concentrate looking for the outline of the runway in the snow to make sure he did not run off and hit something on the side. As usual, the co-pilot was watching the instruments and calling out the "V" speeds as the huge black bird accelerated down the runway. When Steve called out "VR" Stoney once again pulled back on that yoke and the Constellation reached for the black void ahead.

"Ok, Captain, where do you want to go?" asked Stoney as he leveled out at 25,000 feet.

"Turn to a heading of forty degrees and tune your A.D.F. radio to 359 Kilohertz. In a while we will hear a beacon that you will fly toward. Forty degrees will get us headed in the correct direction," said Leshev.

"Steve, tune in the beacon and put it on the speaker," said Stoney as he turned the aircraft to Leshev's heading.

Static filled the cockpit from the A.D.F. receiver so Stoney turned the volume down to where it was just audible in the background.

Turning on the autopilot, Stoney said, "Steve, go ahead and take a navigational reading we can use as a starting point."

"Can do," replied Steve as he started to get out of his chair.

"Where do you think you're going?" asked Leshev, seated in the jump seat.

"I need to find out where we are. To do that I have to use that glass bubble, above your head, and my sextant to take a look at the stars so I can determine our position."

"Go ahead but I warn you not to try anything funny," and as he said that, Leshev got out of his seat and stood at the back of the cockpit where he could still see everyone and all goings on.

While Steve was getting his equipment out, Stoney turned to Lee and asked, "Lee, how's that number three engine looking?"

"It's purring like a kitten sir, everything looks great."

Steve, sextant in hand, stood on his stool and stuck his head up into the glass bubble and within five minutes he had an initial mark on a chart to show where they were. Using his ruler and pencil he made a course line at zero-four-zero degrees and when he took his next reading, if all was well, the new dot would end up on that line, or at least very close to it. The difference would show them what the winds at their altitude were doing to their course. To keep an aircraft on track, the pilot has to compensate for the winds. In reality the aircraft may be flying sideways through the air, but its track along the ground would be along the desired course.

After Steve returned to his seat, Stoney motioned for Leshev to come forward.

"I have to hit the head," said Stoney.

"What do you mean? I do not understand," replied Leshev.

"Sorry for the slang, I need to go to the bathroom."

"Corporal Vavilov will accompany you,"

"Exactly what do you think I can do to you in an aircraft bathroom? I prefer to go by myself!"

"Da, Corporal Vavilov will wait outside the door. You see, we Russians are not all that bad?"

"Yes, allowing me to go to the bathroom by myself shows the level to which you will go to be kind to your hostages. Thanks!"

"Better to go now and stop talking or I will change my mind and keep you in that seat!" said Leshev.

"Vavilov, follow him to the bathroom!" barked Leshev to Vavilov who was seated near the cockpit.

"Steve, you have the aircraft. I'll be back in a minute," said Stoney.

"Yes sir. Take your time!"

With control of the aircraft turned over to his first officer, Stoney got out of his seat, squeezed by Leshev who was sitting in the jump seat, and made his way to the bathroom. Vavilov waited at the cockpit door then followed him the ten steps to the lavatory.

Good grief, we're barely on our way and already Danshov and crew have broken out the booze. Drink up boys . . . while you can, thought Stoney as he surveyed the cabin. After a prod from Vavilov, Stoney opened the lavatory door, stepped in, and shut it. He really did have to go, and once he finished, he pulled out a pen he had managed to sneak into his pocket and he wrote a note on a small piece of toilet paper.

Follow my lead: 'Boy, the stars sure are bright!' Take three deep breaths and hold.

After he wrote the note, Stoney rolled it up into a small ball and opening the paper towel holder he stuck it under and behind the supply of paper towels where it was not readily visible. He then flushed the toilet, stood there, and watched as the blue water swirled around the bowl before disappearing into the holding tank. He washed his hands and face in the sink and afterward stood there staring at himself wondering if the plan would work. He was planning to activate the anesthesia gas system while he and Steve held their breaths long enough for the Russians to pass out. No one had ever used the system, and he didn't know how long that would take. He hoped the two of them wouldn't pass out first. The main question in his mind was, *Can we hold our breaths until they become groggy enough so we can put on oxygen masks without interference from Leshev?*

Just about then, his minder started banging on the door demanding that he come out.

"All right, all ready! Keep your knickers on, I'm coming out," Stoney said as he opened the door.

Once he started heading for the cockpit, Vavilov went into the lavatory and began to diligently search it. Stoney hoped Vavilov wouldn't find his hidden note.

Entering the cockpit, he turned to Leshev and said, "I hope your corporal leaves the bathroom where it can be used again. It sounds like he is tearing it apart!"

"Just take your seat and fly the plane," said Leshev in a somewhat exasperated voice.

"Steve isn't it time for another navigational fix?" asked Stoney.

"I believe it is, sir. The aircraft is yours," Steve said as he began to unbuckle his harness.

"What are you doing—NOW?" demanded Leshev.

"I have to plot another point on the map to see if we are headed in the right direction and are adequately compensating for the wind. You do want to eventually get there, don't you?"

Leshev again stood up and moved to the back of the cockpit. Steve got out his equipment and standing on the stool, took his sighting and then turning to his chart he plotted their current position. When he placed the dot on the chart, he put it to the right, or south of their projected course. This indicated that there was a north wind blowing them southward so they would have to increase their heading to the north to compensate. When he had finished, he told Stoney they needed to crab about ten degrees to the north. He then told Leshev he needed to go to the bathroom and since he was up now was a good time.

"What is with you pilots and the bathroom?" asked Leshev.

"It is all that coffee we drank trying to warm-up at the airfield," replied Steve.

Turning to look out the cockpit door, Leshev said, "Vavilov, *this one has to go now.* Keep an eye on him!"

Several minutes later, Stoney saw Steve climbing back into his seat. "Looks like all is well; I see we haven't entered a death spiral," joked Steve as he sat down.

"No, I managed to keep the wings level while you were gone. You probably had more excitement in the lavatory that I did up here!" said Stoney.

"Yes, I've always found toilets fascinating!" replied Steve.

"You two have definitely got a case of air sickness. I can't remember the last time I heard such dribble. If you all keep this up, I will have to report the two of you need psych evals!" exclaimed Lee.

"Enough of this nonsense! No more talking unless it is about flying this aircraft!" commanded Leshev.

The entire time Steve was gone, Stoney had been contemplating his next move. He had thought about "accidentally" de-pressurizing the cabin, but the controls to do that were on Lee's panel. No way to get there without causing Leshev to shoot him and no way to tell Lee to do it. He also had begun to hear the faint dot-dash pattern of the Non-Directional Beacon (NDB) that would lead them to Soviet airspace and the gulag. Whatever he was going to do he had to do it fast. Once inside Soviet airspace he was sure they would scramble fighters to make sure he landed at their convenience.

The Northern Star engineers had cleverly disguised the anesthesia gas controls as a radio panel so it seemed natural when Stoney reached down and dialed in the "correct" frequency to get the system ready. He looked over at Steve and said, "Boy the stars sure are bright. I can never get used to seeing them this far north."

As he said 'north' he took three deep breaths holding the last one as he reached down and pressed the radio's Squelch Button four times in a row. With a loud hiss, the gas system activated. Stoney, still holding his breath, could hear Leshev and Lee gagging behind him when all at one he felt a pair of hands close tightly around his throat as if trying to squeeze the life out of him. As the hands tightened they began to drag him over the back of his chair.

Stoney's vision began to blur as the hands continued to squeeze his throat. Out of the corner of his eye Stoney saw Steve stand up on his seat, lean over and repeatedly punch Leshev in the face. Leshev finally let go of Stoney's neck as he moved to repel Steve's attack.

As soon as the hands left his throat, Stoney immediately pressed his seatbelt release button, jumped up and stood in his seat momentarily before diving over the seatback throwing his body weight into Leshev as he continued to fight Steve. Stoney and Leshev fell to the floor in a heap with Stoney on top. They struggled on the floor, as Steve stood in his seat unable to help Stoney when all of a sudden Leshev's pistol went off.

Stoney heard Steve scream and an instant later all sound was drowned out by a deafening howl that filled the cockpit along with a fog-like vapor as the aircraft rapidly depressurized. Finally Leshev passed out from the gas as well as the lack of oxygen. Stoney was starting to black out but managed to grab an emergency oxygen mask. He quickly put it on looking toward the co-pilot's seat to check on Steve.

To his absolute horror, Steve was gone and blood covered the windows surrounding the one that shattered. As he sat there in the fog of oxygen deprivation his brain told him the rapid decompression had caused Steve to be sucked through the shattered window. As the oxygen from the mask cleared the fog from his mind, he realized that alarms were going off all over the panel. He jumped back into his seat, turned off the autopilot, pushed forward on the control yoke starting a rapid descent to 10,000 feet where everyone could breathe.

Once he had the autopilot set and the alarms silenced he climbed out of his seat and put an oxygen mask on Lee to speed up his recovery. Fortunately, Lee came around quickly and Stoney told him to tie up the Russians and collect their weapons while he flew the plane.

"Why in hell didn't you warn me you were going to use the gas? Where is Steve?" Lee yelled through the howling wind blowing through the missing window.

"There wasn't time and I knew it would knock out the Russians. Steve was sucked out when Leshev's gun shot out the window. Quickly, get them tied up." Stoney hollered back.

Grabbing a portable oxygen system, Lee dragged Leshev into the main cabin and made sure he didn't have any weapons on him. He took Leshev's knife and a small pistol hidden inside his boot both of which Lee stuck in his own belt. He propped Leshev into a seat and tied him tightly to the seat. He then grabbed all of the rifles and put them in the lavatory. Using seatbelt material that he had cut from the extra seats and some rope he found in a survival kit he repeated his exercise on each of the Russians. He also used duct tape and taped their mouths shut and used it to help secure them to their seats. He found Dashov's pistol and checked it for ammo then he stuck it in his belt with Leshev's weapons. While Lee was working on their "passengers" he suddenly felt the aircraft start a right turn and he assumed Stoney had turned back to 'Q'. Lee agreed that was a good idea since Leshev had damaged the aircraft.

Damn, if the window hadn't been shot out I could put my plan into action. Lee thought as he finished tying up the Russians and then headed back to the cockpit.

Once Stoney had the autopilot's new heading set he noticed that they had just about reached 10,000 feet and he removed his oxygen mask. There was a terrible roar in the cockpit as wind blasted through the missing window with the force of a hurricane. He tried not to look at the blood which covered the co-pilot's side of the cockpit. He knew the force that sucked Steve's big body through that small window had shredded him as he went through.

However, knowing Steve was dead before he made the long fall to Earth provided little comfort. Stoney had to work very hard to suppress the emotional stress associated with such a brutal loss of a friend and co-worker. As long as he had been flying, death had always been a possibility but until this trip, he had kept the Reaper at bay. His natural instinct was to preserve his aircraft and crew at all costs. Normally, that would include anyone on the aircraft, but he didn't care at all what happened to the Russians sitting in the cabin.

His first instinct was to asphyxiate them all especially after what had happened to Maria and now Steve, however, his conscience would not allow him that luxury. Mentally kicking himself back to reality, he put on his headphones, but he couldn't hear anything on the radio.

Static filled his ears though he could make out the strange noise that they had first heard when trying to contact Polar Control at the beginning of this nightmare. Actually, he was surprised he could hear anything over the roar. About this time Lee reappeared in the cockpit.

"Turn up the heat as high as it will go and hand me my parka. I am freezing!" Stoney shouted over the howl of the wind. Lee handed him the parka which he put on. He motioned for Lee to sit in the co-pilot's seat.

Lee wiped the blood from the co-pilot's seat and the windows using a rag he had found in the galley. He then climbed into the seat and put on his seatbelt.

Stoney had begun to worry that they might not find the airfield in the dark. Just because he was on a reciprocal heading and was trying to compensate for the wind, his level of confidence was not high. He knew that with the airfield's beacon, radar, and radios destroyed they couldn't help him from the ground.

He was not sure why he did it, but he reached down and dialed in the international emergency frequency on the radio. This frequency also happened to be the military "Guard" frequency of 121.5 MHz. He knew that the military monitored that frequency as well as all rescue centers worldwide and aircraft in flight would monitor it as well. He crossed his fingers and began to send out a mayday signal hoping and praying that someone would hear him.

"Mayday, mayday, mayday! This is Atlantic Pacific Air Flight 28-Alpha. Anyone that hears me, please respond!" He had the volume on the radio turned up all the way and all that he heard was static, the strange noise, and the howl of the wind. He continued the sequence every minute on the minute. In between mayday calls, Stoney asked how the pax were doing. Since Lee had propped open the cockpit door, he was able to look out into the cabin.

"Seems the natives are getting restless; guess they didn't get a strong enough dose of the gas. Leshev is already awake and trying to thrash around," Lee reported.

"Take one of those pistols you have and go knock each one on the back of the head. For God's sake don't kill them, just knock them out!"

Climbing out of the seat, Lee walked out of the cockpit door and saw Leshev and Danshov both struggling with their bonds.

You get it first, comrade captain, thought Lee as he walked up to Leshev with the pistol in his hand. Leshev was desperately trying to get out of the bonds and Lee could hear muffled sounds of anger coming through his duct taped mouth. Lee just stood there and watched him struggle for a few seconds then he took the pistol and put it between Leshev's eyes. Leshev suddenly became very still and quiet as Lee just stood there with the pistol's barrel making a round circle on the skin between Leshev's eyes as he forcefully pushed it against the skull, all the while thinking, *I am not normally prone to violence, but after what you've done to Steve, Maria and the two 'Q' guys I'd like to do more with this pistol then whack you on the head. I'd like to shoot you right where you sit; feeling as helpless as we have these last few hours! Stealing this aircraft is one thing, but killing and maiming innocent people is something quite different.*

With one last look at the defiance in Leshev's eyes, Lee took the pistol walked behind his captive and with a single forceful blow sent him to dreamland. Moving on to Danshov and the two corporals, Lee let them have it with the same pent up rage he'd used to knock out Leshev.

Heading back to the cockpit, he stopped at the front of the cabin, turned around and surveyed his handiwork while thinking, *Well, on the bright side they'll wake up with one hell of a headache and a stiff neck to boot.*

The ropes held up each man's body in the seat, but their heads hung forward against their chests, so with a smile on his face he continued on into the cockpit, put on his overcoat and climbed back into Steve's seat.

"What did you do with their weapons?" asked Stoney over the howl of the wind.

"I put them all except these pistols into the lavatory and used the Stew's keys to lock them up."

As they talked he looked over at Stoney and he could tell that his teeth were chattering as much as his boss's were. Boy, what he wouldn't give for something hot to drink or at least something warm for his hands!

Picking up the microphone, Lee continued the mayday calls.

"Mayday, mayday, mayday. This is Atlantic Pacific Air flight 28-Alpha. Please respond if you hear me!" He let up on the mic button and sat shivering while listening to the static.

"Atlantic . . . . Air . . . . this is . . . United States . . . . 24—please respond." Both Stoney and Lee looked at each other and they both yelled "All right!"

"This is APA flight 28-Alpha, responding United States aircraft please say again. We are only getting a few words. Please respond!" Lee anxiously yelled into the microphone.

The minutes that followed seemed to last an eternity for Stoney and Lee, Stoney was concentrating on holding a good heading back to airfield 'Q' and Lee was staring at the radio as if trying to make it respond again through willpower alone.

After what seemed like hours, the radio suddenly crackled to life: "Atlantic Pacific Air Flight 28-Alpha, this is the United States Air Force call sign Snowbird 24 calling; how do you read us?"

Both men almost jumped out of their seats at the clarity of the signal. Stoney intently listened to the ensuing radio conversation through his headphones.

"Snowbird 24, this is APA flight 28-Alpha. We read you loud and clear," Lee said into the microphone.

"Roger, APA 28-Alpha, this is Snowbird 24; we read you loud and clear as well. Please say position and conditions on board."

"Snowbird 24 this is 28-Alpha, best guess is we are fifteen miles from Emergency Airfield Quebec. We have bound and gagged guests on board and have suffered minor damage to the aircraft. We are hoping to land at back at Quebec. Please say your position."

"28-Alpha this is Snowbird 24, we are located on the field at Quebec. We have assets to help you with your guests. We will attempt to light the runway for your approach. Cross the runway at the midpoint and make right downwind traffic for the runway. Good Luck!"

"Snowbird, turn on every available light to help guide us to your position."

"Roger, WILCO," came the reply.

Lee reached over and patted Stoney on the shoulder. Conversation in the cockpit was hard at best with the wind howling through the broken window. Lee noticed that Stoney had started descending down to the published minimum altitude on the 'Q' approach chart. Lee knew that altitude would keep them clear of the terrain below.

Both crewmembers were staring out into the darkness looking for the lights they hoped Snowbird would turn on for them. All at once they both saw the faint glow of lights just in front of the right wing. Stoney yelled to Lee that he guessed they were at least ten miles out and to start the Pre-Landing Checklist as he turned the aircraft toward the distant lights.

As the glow of the lights became brighter, they concluded the checklist and were relieved when they felt the landing gear lock into position and saw those three green lights on the panel which confirmed it.

Lee picked up the microphone; "Snowbird 24 this is 28-Alpha; we are on a two-mile final, have the runway in sight. All indications are green for a normal landing."

Stoney lined up the Super Constellation with the runway outlined by orange/red flares. Lee thought to himself, *I don't think I've seen a more beautiful sight in my life!* Lining up, dropping flaps and setting the engines for touchdown, the aircraft slowly sank toward the ground. Crossing the end of the runway, Stoney pulled out all of the power and the big bird settled down at airfield 'Q' once more. As the aircraft slowed, Stoney shutdown the outboard two engines and upon reaching a safe taxi speed he performed a U-turn on the runway and taxied to the tarmac. That's when Lee noticed the USAF C-130 sitting there. When they reached the tarmac, they parallel parked next to the 130 and once again, the engines were shutdown at airfield 'Q'. Stoney slumped over the controls in complete exhaustion as Lee got up and opened the cabin door. By now the Russians had regained consciousness and displayed no reaction when several U.S. Marines entered carrying M-16s at the ready.

CHAPTER 17

The teletype machine started to sound like a large electric typewriter as the striker arms began to bang out a message on the yellow paper. Train, Burton and Smith all ran over to see what was coming out. The machine continued to pound the message into the paper and finally a little bell dinged indicating complete receipt of the message. Tearing the paper off the machine Train began to read.

***BEGIN MESSAGE

APA flight #28A returned to Airfield 'Q'. Successful landing. 1 crewmember killed during altercation with hostiles in flight, 1 crewmember killed during initial takeover. 2 'Q' personnel killed. Aircraft cockpit windshield severely damaged. All hostiles in custody. No rescue team casualties. C-130 departs in two hours will rtn to home base with pax and crew. Please advise on protection of assets.

Tyler Noland, Acting Airfield Chief sends.
EOT (End of Transmission)***

Both Train and Burton whooped with relief that the aircraft, crew and passengers were safe though the loss of several lives dampened their spirits. Turning to Train, Burton asked, "How do we deal with a broken aircraft sitting in the Arctic?"

"We will have to dispatch a crew and repair team with appropriate parts to fix the windshield and fly her home. We'll need to have the Marines stay on site to secure the aircraft until it is safely in the air once more. No telling if the Russians would try again with it stuck on the ground. However, closer to home, we are going to have to put all of this in an after action report for the leadership to digest. I will put an interim report together until we can personally interview the crew. There is one major problem we need to address immediately; the passengers. I will bet they are hopping mad, and we will have to do a lot of 'smoothing of wrinkled feathers' to prevent them from going to the press and spilling the whole incident across the front pages of <u>The New York Times</u> and the <u>London Daily Telegraph</u>. I guarantee this incident is the death knell for our program. Even with no passenger deaths, Congress will not be able to stomach what has happened and will kill it before it can happen again," said Train.

"You and I along with a 'company' psychologist should get to Elmendorf as soon as possible. The passengers will want to quickly resume their journey. If we don't intercept them now, there is no way we'll be able to contain the story. The political fallout from this incident will last for years! I'll contact the maintenance people out at Victoria and tell them to get ready to go out to 'Q' to fix 28-Alpha. I'm going to have APA send a co-pilot and skeleton maintenance crew as quickly as possible to Elmendorf where they will catch a C-130 to Quebec. Once repaired, Stone and his crew will fly 28-Alpha to Elmendorf from Quebec, refuel and return to Los Angeles. I am going to request that several of the Marines remain at Quebec for asset protection," Burton replied.

"If you take care of all of that, I'll finish the interim report and forward it to you and my management. I'll also get hold of Andrews AFB and have a jet standing by to get us to Elmendorf ASAP. Bring one of your shrinks and meet me at Andrews in two hours."

Burton headed out the door to take care of his 'do list'.

Just before leaving Train said, "Smith, please send a message to Polar Control that 28-Alpha has been found and is OK. We will advise if we require further assistance from them. Also thank them for their help."

"Yes sir, I will take care of that ASAP," said Smith.

Holding out his hand Train said, "Thank you for all of your work and help. Your quick action may have saved the day."

"Glad to help sir, good luck, but I think your work is just beginning," said Smith as he shook Train's hand.

"I think you're right," said Train as headed out the door and back to his office. He had to finish that interim report and tell his wife he wouldn't be home for dinner for the next several nights.

Stoney started to get up out of his seat and realized that he ached all over. *No doubt from the adrenaline rush and stress of the last hour*, he thought. As he climbed over the center console he saw the Russians being marched out of the aircraft and down the stairs. As the last one went down the stairs a Marine came over and held out his hand.

"I'm Captain Pete Jones."

Extending his hand Stoney said "Captain Victor Stone, though my friends call me Stoney. Believe me, you are one of my friends. You cannot begin to understand how happy we are to see you and your guys! This has been an ordeal and a half."

"Nice to meet you Stoney! Very impressive how you and Lee managed to subdue and secure a squad of Spetsnaz troops. How did you do it?"

"Unfortunately, you may not have a high enough clearance for all of the details, but suffice it to say that I will be forever in debt to the engineers that designed the systems in this aircraft. Without their foresight, Lee, Steve and I would be in Russia about now."

"Who is Steve?" asked Jones.

"When we tackled Leshev, his pistol went off in the struggle. The bullet grazed my co-pilot, Steve, before it hit the window behind him. The bullet shattered the window causing rapid decompression which sucked Steve out the hole."

"I am sorry to hear that, but I am glad that at least you, Lee and the aircraft made it back here. How did you find the field?"

"We dead reckoned a course back and had it not been for Snowbird 24 talking us down we probably would have missed the airfield and searched until we ran out of fuel and put her in the snow. I want to shake that man's hand!"

"I am sure Captain Marcus will want to say 'Hi' as well. He should still be in the 130, let's walk over and see."

"What are you going to do with the Russians?"

"My men are handcuffing them and securing them for the trip back to Elmendorf. I am sure the State Department is going to love having a handful of Russian Spetsnaz troops to deal with; would love to hear those discussions. Let's go see Captain Marcus."

Descending the stairs, after they closed the cabin door behind them, they walked across the ramp to the C-130. Captain Jones opened the door and they climbed into the 130. Turning left they entered the cockpit and saw the two pilots hunched over the center console entering data into what Stoney guessed was the INS.

"Captain Marcus, this is Captain Victor Stone of APA Flight 28A," said Jones as he made the introductions.

"Please call me Stoney. You don't know how happy I am to meet you. Thank you very much for sending out that radio call. That really saved our bacon."

"Nice to meet you Stoney, that is Lieutenant Bryan. He is the one you talked to on the radio. That strange noise on the aircraft frequencies has us baffled and it made it nearly impossible to hear you. Glad you were already headed in this general direction since the closer distance allowed us to hear you much better over the interference. When we landed we learned of your departure with the Russians. We had hoped you would be able to re-take control of the aircraft once airborne, but how you managed to subdue a small contingent of Spetsnaz is beyond me. How did you do it?"

"Nice to meet you Lieutenant I would love to tell you but like Captain Jones, here, I can't reveal certain secrets of the aircraft without an appropriate clearance. Let's just say that the engineers who designed the systems made it possible for us to retake the aircraft."

"Well, however you did it, congratulations. Is there any damage to the aircraft?"

"Yes, the cockpit window was blown out when the Russian captain's gun went off during our struggle on the cockpit floor. The bullet shattered the window and the decompression sucked my co-pilot out."

"I am sorry to hear that. Given the circumstances, I am glad we didn't arrive to find everyone here dead. Guess you and your passengers will be guests of the U.S. Air Force aboard our luxurious C-130 back to Elmendorf," said Marcus.

"Looks that way, but there is the problem of securing and safe guarding the Northern Star. We can't leave it unattended out here. Has Washington been notified of our return?"

"Yes, we had the local station manager send out a teletype message once you landed and we determined your status; so far, no response that I know of," said Jones.

"I know that the Russians killed James and Hudson before we left. Who is in charge now? By the way, how are the rest of my crew and passengers?" asked Stoney.

"Tyler Noland is the next ranking civilian. Your crew and passengers are safe and sound. We have them in the cafeteria. It seemed to be the most comfortable place to put them. I am afraid that some of them are getting agitated and want to contact loved ones at home. So far I have told them communications to the States and England

201

are impossible since the Russians destroyed most of the radios and there is no phone service here."

"That was wise. I am sure Washington will have instructions regarding them as well when we hear back. Captain Marcus, Lieutenant Bryan, thank you very much for your assistance. We probably would not have made it here without you."

"I am glad we were able to assist. You get to buy the first round at the O'Club when we get back to base!"

"You got it! Captain Jones, let's go find Mr. Noland," said Stoney.

Once again Stoney and Jones braved the cold winds of the Arctic and headed for the main building. Entering the building, Stoney said, "I am going to stop off in the cafeteria and see my people."

At that moment, Corporal Dane walked up and said to Jones, "Sir, the passengers want to talk to you."

"I'll go with Captain Stone to see them. In the mean time find Tyler Noland and see if he has received a reply from his status report."

"Yes, sir, if there is a reply I'll bring it to you in the cafeteria," said Dane who pivoted on his heel and headed to the communications building.

Entering the cafeteria, Stoney was surprised with the change in atmosphere. Everyone was talking and the stress level was definitely lower. However, he could sense some anger in the tone of some of the conversations.

"Ah, Captain Stone glad to see you made it back safely," said a loud voice from across the room. Turning in the direction of the voice, Stoney recognized Mr. Gooseman coming toward them. Additionally, Virginia and Brad jumped up at the mention of Stoney's name and ran over to them as well.

Virginia gave Stoney a great big hug and Brad reached out to pump Stoney's hand and slap him on the back. "Stoney, it is great to see you. Brad and I thought that we wouldn't see you guys ever again. Where are Lee and Steve?"

"Steve was killed, and I don't know where Lee is. I am glad to see everyone is still OK."

"Captain Stone and Captain Jones," said Mr. Gooseman, "Now that the reunions are over can you please tell me when we will leave this God-forsaken place and get to London? I have business there as do several of the other passengers."

"Mr. Gooseman, it is nice to see you again. If you will allow me, I will address the entire group at once." Projecting a loud voice, Stoney said "ATTENTION EVERYONE! If you will quiet down I'll fill you in on current events."

Slowly, the chatter in the room became silence as everyone turned to look at the small group at the front of the room.

"First of all, let me say that I am glad to be back here and not in Siberia. I know things have been terrible since this ordeal started and I want to commend everyone for their strength and endurance. The nightmare is finally over! I am sure each of you are wondering what will happen next. Before I get into that, let's have a round of applause for our rescuers Captain Jones and his Marines!" The room erupted in applause and Stoney let it go on for a short time then he held up his hands for quiet and continued.

"We sent a status message to APA headquarters and we are waiting on a response from them. I regret to inform you that in the process of re-taking the aircraft there was a gunshot which killed my co-pilot, Steve Valdochi and damaged the aircraft. The gunshot caused the cockpit window to blow out and as such the aircraft is grounded. I suspect headquarters will want us to return to Elmendorf AFB, Alaska, on the C-130 that brought the Marines here. APA will send a flight crew and maintenance team to repair our aircraft before they fly it back to California."

"How about getting us to England?" asked Mr. Gooseman.

"Captain Stone, I have a more fundamental question I would like to ask before you go any further," said Robert Deems as he made his way to the front of the room.

"Mr. Deems, what is your question?" asked Stoney.

"It seems to me, that the Soviets have spent a lot of time, energy, and most likely a fair amount of political capital to get their hands on an aircraft most airlines consider as surplus equipment; now why would they do that?"

Stoney noticed the room had become deathly quiet and he felt the eyes of everyone in the room fixated on him as he debated on how to answer that question. *Of course, the one question I can't truthfully answer. I owe them a reasonable explanation for what has happened but I can't divulge national secrets,* thought Stoney.

"Captain Stone, maybe I can help," said Brad.

"Robert, as a member of the crew my primary job is to handle the long range communications with air traffic control when we are out of radar coverage. Aboard the aircraft I sit in a communications room in the tail. That is why no one saw me during the flight. From that compartment, I use specialized radios to talk to air traffic control giving them position reports and passing any airborne traffic information to Captain Stone in the cockpit. However, it just so happens that those same radios have the sensitivity to intercept radio communications from submarines and other aircraft within a several hundred mile radius. As we fly the polar route, I am intercepting those radio communications, recording them on magnetic tape and when we reach our destination representatives of the U.S. Department of Defense come aboard the aircraft and take those tapes for analysis. Undoubtedly, the Soviets have discovered what we are doing and they were after those radios so they could build a defense against our prying ears."

"So you mean to tell us, that we paid money to fly on a U.S. Government spy mission?"

"No sir, I am telling you that APA agreed to this arrangement as a patriotic company willing to do its part to keep the Soviets at bay. What the Soviets don't realize, is that the radios they were after are readily available on the open market. Their communications systems are so under-engineered that just about anyone could receive the transmissions if they were close enough to the source. It just so happens these flights cover large swaths of the polar ocean where their subs happen to be. It's nothing more than being at the right place at the right time."

"Mr. Deems, Brad is entirely correct with his explanation. We're all patriots at heart and keeping one step ahead of the Soviets might just keep our kids safe at night," added Stoney.

"I am still not happy about this at all, but I will accept your explanation for now. I don't know about the rest of you, but I will be seeing a lawyer when we get back to civilization," said Deems.

"Mr. Gooseman, you asked about England?" said Stoney changing the subject.

"Yes, I did. How do we get from here to there?" said Gooseman.

"Sir, I assume APA will send a charter flight to Elmendorf, and it would return everyone to California where all of you will be given complementary tickets, first class of course, on the first flight to London. I have asked Mr. Noland to let me know as soon as we get a response from APA headquarters. In the mean time, please make yourselves as comfortable as possible. If anyone wants to try and sleep, I am sure the folks here at 'Q' will do their best to accommodate that wish. Does anyone else have any questions?"

"Captain Stone," said Mrs. Whiteman, "What will become of our luggage and will we be reimbursed for our tickets?"

"Mrs. Whiteman, we will make sure your luggage travels with you to Elmendorf, as far as ticket refunds, I will have to leave that to APA to determine. My crew and I will do everything we can to make your stay here as well as your travel arrangements as quick and as smooth as possible."

Stoney felt a tap on the shoulder and turning around he asked the man standing there, "Are you Mr. Noland?"

"Yes, captain, it is nice to meet you. I have a teletype message from APA headquarters. If you will step outside with me we can discuss their instructions."

Turning back to the group, Stoney said, "Everyone, I have a message from APA headquarters. If you will excuse me I'll see what it says and then report back to you."

He turned and followed Tyler out the door assuming Jones wouldn't be far behind.

After closing the door, Tyler pulled a piece of yellow paper from his pocket and handed it to Stoney. Unfolding it, Stoney began to read:

****

"This message is for Captain Stone and Captain Jones.
Captain Stone:

Glad all is well, under current circumstances.

Return all pax/luggage to Elmendorf via Snowbird.
Inform pax transportation to San Francisco will arrive
in 3 days. DO NOT allow communication from pax to
outside world.

Consider them quarantined to prevent spread of
information.

Provide assurance all will arrive at final destination
ASAP.

You and flight engineer to remain at 'Q' until aircraft
is flyable.

Maintenance crew, repair materials, replacement
co-pilot to be dispatched to your location ASAP.

When possible fly to Elmendorf to refuel then return
to home base via most direct route ASAP.

Send non-essential aircrew to Elmendorf via
Snowbird.

#####

Captain Jones:

Return all prisoners to Elmendorf aboard Snowbird.

Leave contingent to guard Northern Star assets.

Remaining personnel will return aboard Northern Star.

Secure all communications assets to prevent
unauthorized information leakage outside of military
channels.

Consider all information regarding current situation as
"TOP SECRET/NOFORN" until further notice.

####

Have 'Q' comm. officer signal acknowledgement and
compliance upon receipt of this message.

####
This is an NSA/CIA/HQ USMC/HQ USAF/Elmendorf-CC coordinated message.
####
Tom Train, NSA/SES-1 sends."
###EOT###
****

"Well Pete, looks like you and I have our orders. Tyler, looks like you all will have company for a few more days. I don't have anything to add to an 'ACK' message to HQ."

"Stoney, I agree. I don't like the quarantine issue. I don't think your pax will like it one bit. I will stay with you and keep Daniels and Maxwell. The others can handle the Russians on the return trip to Elmendorf. Tyler go ahead and send an 'ACK' message to HQ."

"Can do, sirs," responded Tyler as he headed back to the communications building.

"I agree Pete; I know the pax are not going to be happy at all about not being able to contact families and such. As of several hours ago, we were officially late into London. I am sure the APA office has informed them that we are safe and no harm has come to anyone, however, keeping them at Elmendorf for three days is going to be rough. In the mean time we have to break the news to them."

"Glad that is your job, I sure wouldn't want to have to break that news especially after that grilling from Deems. Good luck, buddy. I'll catch up with you later. I need to check on our 'guests' and make sure they haven't given my Marines a reason to shoot one of them; talk about a diplomatic mess," said Jones.

"Right now, I think your job is much easier than mine. Your hostile audience is all tied up!" retorted Stoney as Jones headed off.

Stoney stood in silence for several minutes to compose in his head what he would tell his passengers and crew. He knew they would be furious at the three-day delay but this was out of his hands. He reasoned the delay was to allow time for CIA/NSA to debrief the pax and figure out how to keep them from spilling the story to the closest reporter once they left military hands.

He was sure if he were in their situation that is exactly what he would want to do. On the operational side, he wondered who they would send to replace Steve. He had known all along this job would have certain inherent risks, but he never imagined it could result in the deaths of innocent people like Maria, Steve, James and Hudson. Standing there, he began to realize just how tired he had become. It seemed like an eternity since that Beep . . . Beep . . . Beep of the alarm clock back in Victoria.

Standing straight up, clearing his throat and his head he reached out and opened the cafeteria door and walked in.

"Ladies and Gentlemen, if everyone would have a seat and let me have your attention once more. I have some information to pass on that will be of interest to everyone."

Everyone found a seat and the room became quiet with anticipation.

"I have received instructions from APA Headquarters. All of the passengers and the flight attendants will return to Elmendorf Air Force Base to await transportation back to San Francisco. Unfortunately, the Russian prisoners will return with you aboard Snowbird 24 along with several

Marines to guard them. The Flight Engineer, Lee, and I will remain here at 'Q' until our maintenance personnel arrive with spare parts to repair our aircraft. Once repaired, we will fly it and the remaining Marines to our home base in California. Your luggage will accompany you on the Snowbird. That is all of the good news. The not so good news is your transportation to San Francisco will not arrive in Elmendorf for three days. I have been assured that all of your families and anyone that had gone to the London airport to meet you have been informed by APA personnel that everyone is safe and sound but that it would be a few more days until you arrive back in San Francisco. Once in San Francisco you will be booked in First Class on the first possible flight to London or wherever it is you would like to go, all courtesy of APA. No one has any questions, right?"

Stoney hadn't even taken a breath when the entire room erupted in conversation. Mr. Gooseman jumped up and tried to shout something to Stoney, but with so much noise Stoney couldn't hear him.

"QUIET!" shouted Stoney, "Mr. Gooseman wants to ask a question. If everyone will quiet down, I will try to answer all of your questions. However, keep in mind that I can only pass on the information I currently have which I will admit is not much. Mr. Gooseman, your question."

"Captain Stone, as you are well aware we have been tied up, starved, scared half to death with guns in our faces and now you tell us it will be three more days till we can continue on our way. I believe I can speak for everyone here and say that is ABSURD. Do you honestly expect us to sit for three days in Alaska waiting on an aircraft? Surely, APA has additional airplanes they could send to meet us when we arrive on the Snowbird!"

"Mr. Gooseman, please believe that I sympathize with your feelings and those of everyone who has been involved in this whole affair. I cannot begin to guess why APA is taking three days to get you out of Alaska, but I can assure you there must be a very good reason. It is only logical that they would want to get you on your way as soon as they can. I know everyone here has been patient and I am sure that your patience is wearing quite thin, however there are certain things out of my control."

"Captain Stone, I have a question as well," said Ms. McQuinn, in her thick Scottish accent.

"Yes, Ms. McQuinn."

"What assurances do we have that the Marines we have on board will be able to handle the Russians? I, for one, don't like the idea of being on the same airplane with those animals."

"Captain Jones assures me his Marines can handle the Russians since they will be secured and guarded just as they are now. They will not be in any position to cause problems. If it would make you feel better, I can ask Captain Jones to talk to the group about that concern as soon as he can."

"Captain Stone," said Mr. McNeely, "when will the Snowbird leave for Elmendorf?"

"Ah, good question, Mr. McNeely, I am told it will leave in about six hours, at dawn."

For the next thirty minutes, Stoney continued to try to allay their fears about the trip to Elmendorf as well as the delay in returning them to San Francisco. Finally, when he had answered everyone's questions he suggested they all turn in for some much needed rest. Since their luggage would have to be unloaded from 28-Alpha he asked the 'Q' personnel if that could be done ASAP to allow the pax to shower, get some sleep and get ready for the trip to Elmendorf.

After working with the facilities manager, Stoney made sure everyone had a place to shower and sleep and with all of those arrangements settled, he headed to the room he would share with Lee.

Entering the room, Stoney realized that the regular inhabitants of 'Q' had given up their personal space for the crew and pax from 28-Alpha. Making a mental note, Stoney would put in a request with the NSA/CIA managers to figure out a way to give all the personnel at 'Q' a large bonus for the outstanding work they had accomplished under extremely difficult conditions.

As he looked over the room, he realized someone had brought in his overnight bag from the aircraft and placed it next to one of the two beds and Lee's bag was sitting next to the other one. Stoney stripped down to his underwear and hung up his uniform. He would have to see if there were any laundry facilities since there was blood on his shirt.

Seeing the blood spatter reminded him of his friend Steve and the horrible way in which he had died. He would have liked to grab a weapon and shoot every last one of those Russian bastards for what they had done to his crew. He walked over to the wall switch, turned off the light, and climbed into bed. He fell into a deep sleep just as his head hit the pillow. Stoney had a restless sleep since his mind kept playing the scene of Steve going out the cockpit window and the look on Maria's face when he cut her loose. The same scenes played over and over like a movie projector caught in an endless loop.

CHAPTER 18

I n the midst of those dreams, Maria kept saying "Captain Stone . . . Captain Stone . . ." then Stoney came to realize it wasn't the dream it was someone trying to wake him. Slowly opening his eyes he saw the familiar face of Tyler Noland looking down at him and gently shaking his shoulder.

"Is it that time already?" he groggily asked.

"Yes sir, the passengers are being awakened as well and the C-130 crew has the aircraft ready to go. All of the luggage has been loaded and everyone is eating in the cafeteria. You have enough time to run through the shower before they'll be ready to board."

"Thanks Tyler, don't wake up Lee. I'll be ready in about fifteen minutes," Stoney said in a whisper.

"Sir, here is a set of clothes for you to wear, I will see about getting your uniform cleaned in the mean time."

"Thanks Tyler, all of the folks here at 'Q' have been outstanding, we really appreciate the help."

"There should be clean towels in the bathroom. We are gathering everyone in the cafeteria before loading the aircraft. I'll see you there," said Tyler as he left the room.

Stoney got out of bed and noticed that even with the talking and the light on, Lee had not so much as budged or rolled over. He opened his overnight bag grabbed some clean underclothes and his shaving kit and made his way to the bathroom. Climbing into the shower, Stoney didn't realize hot water could feel so good. It seemed like an eternity since that last shower in Victoria.

Dressed and feeling much better, Stoney made his way to the cafeteria. As he was walking down the hallway, he ran into Mike Whiteman. "Good morning Captain Stone," said Mike.

"Good morning, Mike. How are you doing?"

"Well, sir, I'm fine, however I'm afraid that Lillian McNeely is having a hard time with this whole situation. She is afraid to get on the C-130 with the Russians. She understands they are tied up with no way to get loose and the Marines will be guarding them, however I still can't convince her it will be a safe trip. I'm afraid many of the other passengers feel the same way. We're all anxious to get home, but not about this next part of the trip."

"Thanks for telling me Mike, I really appreciate your concern and I wish that I was going with all of you, but I have a responsibility for my aircraft as well as my passengers. I'll have Captain Jones talk to everyone prior to boarding. He should be able to allay their fears. Please tell everyone that I'll be there as soon as I find him."

"Thanks captain, I'll let everyone know."

Entering the main administration area, Stoney found Jones talking to Tyler and drinking a cup of coffee. "Hi guys, where did you get that coffee?" inquired Stoney.

"The pot is on that table help yourself," said Tyler as he pointed to an adjacent table.

Walking over to the pot, Stoney poured a cup and rejoined the two men. "Pete, I think we have a small problem concerning the Russians, my passengers, and this flight. I just talked to Mike Whiteman and he voiced a concern many of the passengers have. They are afraid of traveling with the Russians in the same plane. They realize all of the security measures you have taken, but they are naturally concerned about being confined with their previous captors and not a whole lot of folks to guard them. I need you to talk to the passengers and see what you can do."

"To be honest, I am not surprised they are concerned. I am not exactly happy with the arrangements either. I would like to knock them all over the head and put their lights out for the trip."

"How about putting them all to sleep?" asked Tyler.

"How do you propose to do that?" asked Jones.

"We have a small pharmacy and I am sure there is something there we could use to put them out for the trip. If you would like, I can find the medic we have and see what he can cook up."

"I think that would go a long way to allay their fears. A group of snoring Russians isn't a threat to anyone. What do you think Pete?" asked Stoney.

"If they have something in the pharmacy that we could slip to them in coffee or something, I am not in favor of giving them injections of any kind. I realize the fear that the passengers must have, but that could cause serious problems with the State Department and it would not play well in the news. You know as well as I do the Soviet propaganda machine would have a heyday with that information. I can just see the headline on the front page of Pravda—'U.S. Marines Kidnap and Inject Soviet Soldiers with Experimental Drugs!' Tyler, go ahead and get with the medical folks and see what they have. Let me know ASAP, we want to get the Snowbird airborne soon as we can."

"I'll have an answer for you in minutes." Tyler took off running down the hall to the medical facility.

Calling it a medical facility was a stretch at best, thought Tyler as he ran down the hall. The medical facility consisted of a military trained medic and a couple of cabinets of pharmaceuticals, bandages and Band-Aids. Entering the room, he saw Jake Thornton.

"Hey Jake, what do you have that would knock a big guy out for a couple of hours? Preferably something that could be dissolved in coffee or sprinkled on food."

"Hey Ty, let's take a look and see what we can find. To be honest I am not surprised you're here, I wouldn't want to be confined in a plane with those Commie bastards after what they've done." After looking through the pharmaceutical cabinets Jake held up a bottle of pills.

"Here are some sleeping pills. They're somewhat potent and should do the job. It seems I have quite a lot of them. Guess the supply folks think all we do is sleep around here. We can grind these up and put them in the coffee pot. It might take a while but, I believe it will put them out for a few hours."

Grabbing a small dish and a heavy glass jar, Jake smashed the pills using the jar. As he ground up the pills, he gathered the powder and poured it into an empty bottle. Soon the bottle was about three quarters full of ground up sleeping pill powder. Handing the bottle to Tyler he said, "That should take care of the problem. Make sure you tell Captain Jones that it might take a short while for them to kick in. Good luck!"

"Thanks Jake, I'll get this to them ASAP," Tyler said as ran out the door to find Pete Jones.

A little while later in the cafeteria, Jones and Stoney were talking to some of the passengers when Tyler walked up to them.

"Captain Jones, I have the item you requested. Can I see you outside?" asked Tyler.

"No problem Tyler. Please excuse us for a minute," said Jones as he followed Tyler out the door.

Stoney was talking with Mr. Gooseman when he saw Noland and Jones re-enter the room and head for the kitchen. Quickly ending the conversation, he excused himself and went into the kitchen to see what was happening.

"Hey guys what's up?" he asked.

Jones explained the plan as Tyler made a large fresh pot of coffee.

"That is an awesome idea! And It might just work," Stoney replied.

Stoney helped Jones gather up a supply of Styrofoam cups along with milk and lots of sugar. Stoney had learned that Europeans liked their coffee with lots of milk and very sweet during his intercontinental flights. Meanwhile Tyler was mixing the sleeping powder into the freshly brewed coffee.

Once everything was ready, they hustled to the holding area where the Russians were sitting on the floor with their hands bound behind them. Several of the Marines were standing around with their weapons at the ready,

Stoney placed the items he was carrying on a table and said, "I am going to let the pax know that we have a potential solution to their concern and I'll catch up with you in the loading area."

"Don't give them too much information; again they need plausible deniability should they be confronted by the press," Jones whispered back.

Hurrying back to the cafeteria Stoney said loudly, "Ladies and gentlemen, if I can have your attention again for just a minute. I believe Captain Jones has found a solution to your fear of the Russians flying on the 130. I cannot give you the details, but Captain Jones has assured me the prisoners will be quite subdued during the flight. You have his word that they will not be a problem once airborne. We will plan to head out to the aircraft in about half an hour. Why don't you take this time to make sure that you have warm clothes, unfortunately, 130's can be quite cold at altitude. I am sure the folks here will be able to supply you with some blankets and if needed we can raid our aircraft for additional ones. Virginia, if you could be in charge of that and if you need to go to the aircraft, please let the maintenance folks know and they can get the blankets off the Constellation. If you all will excuse me, I have some arrangements to finalize. I will be back when it is time to load up." Stoney headed toward the door and went to talk to Jones in the secure area.

"Pete, there you are," Stoney said as he entered the secure area surprised at seeing the Russians were not restrained but were standing around drinking coffee. Marines, weapons at the ready stood watching the group.

"We wanted to show the Russians that Marines can be humanitarian on occasion. I told them the heat on the 130's doesn't work very well and the coffee would help warm them up prior to the trip. Also wanted to let them up to get the blood flowing in their legs. They have been bound, gagged and sitting on the floor since we arrived."

About that time, Captain Leshev walked over and as he did so, one of the Marines stepped between him and the two captains blocking his way.

"It's OK Marine, I don't want to do anything, I just want to talk to your captain," said Leshev.

"Let him through," said Jones and the Marine stepped out of the way, but not too far out of the way.

"Captain, I am wondering what will become of my team once we return to your base?"

"All of you will be put in the stockade for safe keeping, but other than that I have no idea. That will be for the diplomats and folks at a much higher pay grade than I am to determine."

"Will my men be able to contact their families? I believe the Geneva Convention allows communication to their families."

"I'm not a lawyer, but I don't believe the POW rules apply to you and your gang of marauders. If I'm not mistaken there has not been a declaration of war between Uncle Sam and the U.S.S.R. But who knows, that is for the lawyers and diplomats to argue about. I am sure if our roles were reversed, your treatment of us would be a lot worse. I imagine we would end up as guests of the KGB in Lubyanka prison with no hope of communicating with our families."

"Comrade captain I am sorry that you have such a dim view of Russian hospitality. We also have been told that you Americans have places that are similar in nature to Lubyanka, so I don't think you have much to complain about."

"Well, comrade, I know you will be pleasantly surprised with how we treat our prisoners. Now I must request that your men finish their coffee and place their hands behind their backs. We need to board the 130."

"Very well, captain we will do as you ask, however, I am formally requesting to be allowed to contact the Russian Embassy in Washington DC as soon as I can." Leshev turned to his fellow Spetsnaz troops and in Russian barked orders to his men who immediately started to throw their cups away. They then formed a line shoulder to shoulder with their hands behind their backs. Corporals Maxwell and Dane proceeded to tie the Russian's hands securely. When they got ready to put duct tape across their mouths Captain Leshev spoke up.

"Captain, is this really necessary? I assure you my men will maintain silence if you will agree to not tape our mouths."

"As long as they do not say a word, I will honor your request. However, my men will be given strict instructions to tape everyone if your promise is broken."

"Agreed," was all that Leshev said.

"L.T. and Gunny, once you verify their bonds, take them out to the aircraft and seat them at the rear. If during the flight they sneeze too loudly, tape them up."

"Yes, sir," the L.T. replied.

After they left the room, Stoney asked Jones, "How long do you think it will take for the pills to kick in?"

"Since they haven't eaten in a while, they should start to get sleepy within the next thirty minutes or so. I hope that by the time the 130 taxies to the end of the runway you won't be able to hear the engines over the snoring."

"I sure hope this works," was all Stoney said. About that time, the door opened and the Russians filed out of the room, Leshev in the lead with the Marines escorting them, weapons at the ready. Stoney and Jones headed back to the cafeteria to make sure the passengers were ready to board.

"Ladies and Gentlemen, we are ready to board the 130. Please gather anything you need and let's head on out." Stoney announced to everyone. The passengers dressed in their warmest clothes and wrapped in their blankets filed out the door as Stoney held it open for them.

Virginia and Brad walked with Stoney as the whole group headed down the hall. "Stoney, I hate to leave you and Lee here while we head back to civilization," said Virginia.

"I second that opinion," added Brad.

"Thanks for your sentiments, but APA was adamant that only essential aircrew remain here. I wish you all could stay as well, but in the long run I think it is better that you go with the passengers. It may also serve to keep their spirits up since they'll have familiar faces riding along with them."

When they reached the main door, Virginia hugged Stoney and tried to hide the tears in her eyes. Brad shook Stoney's hand and then they all headed out the door and to the waiting 130.

Climbing up the stairs into the 130, Stoney saw Sergeant Smythe and Virginia helping the pax get into their seats while showing them how to fasten their shoulder harness and seatbelts. Webbed seats made of red nylon straps lined both sides of the cabin. The passengers sat shoulder to shoulder down both sides of the 130 facing the middle of the cabin. The Russians sat in the rear of the cabin on the last few seats on both sides to minimize eye contact with 28-A's passengers. In the middle of the cabin was the pile of luggage securely strapped to the floor. As soon as everyone was seated and belted in, Stoney took the PA microphone.

"Ladies and gentlemen, this is not how I wanted to say good bye to all of you. Normally I make this speech from the cockpit as we taxi to the terminal at Heathrow. However, I would still like to wish everyone a safe trip home and I am sorry for the circumstances that have brought us here. I hope the rest of your trip goes smoothly and I thank you for your patience and understanding during this trying time. An APA representative will be meeting the aircraft at Elmendorf AFB and he will make sure that all arrangements are in place to get everyone to their final destination. Virginia and Brad are traveling with you to help in any way possible." As he finished his speech, there was a chorus of applause.

Stoney said "thank you" and went into the cockpit to say goodbye to Captain Marcus. As he turned to head out the door, he looked toward the aft section of the plane and saw the Russians strapped to their seats noting that several of them had started to nod off. *Great*, thought Stoney, *the pills are working.* With that thought, he descended the stairs and helped pull them away from the side of the aircraft and immediately he could hear the starter's whine as one of the propellers began to turn. Stoney and Jones then stood out of the way of the aircraft as one by one all four engines roared to life and Marcus turned the aircraft to head out to the runway. Stoney and Jones walked to the communications building and climbed the stairs up to the Control Tower Cab. When they reached the cab they saw Tyler Noland talking on a portable radio to Captain Marcus. Stoney and Jones saw the 130 reach the end of the runway and as it lined up for takeoff all of its landing lights came on and seconds later it began to accelerate down the runway. About half the way down the runway, it leaped into the air and the wheels retracted into their wells. After reaching a safe altitude it turned left and began the trip to Elmendorf AFB, Alaska. Reaching for the mic, Stoney said, "Snowbird, thanks again for all of the help and have a safe flight home."

"Thanks Stoney, I just got a call on the interphone that all of our 'guests' have dozed off and are sleeping like babies. Best of luck; first beer is on me at the O'Club when you stop to refuel. See you soon."

CHAPTER 19

"**L**adies and gentlemen, greetings from the flight deck; we are about fifty miles out of Elmendorf Air Force Base and should be on the runway in about fifteen minutes. Please buckle up and prepare for landing," said the captain of the U.S. Government Gulfstream jet as it glided through the crystal clear Alaskan sky.

Tom Train looked over at Glen Burton who was just waking up from a nap. Katie Fuller, the CIA psychologist, sat in the front of the cabin sipping a drink. Before departure, Train met with his higher management and they authorized him to 'pay for the silence of the passengers', if necessary, and to cut limited deals to ensure their silence.

He wasn't sure what the term 'limited deals' had meant, but he knew he had the backing of the National Security

Advisor to the President to do what was necessary to keep the Northern Star program and the events surrounding APA Flight 28A out of the press. The last thing that the U.S. Government wanted was a full fledged scandal in the newspapers revealing the nature of the Northern Star program, APA's connection with the Government, and the fact that the Constellations had been covert surveillance missions with fare paying passengers.

Needless to say, Train had his work cut out for him. As with any randomly chosen group of people thrust together by chance, each would be unique and would respond to a given situation differently. Train was well aware of this fact which is why the team included a psychologist. Her job was to get to know the passengers and help find ways to keep them quiet.

Time was their biggest enemy since they only had three days to accomplish their task. That was as long as they thought they could sequester the passengers with the pretense of awaiting an aircraft to fly them back to San Francisco. The Air Force would wine and dine them as much as possible. Above all there could not be any interaction with non-cleared base personnel and there would be absolutely NO phone calls or mail service.

Concluding his meeting with the Director of the NSA and the DDO, Train had hurried back to his office to get the overnight bag he kept in his closet. He had learned years ago that NSA employees went on business trips with minimal or no notice, so like most everyone else in the agency he kept a bag packed at all times.

As he hurriedly gathered up everything he would need for the trip, he gave his secretary instructions on how to contact him in Alaska as well as other information vital to keeping his office running smoothly while he was gone. When he finished, she mentioned that Glen Burton had requested Train pick him up at the office for the ride to Andrews Air Force Base. Before he raced out the door, Train took time to call his wife once more and say, "Good-bye." Thanking his secretary for all of her quick work in putting the trip together, he grabbed his bag and briefcase and headed for the parking garage where his driver was waiting.

Throwing his bag in the trunk, he asked the driver to swing by CIA HQ to pick up Mr. Burton. As the government sedan weaved and dodged through the Washington, D.C. traffic, Tom was deep in thought building a plan to accomplish his mission. He hoped that Glen was able to find a competent psychologist, with the appropriate security clearance, to accompany them on the trip. There was no doubt he or she would be a key member of the team. Staring out the windows but not actually seeing, he didn't notice their arrival at CIA HQ until the car screeched to a halt.

Tom saw Glen hustle out of the front door and throw his bag into the trunk. Glen climbed into the back seat next to Tom and as he was shutting the door, the car peeled out of the parking lot and raced towards Andrews AFB.

"Glen, did you find a psychologist for us?" Tom inquired.

"I did. Her name is Katie Fuller. Here is her dossier which I though you might want to look at on the way. While you're browsing, I will give you the 'Reader's Digest Condensed' version of her credentials and career."

"She is not just any run-of-the-mill psychologist. She has been working for CIA for several years and has worked cases that involved Russian and Soviet Block defectors as well as CIA case officers that had been 'damaged' in the field. Her job has been to analyze their psyche and then determine a course of action to either help them assimilate into western society or, in the case of the damaged spooks, to help them back to a somewhat normal life. As you can tell from her commendations, her success rate has been quite high."

"Her talents will be truly tested in Alaska since she has only three days to convince twenty people to keep quiet about a very traumatic event in their lives. Given her record of success, what is her background?" said Tom.

Glen continued, "Unlike most psychologists, she has a passion for technology and the human psyche and as such she did her undergraduate work at MIT. To be frank, I didn't even know MIT had a psyche department until I met her a few years ago. I got to know her fairly well when we worked on a CIA project together in Japan. I am sure you have heard of the MIG-17 pilot that defected, with his plane, from North Korea to Japan. I happened to be the CIA station chief in Japan at the time and she came over to help us work with that pilot. She was able to convince the pilot that the North Korean view of western society was a total sham. Likewise, over time she was able to convince him that the CIA did not built Tokyo just to fool with his mind. She later described her interest as more behavioral science rather than straight psychology. The CIA directly recruited her during her last year of school. I am sure if anyone can handle the passengers and obtain their cooperation, it will be her. I tracked her down at the Pentagon and asked her to meet us at the VIP terminal on Andrews. With this traffic, she will probably beat us there."

"Sounds like you picked a good person for the job. I'm sure she'll do fine," replied Tom as he handed the folder back. Glen was returning the folder to his briefcase when the car slid to a halt at the Andrews AFB VIP terminal.

As Tom and Glen gathered their bags and briefcases, a tall slender woman in a tailored suit walked up.

"See Tom, I told you she would make it here ahead of us. Katie thanks for coming on such short notice. This is Tom Train, the Northern Star Program manager."

Holding out his hand Tom replied, "Ms. Fuller, very nice to meet you. Thank you for agreeing to such a short notice trip."

"It is nice to meet you as well, Tom. Please call me Katie."

"Let's get a move on, the plane should be waiting for us on the ramp," replied Tom as he led the group inside the terminal.

Just then the Gulfstream thudded onto the runway. The ex-naval aviator that was driving had never quite gotten the idea that not every runway was as short as the one on the aircraft carrier, USS Enterprise. The landing didn't quite jar their bones, but there was no doubt in any passenger's mind they had arrived on the runway. *Seems, this guy is a student of the old saying 'Any landing you can walk away from is a good one',* thought Tom as they taxied up to the Elmendorf AFB VIP ramp. As the engines spooled down, an Air Force Lieutenant opened the door and stuck his head in the cabin welcoming them.

After the team exited the aircraft, the L.T. said, "Mr. Train, there are rooms booked for you in the VIP quarters. I will have your luggage delivered there."

"Thank L.T. is there anyone here to pick us up?" asked Tom.

"Yes sir, Major Cooper the base commander's executive officer is waiting for you in the VIP lounge."

The group continued across the ramp to the doors leading to the VIP lounge.

"Major Cooper, this is the group you were waiting for. This is Mr. Tom Train," said the Lieutenant as they walked into the lounge.

"Thanks L.T., I'll take it from here," said Cooper.

"Mr. Train, I am Major Erik Cooper and will be your liaison officer while you are here."

Shaking the offered hand, Tom introduced the rest of the team.

"If you all will follow me, we need to get moving to make your appointment with the base commander, Colonel Tomlinson," said Cooper.

Cooper led the group outside to a van. As the major climbed in and sat down in the driver's seat, Glen asked, "Major Cooper, do we have an expected arrival time for the Snowbird?"

While answering the question, Cooper fired up the van and drove quickly toward their destination. "Yes, sir, they lifted off about twenty minutes ago. Their ETA is about two hours from now. The Base Commander is anxious to see you and get a quick brief on your mission. He is also curious about the quarantine requirements for the pax. As his Executive Officer I can pretty much offer the full services of the base to you and I have the commander's authority to do so. I am here to grease the skids, if you will. Mr. Burton, in the seat beside you there are three manila envelopes, one for each of you. If you don't mind, please pass them around. Inside you will find your room key and a pre-programmed Land Mobile Radio for use around the base. Each radio has one channel programmed into it. There is an Air Force communications specialist at the other end of the radio and he will be able to connect you to anyone you need to talk to. These radios are cleared for up to SECRET level communications as is the communications operator. Please feel free to use them to call anywhere you need. We hope this will make it easier for you while you are here. Don't hesitate to call me, regardless of the hour. We should be at the colonel's office in another minute or so."

"Thank you Erik, on behalf of the CIA and NSA we really appreciate your efforts on such short notice. Where will the passengers be staying?" asked Tom.

"We have an alert facility that is a self-contained complex isolated from the rest of the base. The quarters are excellent and there is a cafeteria and recreation rooms. By design, the facility is self-contained. I think they will be very comfortable there. There are rooms available for you to use for the debriefings as well. We are trying to make them as comfortable as possible. Our other 'guests' that are arriving will be put in the base brig and kept isolated from everyone else. I'm expecting to hear from the State Department at any time. I'm surprised they didn't send a rep on your flight."

Cooper safely and carefully ignored traffic lights and stop signs as the van hurled through the streets of the Air Force base towards its destination.

"We contacted them, but they could not meet our departure timeframe. I expect your boss will be getting a phone call from them anytime now. Fortunately, that is not our problem at this time. Thanks for the radios; they will make life easier with our tight schedule. Will the base operations officer contact us as soon as the 130 is on approach?" said Tom.

"Yes, sir, as soon as the Snowbird contacts the tower they'll let us know. Colonel Tomlinson and I will meet the passengers. We think it would be better if you wait for them at the alert facility. I expect they will not be happy when they realize their first stop is not a telephone. We'll bus them over to the alert facility and turn them over to you. We'll deliver their luggage there as soon as possible and will put it in the main lounge to allow everyone to claim their bags."

"Major, I think it would be better if our luggage is taken over there as well. It'll be easier to conduct our business if we stay in the same quarters as the pax," said Glen.

"Yes sir, I'll have billeting bring your luggage over there as soon as the pax are settled in. I should have thought of that, but when VIPs arrive they are automatically booked into the VIP Officer's quarters."

Just then the van pulled up to the front door of what appeared to be the base command building. Tom noticed that it was a standard brown Air Force building except for an overhang that extended across a circular drive. The van stopped under the overhang and everyone got out.

As they walked inside the building It looked like every other military facility Tom had visited. The floor had plain off-white tile and the typical drab grey walls decorated with framed pictures of USAF aircraft. The 673rd Air Base Wing unit crest occupied the middle of a large wall and surrounding it were the unit crests for all the individual units

231

located on the base. A quick scan of the crests showed all but one belonged to USAF organizations. The odd crest was red and gold indicating it belonged to a unit in the U.S. Marine Corps and undoubtedly represented the contingent of Arctic trained Marines put there by the Northern Star Program.

Pausing a moment to look at the crest, Tom thought, *I had hoped this day would never arrive, but as the program manager for Northern Star, I paid for you guys to be here just for a contingency like the one facing us now. I know I am sending you into harm's way, but a lot of lives and national security interests are at stake. I wish you good luck and a safe return.*

"Mr. Train, the colonels are waiting for us," said Major Cooper.

"Sorry," said Tom as he followed the group up the stairs.

NSA/CIA received a yearly bill for all services provided by the 673rd Air Base Wing to the Northern Star Program and this year's bill would include additional fees for use of the alert facility and the cost to host the passengers and the NSA/CIA team during their stay. Walking into the "Command Section" also known as the headquarters, Tom and his fellow travelers were surprised at the nicely carpeted area as compared to the front entrance. The base commander's secretary was at her desk and as soon as the group entered the area, she told Major Cooper that the colonel was waiting for them and to go on in.

As they entered the office, Colonel Tomlinson stepped from behind his desk and Major Cooper proceeded with the introductions. After the appropriate handshakes the colonel sat down behind his desk in his large leather chair. Framing his desk on the left side was the U.S. flag and on the right was the USAF flag. Mementos from the colonel's various assignments during his tenure in the USAF covered the wall between the flags. He invited everyone to take the chairs arranged in a semi-circle in front of his desk. In the middle of the semi-circle was a small table. The traditional small talk began about their flight up and as they were talking, the colonel's secretary entered carrying a coffee service which she sat on the small table in front of the chairs. Everyone helped themselves to the coffee and once the secretary departed the room the real discussion began.

"Sir, may I start off the meeting by offering a sincere 'thank you' on behalf of the NSA and CIA to you and your people for the expeditious work and hospitality you have shown us. This is a very touchy situation with the passengers, and the need to keep this out of the newspapers is of paramount importance to national security. By the way, as far as the pax are concerned, we are representatives from Atlantic Pacific Air, it is vital that our connection with the U.S. Government be kept under wraps," explained Tom.

"I understand the need for secrecy. It would surely be a political nightmare should the real nature of the Northern Star Flights ever be revealed to the public. I'm curious as to how you plan to keep them from filling the newspapers with stories of the recent events."

"That is where Ms. Fuller comes in. She is a clinical psychologist and she specializes in debriefing defectors as well as long time undercover spooks. Her job is to work with the passengers as a group as well as individually to determine how to convince them to remain silent."

"The challenge," continued Katie, "is the short amount of time we have to work with them. Their transportation back to the lower forty-eight will be here in three days and it will take all of that to accomplish our goals. Since not all of them are U.S. citizens we cannot threaten or coerce them with imprisonment, so we have to find a way to appeal to them that ensures their silence for years to come."

"You certainly have your work cut out for you. Major Cooper, how much longer till the Snowbird lands?"

Looking at his watch, Cooper replied "About an hour sir."

"You better go ahead and take these folks out to the alert facility and get them situated. Mr. Train, Ms Fuller, Mr. Burton, thanks for stopping by. If there is anything me or my folks can do for you please let me know," said Tomlinson.

As everyone finished their coffee and stood up, Glen said "Colonel, thank you again. If CIA can do anything to help you in the future, please let me know."

"The same goes for the NSA, sir. Thank you once again for everything," added Tom as everyone started heading for the door.

Walking back to the waiting van, Cooper said, "We'll have to hurry if we are going to do a quick tour of the facility before the Snowbird arrives."

"Agreed! I really want to see it before hand," replied Tom as the group almost broke into a jog for the front door. As everyone else quickly entered the van, Cooper dived into the front seat and was starting the engine just as the doors slammed shut. Pressing a button on the dashboard, he turned on the blue flashing lights on top of the van. Quickly putting it into gear he gunned the engine and took off toward the alert facility.

CHAPTER 20

nce the Snowbird was airborne and climbing through 10,000 feet, Marcus said, "L.T. try to contact Polar Control."

"Can do sir."

Pressing the transmit switch on his control yoke Bryan said, "Polar Control this is Snowbird 24, how do you hear us?"

"Snowbird 24 this is Polar Control. We hear you loud and clear. Seems that whatever interference that was preventing contact with both you and APA FlIght 28-Alpha has disappeared. Communications have been normal for the past hour. Please say position."

"Polar Control, this is Snowbird 24 glad to hear that communications have returned to normal. We are presently Southwest bound for Elmendorf Air Force Base. We departed airfield Quebec moments ago. We anticipate two hours en route to Elmendorf."

"Snowbird 24, you are cleared present position direct Elmendorf. Squawk 3123 and say airspeed and altitude."

"Polar Control, we are at flight level two-eight-zero and three hundred and twenty Knots airspeed. Copy cleared present position direct Elmendorf."

"Snowbird 24, that is correct; we will advise when you are in radar contact; please continue normal position reports until then."

"Polar Control; roger; WILCO; Snowbird 24 out."

Looking over at Marcus, Bryan said, "Well, seems that whatever was causing interference with the comms has cleared up."

"Or, which is more likely the case, been turned off. Based on events with the Russians and 28-Alpha, I am convinced the interference was manmade, or rather should I say Russian made. I think they had the frequencies jammed so they could force 28-Alpha to land at an alternate field and no one would be the wiser. That would have given them several hours to remove the classified equipment before anyone realized they were missing. I do wonder how Stoney kept them from just gutting the equipment and disappearing into the snow. I am sure they had a submarine standing by fairly close. He didn't mention it, and it didn't occur to me to ask."

"Bet all of that information is above our clearance level anyway. When it comes to those NSA/CIA types they classify everything so that 'joes' like us have no way of finding out what is really going on," said the L.T.

"Call the Load Master and see how our sleeping beauties are doing."

Picking up the interphone, Bryan called Sergeant Smythe.

After finishing his conversation with Smythe, Bryan said, "Sir, Load Master reports all of them are out though several are restless. Hopefully they will stay out until we get to base. All of the other passengers are either gabbing or sleeping. Our escorts are playing cards on the floor of the ramp, weapons close at hand."

"First beer at the O'Club is on me," said Marcus.

"I'll take you up on it. Looks like an hour and a half to destination," replied the L.T.

"Captain Stone, looks like the repair crew will be arriving tomorrow," said Tyler as he entered the cafeteria. "I just received a telex from Washington. They will be arriving on a USAF C-130 coming out of Wisconsin."

"Great, I want to get back to the lower forty-eight where it's not so cold," replied Stoney.

"How long do you think it will take to make the repairs?"

"I would guess a minimum of two days. I just hope they have sealant that can cure under these temperatures. The cabin pressure will blow out the window again if it doesn't cure correctly. Did the telex happen to say who the replacement co-pilot was?"

"No, it was very short and just said maintenance crew and equipment would be arriving on the 130."

"Guess we'll find out then," replied Stoney.

Answering the portable radio, the communications specialist informed Tom the Snowbird had contacted Elmendorf Approach and was going to be landing in fifteen minutes.

"When Major Cooper gets back from the latrine we need to head to the airfield," Tom told his group.

A few seconds later, Major Cooper walked into the room. "I just heard the 130 will be landing in fifteen minutes. That gives us just enough time to get to the airfield. If you all are ready, let's go."

They all hurried out to the van, and with Major Cooper driving, they made it to the arrival tarmac in eight minutes flat. On the way, Tom thought, *I wonder if Cooper ever had visions of being an Indy driver,* as everyone in the van held on tightly. Since they were in the command van with the requisite blue flashing lights, the Security Police did not stop them for speeding and ignoring most traffic laws.

"I need to ride with the passengers on the bus. Can you find the way back to the alert facility Mr. Train?" asked Cooper.

"No problem; can I use the lights and ignore the traffic signals like you did?" Tom asked with a large grin on his face.

"No sir, I would not recommend it. The Security Police know me; however, they don't know you and being pulled over would not be a good idea. Once the bus leaves the tarmac it will take an extra five to ten minutes to get to the alert facility. If you hot-foot it back to the van you can make it to the facility and be there when we arrive."

"No problem, we'll see you there."

Cooper parked the van under the awning of the same VIP terminal the group had arrived at several hours prior. Entering the building, they went to the large glass windows in time to see the C-130 land on the runway and begin taxiing to the VIP ramp.

Standing there looking out the windows was the first lull in the action since their Gulfstream landed a few hours ago. Katie was enjoying those uneventful couple of minutes gazing out at the flight line, but her thoughts were on Erik Cooper. *That Erik seems to be a nice guy, not only that he is very pleasing on the eyes,* she thought, *I didn't see a ring so maybe before we leave I'll give him my number and see what happens.* Filing that idea away she returned to the problem at hand. *It will be very interesting to see how the passengers respond to the reason for the three day delay. That may well give me ideas on how to proceed with convincing them to virtually forget what has happened to them.*

There was a yellow "Follow Me" truck leading the aircraft to the tarmac. Waiting on the tarmac were young airmen with brightly colored orange vests and one of them had light batons to guide the aircraft to a parking place. When the 130 pulled up, the airman with the light batons began a series of arm signals to direct the pilot. When the airman crossed his batons above his head Tom and his crew heard the engines shutdown and saw the propellers slow down and then eventually stop their rotation. A couple of the orange vested airmen grabbed a small set of stairs and set it against the fuselage under the main cabin door.

Just as the engines were coming to a halt, Colonel Tomlinson walked past Tom and his group in a huff as he continued through the door to the ramp area. Cooper hurried after the colonel as Tom and his crew remained at the windows and watched the events outside. Two blue Air Force buses, really just regular school buses painted blue with Air Force logos on them, pulled up near the 130 and opened their doors.

The lead bus had a large green "X" on a piece of cardboard taped to the side whereas the second bus did not. Slowly the front door of the C-130 opened and a crewmember stuck his head out to see that all was ready for the passengers to disembark.

Colonel Tomlinson was standing at the foot of the stairs in his dress blue uniform and Major Cooper was standing to his left. The colonel greeted each passenger as they stepped down from the 130 and Cooper directed them to the bus with the green "X" on it. One by one the passengers continued coming out of the door, walking over, and climbing aboard the designated bus. Once everyone was on the bus Tomlinson and Cooper also climbed into the bus and the driver shut the door.

"Let's get moving so we can beat them there," Tom said as he led the group back to the van.

Captain Anatoli Leshev had started feeling a little groggy shortly after he and his men boarded the American C-130 aircraft. He couldn't put his finger on the feeling, but he knew something wasn't right. He had given his word no one would speak so he couldn't talk to Danshov without causing the Americans to put duct tape on their mouths. He knew he didn't want that for him or his men so he remained silent. He remembered seeing the passengers boarding the aircraft and remembered hearing the engines start but after that, nothing until the bump when the aircraft landed and taxied to a halt. He watched as the passengers headed out the door at the front of the aircraft. He was thankful his mind was getting clearer by the minute.

Glancing around at his men, he noticed that they too looked somewhat groggy and as his mind cleared up the reason occurred to him. *They must have drugged us with that last cup of coffee,* he said to himself. Minute by minute his mind became clearer and the rage inside began to build, but he couldn't do anything but sit quietly and wait to see what would happen next.

Suddenly the large cargo door began to open and Leshev had to squint since the reflection of the sun off the snow hurt his eyes. Up the ramp walked an American major brandishing a pistol and behind him were several more men all carrying weapons. The major walked up to the Marine lieutenant while the other men stayed gathered on the aircraft ramp.

"I am Major Jackson, commander of the Security Police Squadron here at Elmendorf."

"Sir, it is nice to meet you, I am Lieutenant Davies and that is Gunnery Sergeant Dane and Corporal Maxwell. We are part of the team that captured these guys at airfield 'Quebec'. I'm more than ready to turn them over to you. By the way, that one," pointing to Leshev, "is their commander."

"Thank you L.T., you and your Marines have done a fine job. We'll take it from here. Welcome home!"

"Thanks Major, we'll be on our way. Let's go Marines," said the L.T. as he walked down the ramp with his men following.

The major took a few steps and stood in front of Leshev.

"Do you speak English?"

"Yes, I do, as a matter of fact," replied Leshev as he stood up eye to eye with the American major.

"Good, then there will be no misunderstandings. I am Major Jackson. My men and I will be taking you and your men to our holding facility. I trust you will not give us any trouble? What is your name and rank?"

"I am Captain Anatoli Leshev of the Union of Soviet Socialist Republics' Red Army Spetsnaz Command. I demand you release us at once! You have no business holding us against our wills much less drugging us with your lousy American coffee. I want to speak to the Soviet Ambassador in Washington, D.C.—immediately!" Leshev thundered back releasing his pent up anger.

"NOW, NOW, captain, there is no reason to yell. As far as those demands, well, there is nothing I can do about them. However, I require that you have your men stand up and walk down the ramp to the waiting bus. I have been authorized by the Base Commander to use deadly force if necessary to assure your cooperation," Jackson replied in a cool calm voice.

"Neyt! I am not moving until I can call the Soviet Ambassador in Washington D.C."

"As I said, I cannot grant any demands. I can, however, shoot your ass unless you do as I say." Jackson pointed his pistol at Leshev's chest to emphasize the point. "Now, tell your men to get off their asses and walk down that ramp—*captain!*"

242

Seeing that he had no other choice, Leshev ordered his men, in Russian, to stand up and walk down the cargo ramp. Once outside, their security police guards ushered them towards the blue bus with blacked out windows. The prisoners did this with minimal prodding from Jackson's troops. Once seated on the bus, Jackson's men took up positions to guard the Russians.

"Yes, it was just like the Americanskys to black out the windows so we cannot see where we are going," said Leshev to his men in Russian. "They want to hide the decadence of this base to avoid being embarrassed at its deplorable conditions."

"Stop talking!" commanded Jackson.

Ignoring the order, Sergeant Danshov continued in Russian, "Comrade captain, how long do you think it will be before they send us back to the Motherland?"

"I do not know comrade sergeant. However, it is imperative that NO ONE give these decadent Americans any useful information. Remember, the Geneva Convention only says we are required to give name, rank, and serial number. I expect the utmost professionalism from all of my troops. We are Spetsnaz, not just a bunch of conscripts!" Leshev specifically aimed that last comment at the two corporals since they were young and hadn't been in Spetsnaz very long.

"We will do our best to honor the Soviet Union, comrade captain!" they both said in unison.

How am I going to explain this to Colonel Sikovski? If we do make it home, then it will be a Siberian outpost or the gulag for me. Leshev thought as the bus continued on its journey.

Several minutes later, the bus stopped, and the front door opened.

"Everyone, on your feet! Exit the bus and stay in a line," barked Jackson.

Leshev and his men stood up in the aisle of the bus and filed down the steps and out the door into the sunshine.

"Follow me," said Jackson as he walked in front of Leshev.

Jackson's troops formed a corridor from the door of the bus to the door of the building through which the Russians were marched. Once inside the jail facility, they continued marching down a hall that opened into a large room that contained many showers and toilets.

"Halt, left face!" commanded Jackson. The Russians stopped marching and made a quarter turn to the left and were standing shoulder to shoulder with their hands still bound behind their backs.

"Does everyone here speak English?" asked Jackson.

"Yes, we all speak English," replied Leshev.

"Good, we will remove your handcuffs and you are welcome to shower and take care of any personal business. Once everyone is finished we will put you in cells where you will be fed and given magazines or books to entertain yourselves."

While several security policemen stood guard, weapons at the ready, another guard removed each man's handcuffs and directed them to a table to get towels, soap and a USAF prisoner uniform.

As they started to undress and get into the showers, Corporal Vavilov asked, in Russian, "Comrade captain, when do you think the interrogations will start?"

"I don't know, but I'm surprised at the way we've been treated," replied Leshev.

Indeed Leshev was amazed at the treatment they were getting. Like all Russian soldiers, especially Spetsnaz, his training said to expect the worst possible treatment from the Americans. *They are just trying to make us think there are no interrogations; trying to get our guard down,* Leshev thought as he showered.

When the Russians finished dressing, they were put into individual cells and within a short while each was served a steak dinner and later on magazines were passed out.

What the devil is going on? thought Leshev as he was eating. *This is certainly not what the unit's Political Officer said would happen if we were ever captured by the Americans. Everyone knows the rumors about the methods KGB uses to get information from traitors and spies at Lubyanka prison and the Political Officer kept telling us that would be nothing compared to the treatment of prisoners by the Americans. He said we would be tortured and put through unimaginable pain to literally drain our brains of any useful information. I can't believe they would feed us steak and then torture us, maybe like so many other things in the Soviet Union, that too was a lie.*

"Comrade captain, what is going on here? This is not how the Political Officer or the leader of my Komsomol group said would it would be if we were ever captured by Americans. How could they be so wrong?" said Osinov.

"I don't know corporal, we can only wait to see what happens. Danshov, what do you think?" said Leshev.

"Comrades, they are just trying to soften us up. You wait, they will come in the middle of the night, put a bag on your head and drag you to their version of hell. The Party said it would be so; therefore it will be. The Political Officers are never wrong. The Party does not lie."

The conversation continued until lights out.

The guards woke the Russians up early the next morning and gave them their uniforms back and told them to get dressed. Afterward, they were fed an American style breakfast and about mid morning they were marched back outside to a waiting bus.

Minutes later, Leshev was following his comrades up the stairway to board an Aeroflot jet back to Moscow. He stopped just before entering the cabin, turned around, looked out over the parts of Elmendorf visible from his vantage point, and said to himself, *I think there are many things the Political Officers either didn't tell us or lied to us about. Some day, I will breathe American air again.*

CHAPTER 21

Sitting at his desk, in the Kremlin, Colonel Sikovski picked up his secure phone and called down to the communications room. After several rings, a voice on the other end said, "Yes comrade colonel, how may I help you?"

"Have there been any additional radio communications from the commander of Operation Dark Night?"

"No, comrade colonel, I was told to bring them directly to you if we heard any news. No one has heard from the team in many hours."

"Call me immediately, if there is any news!" said the colonel as he hung up the phone.

Turing his chair to look out the window, the colonel gazed out over the snow-covered Kremlin courtyard and watched the guards as they marched around the perimeter.

His brow furrowed as he contemplated the lack of current information from his special ops team.

What in the world has happened to Leshev and his crew? Wondered Sikovski, *could the Americans have figured out what was going on and sent in troops to rescue the aircraft, its crew, and passengers?*

As he continued gazing out the window, he organized the information he had so that when Ninski's office called, he would be ready. He also knew that no matter how he presented the information, the admiral would not be pleased. Sikovski had been working diligently for years to build a reputation and the right political connections to finally get that pair of general's stars that he felt he had earned after his exploits during WWII and shooting down and capturing that American U-2 spy plane pilot; it was his engineering troops that had figured out how to shoot down the aircraft in the first place.

Just as he predicted, the Admiral's office called a short while later and ask Sikovski to come up and see the admiral. Sikovski hoped that his reputation and those of his troops would help him save face in the admiral's eyes. He headed up the stairs to the admiral's office with the dread that a condemned prisoner has as he walks down the hall to the gas chamber.

Reaching the admiral's office, he put on his best poker face and making use of the skills he learned in combat he steadied his nerves and calmed his mind as the secretary let him into the lion's den.

When the door opened Sikovski saw Ninski intently studying some papers on his desk. As the room echoed with the sound of boots across a wooden floor, Ninski looked up and said, "Ah, Alexi, please come in and sit down. Please tell me the current status of Dark Night."

"Comrade admiral, as you know Captain Leshev called in several hours ago to receive guidance since the equipment on the Northern Star aircraft could not be removed. Since that time we have not heard from the team at all. I checked with our long range radar operators and there was a target that appeared to come from the direction of the emergency airfield 'Q'. It did not stay on course very long and it suddenly lost altitude and it appeared to reverse course as it faded from the radar screen. There was no radio contact from Leshev to say that he was airborne and heading to Siberia as planned. Since we had no definite information about that long range target we disregarded its importance. It is possible, though I don't think it likely, that it was the Northern Star since it did not continue on its original course but turned just as we picked it up. If it was the aircraft, we have no way of knowing why it turned around. At this point it is impossible to say, with any certainty what has happened."

"Well, comrade colonel, I think it is safe to assume that since we have not heard from Leshev and the submarine has not reported the arrival of the team that something has happened to stop the mission. We have been listening in on the U.S. Government communications channels as well as the news media and nothing has surfaced concerning the capture of Russian troops on American territory or anything else suggesting their capture. We still have significant problems with intercepting their encrypted communications, but we have watched the volume of traffic and there has been no change over the last forty-eight hours. What do you suggest we do at this point?"

"Sir, until we know the status of Leshev's team, I think it would be wise to do nothing. We don't want to alert the Americans, so we can't attempt to rescue the team from

'Q', assuming they are still there. We do know that the Northern Star aircraft did not arrive in London on schedule. I contacted KGB and they agreed to put agents at the gates to monitor any announcements and so far the only announcement said that there was a mechanical problem with the aircraft causing it to divert to an alternate landing place. Our operatives have been unable to get additional information from the Atlantic and Pacific Air gate agents. APA did tell the relatives waiting for the aircraft that it had landed safely but it was impossible to contact anyone at the present time."

"Well, at least we are fairly confident the aircraft didn't crash. I don't like the idea of a missing Spetsnaz team lurking around American soil. I can just see the American's parading them on the evening news channel. Neither you nor I need that kind of publicity."

Seated in a chair in front of the Admiral's desk, Sikovski heard the office door open but without being obvious could not turn and see who had entered. The thudding sound of jackboots hitting against the hardwood floor echoed through the office as they made their way toward the desk. Within seconds the owner of the boots dressed in a black KGB dress uniform was standing in front of the Admiral's desk.

"Comrade Colonel Ivan, good of you to come over on such short notice. Have you met Colonel Sikovski of Spetsnaz?"

Sikovski stood up to shake the stranger's offered hand.

"Nice to meet you comrade colonel, I have heard so much about you it is nice to finally meet you face to face," said Sikovski as he pumped the cold almost dead-feeling boney hand.

"Yes, colonel, I too have heard much about your work as well, we should have shared vodka before now, but alas with KGB it is always work-work-work."

"Yes, maybe we should all have a vodka then get down to business," suggested Admiral Ninski. "Alexi, would you mind to get the bottle and glasses from the credenza? Colonel Ivan if you will have a seat here we can have a quick drink and get started."

As Sikovski got up, his mind was racing at this turn of events. Yes, he knew quite a bit about Ivan and everyone knew his reputation. Unfortunately, it did not center on his charming disposition. He had a reputation for being ruthless and one did not survive long once your name made it onto the comrade colonel's 'list'. *I'm not sure, but even the Admiral's voice seems to have changed since Ivan arrived, very odd*, thought Sikovski as he retrieved the bottle of vodka and glasses. As he walked back across the office Sikovski wondered how this meeting might end. Filling the glasses, he handed them around and at the same time was wondering, *could I be getting ready to toast my political and possibly physical demise?*

"Admiral, if you will indulge me; to your health and the glorious Soviet State!" said Ivan as he held his glass up.

Ninski and Sikovski raised their glasses and there was a chorus of "Here, here!"

All three men downed their drink at one time and then slammed the glasses, upside down on the admiral's desk, as was the Russian custom.

"Good, that is better, eh? Now down to business. Colonel Ivan is aware of our little adventure in the Arctic and he has come to offer a possible solution to our problem. Colonel Ivan, if you would explain for our comrade?"

"Of course sir; ever since the Americans started their Northern Star program and began collecting vital intelligence on the whereabouts of our submarines, KGB has been tasked by the Politburo to either turn an American into an agent or at best plant one of our operatives within the program. Unfortunately all of our efforts to put one of our agents into the program have failed. We lost several agents to American jails during the two years we tried to infiltrate. At the same time we were trying to either obtain information we could use to blackmail a current Northern Star member or sniff out someone who might have conscientious objections to America's role in international politics. We discovered that the U.S. Government's Personnel Reliability Program or PRP was extremely hard to overcome, however we did manage to find one person within the program who has an issue with money. He likes to spend it, but he doesn't make that much. His wife could spend that decadent American, Howard Hughes, into bankruptcy and has put her husband in a serious financial position. Naturally, we have offered to help him and initially he was completely disinterested, however as time marched on he eventually came around to see things our way. We offered to help him with his debts in return for his help with some technical information on Northern Star. The information you used to plan this operation came from that individual. Once the operation was a go, we got word to him that he was not to reveal himself to your troops under any circumstances. However, he was also told that if the operation failed then he was to do anything he could to bring us an airplane or the equipment. Since we now know that the equipment cannot be removed, his job is to get the aircraft to Siberia. His incentive to help us is one and a half million dollars U.S., and transportation to an island nation with no extradition agreement with Uncle Sam."

"That is wonderful news comrade colonel though I have one question to ask. If a squad of my Spetsnaz was unable to hijack the aircraft what confidence do you have that your agent can do it?" asked Sikovski.

"I must be honest with you, I don't have a lot of confidence that he can pull it off, but he is a member of the flight crew and as such he has the confidence of his captain as well as unfettered access to the cockpit. With his financial difficulties, I am sure he will find a way to get us that airplane."

"Do you mind if I ask who it is?"

"Actually, I don't wish to reveal his name; however, he has been on our payroll for some time now. Frankly, I am surprised their PRP system hasn't discovered him yet. At this point we have to wait to see what happens. The traitor has the frequencies needed to contact our controllers once he gets close to Russian airspace. The last thing we want is to have our own forces shoot down the aircraft on its way here. I have placed agents at the airport in Victoria, San Francisco as well as Los Angeles who will watch for the aircraft to return. If it shows up at one of those places we will know that all of our combined efforts have failed."

"At that point, gentlemen, I would expect the Foreign Minister to hear something from the U.S. State Department or the Pentagon regarding the return of or death of certain Soviet troops. At which time we will have to react. Until that communiqué or the arrival of a Northern Star there isn't much we can do. Comrades, I have other pressing matters to attend to, but make sure to keep me informed of any changes," said the admiral as a way to end the meeting and dismiss the colonels.

The colonels stood up and in unison clicked the heels of their boots and turned to leave the office. Sikovski was puzzled as to what had just happened. When Ivan arrived, he fully expected to leave the office in handcuffs headed straight to Lubyanka prison thus becoming this KGB monster's latest form of entertainment and eventually ending up in the gulag.

When they had reached the outer office area, Sikovski said, "Comrade colonel, it has been nice to make your acquaintance."

"Yes comrade; please let me know if I can be of *further assistance* in this little matter," replied Ivan, the tone of his voice much colder than before, as he continued out the door without pausing.

Sikovski hurried out the door and back to his own office. On the way there he stopped in the men's room and scrubbed his hands. *Now I know what it must have been like to shake Heinrick Himmler's hand. Ivan's cut from the same mold as that notorious head of Adolf Hitler's feared SS,* Sikovski said to himself. Back in his office, he decided that he needed another shot or two of vodka to calm his nerves and at the same time hoping he would not have to deal with this Ivan any more. Just thinking his name sent a shiver up Sikovski's back.

Shortly after the colonels left his office, Admiral Ninski received a phone call from the General Secretary's office requesting his presence immediately.

"May I inquire as to the subject the General Secretary would like to discuss?" he asked the aide on the phone.

"Yes, comrade admiral, the General Secretary would like to know why the Foreign Minister just received a phone call from our embassy in Washington D.C. regarding a squad of Spetsnaz troops currently in American custody."

CHAPTER 22

Driving up to the alert facility, the gate guards waved Tom and the team straight through. Tom parked the van and everyone climbed out.

"The bus should be here any minute. Remember we're playing the part of APA representatives and that is the facade we must keep up during the next several days. Katie, please try to get an overall sense of the mental state of the whole group. It will give us an idea as to how difficult our task will be," Tom said.

"Agreed; it is hard to read large groups, but I believe I can get a sense for how they are feeling by the questions they are sure to ask when you address them," Katie replied.

"Well, guys, get ready for our opening act, here comes the bus," Glen said as he looked out the window.

The gate guards waved the blue Air Force bus through as Tom and his group waited in the foyer of the alert facility. They didn't have to wait long for the passengers to start filing into the same area. Tom hoped the passengers would be as impressed with the facility as he was earlier in the afternoon. He had never been in an alert facility, so he was surprised at the deep pile carpeting, the wall decorations, and the furniture which all looked like it belonged in an expensive hotel, not an Air Force facility. As the foyer continued to fill with people, Colonel Tomlinson walked over to where the group was waiting.

"Ah, Tom and company; there you are," said Tomlinson.

"Thank you for taking time to help us with this introduction. I think it will be much more believable coming from you than from us," Tom whispered back.

The colonel slightly, almost imperceptibly nodded an acknowledgement just as Major Cooper walked up.

With his back to the crowd, Cooper asked if everyone was ready and again, the colonel replied with that slight nod.

Turning to face the group, Major Cooper quietly cleared his throat and in a loud voice said, "Ladies and gentlemen, welcome to the Elmendorf Air Force Base alert facility. I am sure that everyone is wondering about the fence and the guards. We use this facility to house our pilots when they are on alert status. What does 'alert status' mean, well, it means that if we were to get an order to launch some fighter aircraft to intercept Russian bombers headed across the pole, the pilots would have just minutes to rush to their aircraft, fire up the engines and get airborne. I cannot tell you the exact amount of time that takes for security reasons, but I can tell you that it is quite fast. To achieve this quick response, the pilots and other crewmembers live here for a one week period then they swap out with the next alert team. The fence and guards protect the pilots as well as their fighter aircraft parked on the flight line side of this facility. As soon as we finish this introduction we'll get your room assignments and let everyone freshen up and relax. Since we lock up our pilots for a week at a time, this facility was designed to make it feel as close to a luxury hotel as the taxpayers would allow. I really think you will be quite comfortable as we await your transportation back to San Francisco."

Once Cooper finished, he turned to Tomlinson and again introduced him to the passengers.

"Again, I would like to welcome you to Elmendorf. We will do everything we can to make your short stay a pleasant one. I know you are anxious to continue your journey and APA has assured me they are doing everything in their power to make that happen. I know that everyone would like to contact their families, however, I am afraid that is not possible at this time." With the same reaction as a match tossed into a bucket of gasoline, the entire room erupted in angry shouts.

"Please if everyone would quiet down I will try to answer your questions, but I will not shout over you!" exclaimed Tomlinson.

Once the shouts calmed down, a gentleman near the front of the group whose face, Tom had noticed, was turning redder by the minute, was the first to speak or rather shout, "What do you mean we can't contact our families? Do you think we're just going to stay here for three days with no outside contact? I don't know if you or your major have noticed but no one here is wearing a military uniform except for you! We are not in the military and I don't know if you are aware, but some of us are not even U.S. citizens. You have no right or authority to keep us isolated here! It was bad enough when the Russians had us bound and gagged not knowing if someone was going to get a bullet in the back of the head, but for the U.S. military to keep us figuratively tied up as well makes you no better than the Ruskies! Speaking for me and my wife, and I believe I can include everyone standing here, this is intolerable!"

"Sir, if you will calm down for just a minute, I think we can allay your fears and come to some understanding. I would like to introduce Mr. Tom Train, Mr. Glen Burton, and Ms. Katie Fuller who are all from Atlantic Pacific Air. Mr. Train, will you address the gentleman's concerns?" asked Tomlinson.

"Sir, before I begin, would you mind telling me your name?" said Tom.

"I am Harold Gooseman," replied the gentleman.

"Thank you Mr. Gooseman; as Colonel Tomlinson said we represent Atlantic Pacific Air and we are here to address your immediate needs and to get you home as soon as possible. The information I am about to pass on to you is of a sensitive nature but I have the colonel's permission to pass it on since it will explain the delay in your departure as well as why communications outside the base are currently restricted. It is unfortunate that you arrived when you did. The United States Military and Elmendorf AFB in particular will be participating in a large multinational military exercise that was supposed to begin today. Unfortunately for our circumstances, this exercise occupies vast quantities of Alaskan airspace which causes the FAA and the international aviation organization, ICAO, to close the airspace to all but essential military air traffic due to safety of flight concerns. Participating governments schedule this exercise years in advance and as a result all commercial carriers re-route their flights during this three-day period. As for the restriction on communications, that is also part of the exercise. The military has shutdown all but official military communications for the same three day period to simulate the destruction of the long distance telephone system and the jamming of radio frequencies caused by electromagnetic pulses resulting from the detonation of nuclear weapons. Should this scenario happen for real, then those detonations would completely wipeout non-military communications with the outside world."

Glen Burton added, "When we became aware of the situation at airfield 'Q' we immediately tried to get the Pentagon and the State Department to put the exercise on hold for enough time to get you home with a minimum of delay, unfortunately, the cost of doing so would be in the millions of dollars so we were politely told 'no'. They did agree to a delay of a few hours to get you from 'Q' to this base, otherwise you would still be at 'Q'. I think you will agree, being stuck is bad enough, however, being stuck here is much better than where you were."

"As soon as we had confirmation that everyone was Ok, before you left 'Q' we had the gate agents in London contact everyone that was either meeting your flight or listed as a point of contact on your ticket information to tell them there was a problem, but everyone is Ok. At that time APA also informed them that due to circumstances beyond their control you would be out of communications until three days from now. They were also informed about your flight back to San Francisco and your expected arrival time there," continued Tom.

"Mr. Train, was the British embassy notified of our delay? As non-United States citizens we should be able to contact our embassy to solicit their help in getting us home," said Mr. Clyde-Smith.

"Yes sir, the British Embassy, in Los Angeles, was notified of your predicament and they asked for all British passengers to be patient and understand that since the British Military is part of the exercise, their hands are tied as well," said Tom.

"It seems to me that for whatever reason, and I am not sure that I buy into the ones our esteemed hosts have given, that we are stuck here for three days. I for one, plan to launch a formal and vigorous complaint with the FAA and the Pentagon as well as hire a lawyer to sue APA for every dime they have now and in the future; as soon as I get to a telephone," sighed a resigned Mr. Gooseman.

I think this might be working. Even Gooseman is starting to calm down. Thought Tom as he noticed Gooseman's face slowly losing its red hue.

"I am truly sorry for the delay, but the folks here at Elmendorf and we at APA will do everything to make your stay here as pleasant as possible. I believe Major Cooper has your room keys ready, major?"

"Thanks Mr. Train, yes I do have room keys for everyone," said Cooper.

One-by-one he called out all of the names and handed each their keys. As the passengers walked off to find their rooms Cooper turned to Tom and said, "Your shrink has her work cut out for her. I have never seen a more hostile group than this. I wouldn't be surprised if they ganged up and tried to lynch us all!"

"Yes, she does. However, we have a few cards yet to play. I have a feeling that when they climb the stairs to board that flight home, they will have a much different outlook on this whole affair," said Tom.

As everyone left to find their rooms, Colonel Tomlinson walked over to Tom and the group and said his goodbyes and then he turned on his heels and headed for the door. Cooper was right behind him and said in parting, "Call me if you need me."

As Cooper hurried to keep up with Tomlinson, his mind was preoccupied with the colonel's afternoon schedule but taking a brief second for himself, he thought, *that Katie Fuller, is the best looking CIA agent I've ever seen. I've got some leave coming up so maybe I'll take it in D.C. and look her up, but with my luck she's probably already . . . .* His thoughts were interrupted when Tomlinson said, "Erik, cancel my afternoon appointment with . . ."

Just then, someone tapped Tom on the shoulder and he turned to see who it was.

"Sir, I am Technical-Sergeant Jones, the facility manager here. Major Cooper tasked me to handle any and all of your needs while you are here. You can contact me through the base radio that the major gave you earlier or one of the phones located throughout the facility."

"Sergeant Jones, it is good to meet you. This is Glen Burton and Kate Fuller."

"Please call me George. Normally we serve dinner at seventeen-hundred hours or five P.M. It will unfortunately, be a serving line cafeteria style, but I am pleased to inform you that I have a budding young chef on my staff and he has a knack for creating food that is better than anything an Air Force chow-hall ever thought of serving. I think you and our guests will be pleasantly surprised."

"Great, that is good news. We have a lot to do and if our guests are happy with the food that will go a long way to keeping them happy for the next few days. Would you mind printing out a schedule for the cafeteria so we can give everyone a copy?"

"Can do, I'll have it ready by dinner. Oh, I forgot to mention, that during the meeting, I had everyone's luggage delivered to their rooms. I will make an announcement over the facility PA about dinner. One other thing I neglected to mention, as an alert facility we normally do not keep any alcoholic beverages in the facility, but with the colonel's permission I have a fully stocked bar with both liquor and beer, free of charge, for anyone who cares to partake. Did Major Cooper mention that Lieutenant-Colonel Cheryl Findley from the hospital is coming by tomorrow? She is a nurse practitioner as well as the hospital's chief nurse and the colonel thought it would be a good idea to have her check everyone out."

"No, the major forgot to mention her, but I agree with the colonel. Now, if you will excuse us we have a lot to do to get ready for tomorrow. Thanks again for filling us in and we'll see you at dinner." Turning to Glen and Katie, Tom continued, "Let's go to my room and strategize on how we proceed from here."

"Right behind you boss," they both said in unison. The three of them started towards Tom's room to plan a schedule for the next three days.

Just then, Virginia and Brad walked up.

"We waited until the passengers' issues had been settled before coming to see you. Is there anything you need us to do?" asked Brad.

"Virginia and Brad, I am sorry that I haven't been able to express my condolences on the deaths of Steve and Maria. I know that must have been quite a shock. I, for one, really appreciate your willingness to help us over the next few days," said Tom.

"Mr. Train, thank you very much. Yes, this whole ordeal has been very traumatic. Brad and I want to do what we can to get the passengers safely home. Do you have any information on the status of Captain Stone, Lee and the aircraft?" asked Virginia

"APA HQ dispatched a maintenance team from Victoria to Wisconsin to catch a C-130 to fly directly to Airfield 'Q'. I would expect the team is en route there now. That's all I know, but if I do get an update I'll be sure to pass on the information."

"Mr. Train, do you know if my family in Victoria has been notified of our condition?" asked Brad.

"Yes, they were advised by APA HQ as soon as we received the teletype message from Captain Stone when he landed back at 'Q'. I wish I could allow you to contact them, but given the circumstances and the information we just told the passengers—you understand."

"Yes, sir, I am ex-military so my family is used to getting the bare minimum of information," replied Brad.

"What do you want us to do?" said Virginia.

"I need you guys to put on your 'happy faces' and mingle with the passengers to make them feel as comfortable as possible. We are going to my room for a strategy session and we could use your input," said Tom.

"Tom could you introduce us?" asked Glen

"How rude of me, Glen Burton and Katie Fuller, this is Virginia, the head flight attendant from 28A and this is Brad the Assistant Flight Officer a.k.a. sensor technician.

Brad and Virginia, this is Glen Burton my associate program manager from CIA and Ms. Katie Fuller also from CIA. Katie is a psychologist who is going to help us keep this story out of the papers, regardless of Mr. Gooseman's threats. Let's head on down to my room where we can polish the plan we put into action in the morning."

With Tom leading the way, they headed down the hall to his room. Once they all sat down, Tom asked Katie for her first impressions.

"Well, Tom, we are dealing with fairly rational people. From a normal crowd, I would have expected a lot of threats and four-letter words during your explanation of the delay. We did get some hostile responses, but not nearly the magnitude I had expected. Overall, I think it is a group we will be able to reason and work with."

For the next several hours, Tom and his team strategized how to get the stack of National Security forms lying on the table signed by each passenger.

"Well gang, I think that is the avenue we'll use to try and obtain everyone's silence. It is getting close to dinner time so let's head for the cafeteria; I want to be there before the pax arrive since we didn't have a chance to check it out during our short tour," said Tom.

Arriving at the entrance to the cafeteria they were surprised at the darkness of the doorway until they saw the room bathed in low level mood light, Glen said, "Wow, I am really surprised. I expected a sterile white room with a tile floor and fold out plastic tables, like I had in high school."

"I know what you mean; whoever decorated this place did a bang-up job. It looks like an outdoor Italian Ristorante similar to ones I saw in Rome," said Tom.

"The resemblance to a Piazza is uncanny. From the out door furniture to the gentle sounds of the water fountain they went out of their way to make you feel like you are in a different place. From a psychological standpoint it could make you forget where you are. Which might not be a bad thing after being locked up here for a solid week, just waiting for the alert klaxon to go off," said Katie.

They were standing at the entrance, talking among themselves when several passengers walked up including the Goosemans.

"Good evening everyone," said Tom as they walked up.

"Ah Mr. Train and company, hoped to find you here. I would like to talk with all of you while everyone else gets dinner," said Harold Gooseman.

Pointing to a table in the corner, Tom said, "Let's take a seat at that table and we would be glad to hear what you have to say. Virginia and Brad, would you take over the door greeter duties for me?"

"Yes sir," said Brad, "glad to help."

"Lead on," said Gooseman.

Tom took the lead and walked over to a table in the corner as passengers continued to enter the room and head for the serving line.

Everyone sat down at the table bathed in the red glow of the candle lit centerpiece. The burning candle cast shadows as the fire danced on its wick.

Mr. Gooseman started the conversation, "First, let me say that our accommodations are first rate and the other passengers and I appreciate all of the efforts APA has put forth. Just to be honest, we had a meeting earlier and the majority of the other passengers agreed to let me speak for them as well. Ever since Captain Stone came on the intercom and said that we would have to make an emergency landing, this trip has gotten steadily worse. Even when we thought things were looking up and we would finally get home, we find ourselves here instead. It was one thing for the Russians to tie us up, starve us, and threaten our lives, but we draw the line when our own Government keeps us penned up like a bunch of criminals. This is a very nice prison, but since we cannot leave and cannot communicate with our families we are by definition imprisoned. We believe you are also breaking international law by not allowing our non-U.S. friends to contact their respective embassies."

Starting to lose his cool again, Gooseman continued, "When I get out of here, I am going to contact a lawyer so fast your head will spin. I will sue APA and the U.S. Government for every dime I can get. This whole trip has been an outrage!"

"Mr. Gooseman, let me say that we greatly sympathize with everything that you have said. In your position, we would be as outraged as you and the others are. However, we must tell you that there are forces at play that have forced us to do things we might otherwise not. By the puzzled look on your face, I can tell that you don't understand what I am telling you."

"Stop right there, Train. Do you think I am a complete dolt? The way you are talking to me makes me think that you do!"

Tom noticed Gooseman's face was starting to get red again so in as calm a voice as he could muster he replied, "No, not in the least sir, however in this setting I cannot go into details with you but I can tell you that this whole affair has U.S. National Security implications which are dictating our actions. You may not realize it, but I am telling you the truth. I promise that tomorrow you will see things in a different light; in fact, I guarantee it. However, tonight may I suggest that you enjoy a good meal and a have a drink, if you are so inclined, get a good night's rest and after breakfast tomorrow the three of us will come to your room and will shed some light on recent events. We will be talking to all of the passengers individually and I have no problem putting you at the head of the line. Shall we say eight o'clock?"

"All right, I'll table the rest of this discussion until tomorrow and will pass this information on to the other passengers. I'll expect to see you at eight o'clock A.M. On that note, I'm going to get dinner, something smells wonderful; till tomorrow then." Having said that, Gooseman got up from the table and headed to the serving line.

Waiting until Gooseman was out of ear shot, Tom asked Katie if she stood by her earlier assessment of the passenger's mental state, Gooseman's in particular.

"Well Tom, Gooseman here seems to have taken a leadership role within the group. We have no way of knowing if that extends to everyone, but I would say it is safe to assume it would apply to the majority. With that said, he seems to be quite level headed, a bit boisterous, but beneath that gruff exterior is, I believe, a rational level-headed man. That is a long way of saying, yes, to your question."

"Guess we'll know in the morning. Don't know about you all, but the smell of that food is making me hungry; let's eat," Glen said.

The next morning, Tom and his crew met with Harold and Ida-mae Gooseman. Over the next twenty-four hours they had similar meetings with the rest of the passengers. Eventually, everyone agreed to remain forever silent on the events surrounding APA Flight 28A since departing British Columbia. The official story said the flight had experienced an engine failure which forced it to land at Elmendorf AFB. Unfortunately, a major military exercise had just started causing closure of all surrounding airspace and outside communication. As a result the passengers could not leave Alaska until the military authorized APA to bring in an aircraft and fly everyone to San Francisco. Several of the passengers requested additional compensation which Tom and Glen approved per the DDO's direction. As they left the last passenger's room, Tom said, "Glen and Katie why don't you head down to my room, here's the key. Glen, would you fill the ice bucket? I'll be there in a few minutes I have to go see Sergeant Jones first."

Tom found Jones in the alert facility's administration office.

"Sergeant Jones, I need a bottle of your best bourbon," said Tom.

"Yes sir, I believe I have just what you're looking for. I take it you've been successful?" said Jones as he opened a closet door.

"Absolutely, we are going to celebrate."

"Ah, here it is sir, a bottle of Kentucky bourbon that I know you will like."

"Thank you very much, for the bottle as well as your help over the last couple of days," said Tom.

"Glad to help sir, just leave what ever you don't finish of that bottle in your room and I'll collect it when you all head back to the lower forty-eight. Don't want to waste it!" said Jones.

"Can do, and thanks again," said Tom as he took the bottle and headed to his room.

As Tom entered the room he said, "Hi guys look what I found, with the help of Sergeant Jones, that is," as he held up the bottle for Glen and Katie to see.

Pouring a round for everyone Tom said, "A toast to Katie and her uncanny ability to persuade people into changing their minds and seeing things in a different way," as he held up his glass.

After the clanking of the glasses, Katie said, "Thank you, but it really was nothing Tom, but I will tell you that I was worried about the non-U.S. passengers. Having the head of MI-6 talk to them over a military radio really made the difference. Most people don't realize how much interaction there is between allied countries since you don't read about it in the papers. I'm sure that really helped secure their cooperation. The current state of world affairs played a role as well. What with the Cuban missile incident and the assassination of JFK, and the constant saber rattling by the Soviet Bear, Americans are feeling quite patriotic. Unfortunately, this business with Vietnam could cause a problem if it drags out a long time."

"Bottom line is we have information containment and a stack of signed non-disclosure statements that are internationally binding so once the Northern Star returns to Los Angeles this matter will be put to rest," said Glen.

"Yes and no; I think there will be closed door hearings once Congress finds out what has happened and you can guarantee the State Department has let it slip to their friends in Congress. I have a feeling, our work is just beginning" said Tom as he patted Glen on the back.

"I'm glad that's why you two get paid the big bucks to handle that kind of stuff. In the grand scheme of things I am just a peon and a happy one at that," said Katie.

CHAPTER 23

During the last two days, Stoney kept himself busy checking out various aircraft systems and getting everything ready for the repair team that was due to arrive today. After Leshev's gun fired in the cockpit, he wanted to make sure nothing vital had been damaged. Lee had been a big help during this time and he seemed in good spirits, which Stoney thought was odd given the recent chain of events, but as any good psychologist will tell you, different people react differently to the same situation.

So far they had not detected any issues with the aircraft systems. There was, of course, the broken window and the blood. Stoney and Lee had managed to clean up the blood and when the mechanics arrived they would take care of the window. Trying to keep out the cold and any blowing snow, the local mechanics used some plastic and duct tape to cover the broken windows.

They were just checking out the radios when Stoney heard, "Hi guys, how are things looking?"

Turning around, Stoney saw it was Tyler Noland and said that all was well and it appeared there was no damage to any major systems.

"Have you heard from the maintenance crew?" Stoney inquired.

"As a matter of fact I am glad you asked that question. They are just about to turn on final approach now and should be on the ground in mere minutes. Fortunately we don't have to plow the runway since it hasn't snowed, so everything appears ready."

"Great, well let's go and welcome them to 'Q'," said Stoney. "Nothing against your hospitality, but I am ready to head for the lower forty-eight and some heat. I'm not used to this intense cold weather. I'm sure glad there are folks who like it."

"Yes, most of us prefer the weather here over the lower forty-eight. Even for us though, winters can be brutal. Fortunately, we're only at the beginning of it. In a month or so, it will be in the single digits and the winds and snow will be merciless. Much later then now and it could be a trick getting the Connie out of here."

"Lee, make sure you double check all of the instruments on your FE board. I am going to meet the maintenance folks and see how fast we can get out of here. Don't stay too long, without going in to warm up. I don't want you to get sick. Make sure you minimize any power usage. We'll need every bit of battery power to get her started."

"Can do Stoney, will take about fifteen minutes to check everything out. See you in a few."

Stoney followed Tyler out the cabin door shutting it tight to keep as much cold out as possible.

Lee sat down at his engineer's console and began to toggle switches and turn knobs while noting how the various gauges responded. Once he completed the checks, his thoughts turned back to that day a couple of weeks ago in Los Angeles.

He was having dinner with his wife at their favorite restaurant when the maître d' walked up and said he had a phone call at the bar. Lee excused himself and went to the phone.

Picking up the receiver he said, "This is Lee Wyne, who is this?"

A thickly Russian accented voice on the other end said, "Tonight, eleven P.M. usual place," and then a click indicating the caller had hung up.

Returning to his table, his wife said, "What was that all about?"

"Nothing dear, I have to go into work for a couple of hours tonight. It has to do with that systems upgrade I mentioned to you. They want me there by eleven; we'll need to finish up so I can get you home."

"With you it is always work, work, work, why can't you have a normal nine to five job like everyone else? Oh well, your loss, I was going to suggest we skip dessert—but not so you could go to work!"

"I'm sorry sweetheart, but I have to go; we can't afford for me to lose my job. I'll make it up to you when I get home."

"Don't bother; I won't be in the mood later. Let's just go."

Dropping his wife at home, Lee got back on the highway contemplating the upcoming meeting. *What in the blazes could Ivan want at this hour? I hate these last minute meetings and I sure don't like going to that part of L.A. late at night.*

Working his way down to the L.A. dock area he parked a block away from the sleazy strip club where Ivan liked to meet. Since he was on PRP, he had to be careful that no one was following him so he always parked away from the club and took a circuitous route to get there. Working his way through a couple of dark alleys he kept a firm grip on the pistol in his jacket pocket. More than once thugs had tried to jump him in this area.

Arriving at his destination he opened the door and the blaring music instantly assaulted his ears and as his eyes adjusted to the dim light he saw a topless girl pole-dancing and gyrating to the music. *Ivan is already here,* he said to himself as he spotted his contact sitting at his customary table. Walking over to that table he sat down where they could talk, but he could watch the show as well.

"Ivan, why the rush meeting?" said Lee.

"Sorry, is nature of business," said Ivan.

"Two draft beers," said Lee as the topless waitress walked over.

For several minutes, until the beers arrived, Lee and Ivan watched the pole dancer who had removed her last bit of clothing. Lee sat there contemplating what Ivan would say next.

The waitress set down the beers, Lee paid for them and she left.

"You are working on flight 28-Alpha, yes? Is scheduled for next flight in two weeks, yes?" said Ivan, beer in hand.

"I am and yes the next flight is in two weeks," said Lee as he took his first sip.

"You will bring airplane to Siberia."

The statement hit Lee like a sledge hammer to the head and he just about dropped his glass as he simultaneously tried not to choke on his mouth full of beer.

Recovering his composure Lee said, "First of all, you've got to be kidding! Second of all, how in the hell am I supposed to do that? Third, you don't have enough money to make me want to."

"One million dollars U.S.—cash; how, we don't care as long as you bring airplane in one piece to Siberian airfield."

Lee sat for several minutes thinking about the offer. *That money would pay my debts and let us live like 'she' wants to, but would she agree and can I even pull it off?* "Ivan, I won't do it for less than two million and you must get my wife out of the U.S. and to a Pacific island that has no extradition treaty with Uncle Sam. Also you must get me to the same island with the money."

"One and half million and other stuff is no problem. Here is navigation information you need. Follow directions on back," said Ivan he pushed a folded up piece of paper across the table toward Lee.

After taking the paper and putting it in his pocket Lee took a deep breath and said, "Deal." He then chugged the rest of his beer and went back to his car.

✪

OK, since the Russian's screwed up taking this plane, now it is up to me. I'll need to find one of the hidden pistols and figure out a way to take care of the jarheads that will be flying with us, thought Lee as he got up from the console and walked into the cabin and began looking for the pistols. As a member of the Northern Star program Lee was aware of the multi-layered security protocols incorporated into the aircraft. The theory behind these protocols was to limit the possibility of a crew member hijacking the aircraft as well as give them the tools to prevent a passenger from doing likewise.

The protocols dictated that only the cabin crew or stewardesses had access to the special in-flight 9mm pistols. Similarly the anesthesia gas system, used by Stoney to subdue the Russians, was unknown to everyone but the captain. Though Lee had heard rumors of its existence he was as surprised as the Russians were. No one crew member knew all of the Northern Star's security secrets.

The captain knew the most, but even he was not privy to everything. The cabin crew was in charge of the guns since the flight crew would bolt the bullet proof cockpit door from the inside during an emergency. It was up to the cabin crew to quell a hijacking while the flight crew remained sealed in the cockpit.

Using this information, Lee began a thorough search of the cabin and stewardess areas, i.e. the galley and in-flight storage areas, both forward and aft. After about twenty minutes of diligent searching, he finally found one in the aft storage area. He took it from its hiding place and hid it under his FE console. First, he examined it to make sure it was loaded and a round was in the chamber.

The powder charge in each round was less than a normal round to reduce the possibility of puncturing the skin of the aircraft causing catastrophic rapid decompression at altitude.

✪

Stoney and Tyler were standing with their hands over their ears to protect them from the turbine noise as the C-130 inched its way into the parking area. Glancing over at the Connie he saw Lee hustling toward them. As Lee walked up, Stoney shouting over the roar of the engines, "Did you find something wrong? I thought you'd be out of there sooner."

"No, everything is fine, it just took a little longer than I thought. Far as I can tell she is ready to go." Lee stopped yelling as the turbines began to spool down and the noise abated. The door opened and several people descended the stairs. Walking over to where Stoney and the group stood, the man in the lead held out his hand and gripping Stoney's hand tightly said, "Hi, we are here to fix your broken airplane. My name is Smith, Jonathan Smith. This is Paul Lyman and his sidekick Bob Bell."

"Nice to meet all of you, I am Captain Victor Stone though please call me Stoney, Tyler Noland acting Chief of Airfield 'Q' and Lee Wyne my flight engineer. I thought you were bringing me a co-pilot as well?"

"APA had a co-pilot designated to meet up with us before we left, however, he either ate something or caught a stomach bug a few hours before we took-off. He was throwing up and running out the other end, if you get my drift. There wasn't another Connie qualified pilot close enough to make the plane in time. As it turns out, I am a qualified pilot and even have a multi-engine rating but I am not type rated in the Connie. Since this will be legally classified as a 'ferry trip' APA said I could fill in as co-pilot and Tom Train agreed."

"Welcome to 'Q' guys, I have accommodations waiting for you and our maintenance guys are hanging out in the cafeteria awaiting your arrival," said Tyler.

"Thanks Mr. Noland, a hot cup of joe is just what we need and then we can get started."

"If you all will follow me, let's head that way." Tyler turned and headed toward the main building. Everyone but Stoney followed him, instead, he walked over to the 130 and entered the cabin.

"Anyone home?" he said loudly as he entered the aircraft.

"Can I help you?" came a voice from the cockpit.

Stoney headed on in. "Hi, I am Captain Victor Stone, commander of yonder Constellation."

"Hi captain, I'm Lieutenant Thad Jenkins and this is Lieutenant Mark Cummings."

Shaking hands Stoney said "Nice to meet you. I'm sure glad you're here. I can't wait to get the aircraft fixed and head south! This cold is for the penguins! How long are you going to stay?"

"Well, our orders are to drop off the support guys and head on back to base. We would like to get a cup of hot coffee, empty the bladder, and maybe something to eat before we leave."

"I am sure that can be arranged, finish up what you are doing and make your way to the main building. The cafeteria is just inside. I'll see you there."

"Great, we'll get Technical-Sergeant Chang and be there in about ten minutes."

Stoney headed out the door and over to the main building. He was anxious to get the maintenance people working on the airplane. Entering the building, he walked into the cafeteria which was buzzing with noise. After getting a cup of coffee, to combat the chill, he walked over to where Lee and the maintenance guys were sitting.

"Hi guys, see you found the coffee. How long do you think it will take to get the Connie ready to fly?"

"Well, Stoney, if it is just the window that needs fixing then it will take about four hours since we have to remove the remnants of the window and clean out the sealant, we then have to install the new window and re-seal it. It will take the sealant no less than ten hours to dry and set. We do foresee one potential problem—the temperature," said Jonathan.

"I wonder if there is a way to use the pre-heaters and shrouds," said Stoney.

As they were discussing the rest of the repairs, the 130 aircrew walked up.

Stoney saw them and he stood up to make the introductions.

"Tyler Noland, this is Lieutenant Jenkins, Lieutenant Cummings and Technical-Sergeant Chang. They are the 130 drivers. Guys, this is Tyler Noland the supervisor here. I believe you know everyone else."

"Thanks Stoney, nice to meet you Mr. Noland. I don't want to be rude, but where do we find the coffee pot? It is colder than you-know-what out there and the heating systems in C-130s just don't cut it. We're one step warmer then a popsicle," said Jenkins.

Pointing toward the kitchen, "It's over there, but take a seat and I'll get you some," said Tyler.

"That's Ok, Mr. Noland we're going to see if there's anything to eat as well. We'll be back in a minute," and they headed off in the direction of the kitchen.

Just then the head of 'Q' maintenance walked over and sat down.

"Justin, let me introduce you to Jonathan, Paul, and Bob, they are the maintenance guys that just flew in from HQ," said Stoney.

"Nice to meet y'all," Justin replied in his best southern drawl.

"That is an odd accent to hear from someone who lives in this climate," remarked Jonathan.

"Yep, I'm from deep down Louisiana way, from the bayou. I got tired of all of the mosquitoes and gators and decided that it would be fun to live in a place that didn't make me sweat just to walk out the door. Worst part is the folks that live up here never had any good Cajun food; you know the kind that will grow hair where there weren't none to begin with. Oh well, gotta take the good with the bad. Now I understand you fellas are here to fix that old bird outside. What can my team and I do to help though I must warn you that my team consists of me and one other fellow."

"Louisiana, wow that is a long way from here; no I'm sure the local population doesn't even know what the word Cajun means. But, down to business, we need a way to heat the cockpit and the glass when we go to replace the one that blew out. Our sealant works much faster if the temperature is above freezing, well above freezing. Stoney here, thought there may be a way to use the engine nacelle shrouds and heating equipment to wrap the front of the airplane and heat it that way. What do you think?"

"Well now, that sounds just like a pilot; no disrespect to Captain Stone. They seem to see things as very simple, you know, push the wheel forward—houses get bigger, pull the wheel back—houses get smaller. Generally it takes us maintenance guys to firmly plant those flyboy's feet on the ground of reality. However, in this case the good captain may have accidentally stumbled upon a good idea, no offense sir. I do believe that might work, it will take some doin since I'm not sure how we'll keep the shroud in place since the straps won't reach 'round like on the nacelle, but we may be able to come up with somethin'. I'll head on out and take a look see what I can do."

"No offense taken, Justin; you guys are the tops for getting the 'old bird' as you put it running as you did. By the way, she ran great! Thanks for all the hard, cold work!" replied Stoney.

"I'll see everyone in the maintenance shed as soon as y'all can motivate yourselves back out to the cold," Justin said as he got up and headed out.

"I hope Justin didn't offend anyone, but he is one of the finest aviation maintenance guys I've ever seen. If there's a way to do it, he'll figure it out," said Tyler.

"No, no offense taken. I look forward to working with him. If you fellas are ready, let's down the rest of this coffee and head on out; we have work to do!" Jonathan said as he got to his feet and started putting on his parka.

"Lead on boss. We'll catch everyone later," said Paul as the group headed out the door.

"Colorful group, but if anyone can replace that window in these conditions, I'll bet a month's pay it's those guys!" said Stoney.

"Captain, I need to go see the medic. I have not been sleeping well and I want to get something that will help

282

me since it looks like we'll be southward bound in the next day or so," said Lee as he got up.

"Lee, the pills he gave us to slip to those Russian bastards worked wonders, bet you'll sleep well with those! Good luck, we'll see you later. I'm headed out to the maintenance area after I talk to the 130 crew," Stoney replied.

"Later," Lee said as he walked out the door.

Meanwhile, the 130 crew had joined Stoney and Tyler at the table.

"Mr. Noland, don't know what kind of joe this is, but it sure tastes great. Those coffee pots on the airplanes just can't make a cup worth a damn," said Lieutenant Jenkins.

"L.T. when you were flying in, did you notice a strange noise on your radio and were you able to contact Polar Control while in flight in this area?" asked Stoney.

"Sure thing, no strange noises on the radio and Polar Control worked us all the way here. The airways were clear as a bell. Why do you ask?" said Lieutenant Cummings.

"When we left Victoria and crossed into Polar Control's airspace we were in contact for several miles and when it came time to switch over to the next controller's frequency, there was a strange noise on the radio and communication with Polar Control was impossible. Matter of fact, contact with any other aircraft was impossible."

"Not sure what you encountered, but it was clear as a bell for us. Wonder if the Russians set up a jammer to prevent you contacting control so you couldn't holler for help?"

"That is the same line of thinking that I had, just wanted to make sure it wasn't our comm gear on the aircraft. How about the weather? When we left, a low pressure system was beginning to build over the pole. You all know anything about it?"

"Yes, that's one reason we want to go ahead and beat feet out of here shortly. We want to get out before that front gets nasty. Unfortunately, if you leave in two days you may be in the thick of it. Where are you planning to head once you get out of here?" asked Jenkins.

"We're headed back to the west coast. They'll want to do a complete examination of all aircraft systems back at APA headquarters. Also, I suspect this may be our last flight along these routes. I'm willing to bet the 'powers that be' will cut our funding once they get wind of what has happened out here. We should have enough fuel to make British Columbia and we'll refuel and head down the coast. Based on your experiences, think we can make it out of here on time?"

"If you're headed in a more westerly direction, then it could be a factor, but how much is anyone's guess. Just keep in mind that in this part of the world those fronts can wrap around and do all sorts of crazy unexpected things. You'll need to contact Polar Control Weather service once you're in flight. I understand all of the radios, except the teletype machine are dead here, courtesy of our Russian friends," said Jenkins.

"That sounds like a plan. Yep, I know the weather can do strange things up here. The Connie can only take so much of a cross wind. Not much rudder surface to keep her nose straight if we get straight line perpendicular winds over about thirty-five knots. That's my biggest worry. Once airborne we'll be fine. I sure hope we get out ahead of it."

"We'll keep our fingers crossed. Guess we'll head on back to base once we finish eating. Is there anyone that wants to leave with us?"

"No one has said they'd like to go. We all have work to do here to get this place back operational. There is a lot of work to do in the control cab. Heck based on current events I don't know if they want us to fix the place up or just abandon it. If they kill the Northern Star program, then there is no reason for us to exist. At that point they'll send up a couple of 130's to help us pack out equipment and supplies as well as the remaining personnel and we'll lock the place and leave it for the polar bears," replied Tyler.

"Lieutenant Jenkins thanks again for the weather info. I hope you guys have a good flight back to Wisconsin."

"Stoney, we're actually headed to Elmendorf. We were in Wisconsin to pick up some gear for the communications squadron at Elmendorf. Just happen to be in the right place at the right time to help you guys out."

"Well, then, do you know Captain Marcus?"

"Sure do, he is our flight commander and one of the squadron's check pilots," replied Jenkins.

"If we have to stop for fuel, you'll have to join Marcus' crew and us for a round at the O'Club. I'm buying the first one!" replied Stoney.

"Great! We'll make sure we tell Marcus to let us know. By the way, Mr. Noland, if you all end up packing out of here, we'll probably be one of the crews to help you do it. Well, if no one wants to leave with us, once we finish here we'll head on back to base."

"Before you leave, be sure to stop by the kitchen and ask the cook for a couple of thermoses of coffee for the flight," said Tyler.

"Yes, sir we will. Thanks much for the hospitallty!"

"L.T., have a good flight and maybe we'll see you at Elmendorf. Tyler, I'll catch you later, I'm going to see what's up with the Connie," said Stoney as he got up to leave.

"Thanks sir, we'll see you then. Good luck with the Connie!" said Cummings.

I'd like to buy those guys a beer, but I'd rather get back to L.A. where it's much warmer. Stoney thought as he headed toward the main door. His thoughts turned to James and the tragic loss as he fastened up the parka James had given him.

"How long have you had this sleeping problem?" said Jake.

"Ever since we landed in this place and especially after seeing someone turned into hamburger as they were sucked out a small window," replied Lee.

"Wow, guess I would have sleeping problems after that as well. How many do you think you need?"

"Can I have the whole bottle; I have the strangest feeling that I'll need them for a while even after we get back to the west coast; may take a few days to get back to normal."

"Ok, but, stop taking these things as soon as possible. They are fairly strong and they can become addictive if used over a long period."

"Will do Doc, and thanks much for the help," Lee said as he shook hands with Jake and headed out, bottle in hand and a large smile on his face.

CHAPTER 24

While Jonathan and his team worked to replace the broken window, Stoney volunteered on Justin's team to help them cover the cockpit windows with the heat shroud. Once in place the pre-heaters would warm the cockpit and windows making it possible for the sealant to properly cure.

Once Jonathan replaced the window, Justin fired up the pre-heater and ten hours later after Jonathan inspected the repair, he deemed Northern Star #28A airworthy once more.

Stoney helped the maintenance crew put the shrouds back over the engines and setup the pre-heaters to warm the engines all night in preparation for a dawn departure. Everyone knew that since it had been several days since those big radial engines had been running the oil would

James A. Jack

be thick as molasses and any attempt to start them would cause severe damage. Having them warm up all night would assure that the oil thickness was as normal as possible when they attempted engine start in the morning.

Stoney had a fitful night's sleep. He tossed and turned all night and finally giving up on sleep, he got up quite early in the morning. He took a shower and quietly packed up his overnight bag. Tyler's folks had managed to get the stains out of his uniform and he was grateful to not have a constant reminder of that fateful day. He had been looking forward to a nice quiet flight to British Columbia and then on down to L.A. Unfortunately, the powers above decided that he needed one more challenge on this flight by letting that low pressure system slide south resulting in a winter storm. As he dressed and packed his things, he looked over at Lee sleeping so soundly.

Lee was an odd one. He had confided to Stoney that he was having money problems, and he was afraid it would cause a problem with his security clearance and his status at APA. Lee had said his wife liked to spend money and she managed to rack up a large amount of debt.

He wanted to divorce her and had even threatened to do that if she didn't stop spending. Truth was, he was too much in love with her and he would do whatever it took to maintain the marriage. Stoney had suggested they get financial counseling and Lee had thought that was a good idea and had promised to get started once they returned from this trip.

Lee had begged Stoney not to say anything to management about his problem. That went against all of the security training Stoney had received since joining Northern Star. The security protocols dictated that he report this directly to management but he made a conscious decision not to.

Stoney had known Lee from the moment he started with the program and felt that he would turn his finances around and get his act together, given a chance. Stoney gathered up his things and headed for the door. The 'Q' folks would make sure Lee, the Marines and the APA maintenance folks were awake and fed in time to leave at dawn.

Pulling his coat tight around him, Stoney headed out into the darkness for the Constellation. The wind was strong, putting the wind chill down in the negative numbers. Stoney wrapped a scarf around his head and face but the wind just cut through it. *This wind is at or above thirty knots and I won't be surprised if it has passed the Connie's maximum crosswind capability. It feels like it might not be a direct crosswind; that will help.* He thought as he hurried to the stairs leading up to the front door of the Connie knowing that he could get a bad case of frost bite if he wasn't careful. The door was stuck from the cold, so he really had to work to get it open. He closed it as fast as he could, trying not to lose any of the heat from the cabin.

To facilitate the departure, Stoney and Jonathan had figured out a way to pipe some of the engine pre-heater's heat into the cabin. It was enough to keep everything above freezing which would help the gyros and some of the other delicate equipment warm up faster once the engines were running. After the short walk from the building to the stairs, Stoney was grateful for any increase in temperature, small as it was.

He made his way to the cockpit and turning on the lights he opened the storage closet to put his overnight bag away. He hadn't noticed it before, but Steve's flight case was still in the closet. When he first opened the closet he noticed an odd smell in the cold air. He couldn't place the smell, but it was not an airplane type of smell. Since Steve's case was the only thing in there, he pulled it out and discovered it was the source of the odor.

Taking out a flashlight, he examined the case and saw what looked like signs of high heat and smoke. However, in the dim light of the cockpit he could not be sure of anything. He decided to take the case into the building and really examine it. He set the case aside and began to make sure everything was ready for their departure. Since he didn't have a co-pilot who knew the routine, he made all of the preparations himself. He got out the charts they would need; he completed his pre-flight planning the night before.

They had enough fuel to make Victoria, B.C. with no problem; however, depending on the wind's direction and strength they might have to stop at Elmendorf AFB to refuel. Should they need to divert then Polar Control would alert Elmendorf to expect them. The last thing he checked was the cylinder head temperature and the oil temperature of each engine at the flight engineer's console.

Yep, all of the cylinders and the oil were within the starting temperature range—good to go. Turning off the lights and wrapping himself back up in his coat and scarf, he grabbed Steve's flight case and headed back to the main building.

Walking into the brightness and warmth of the main building, Stoney was shaking off the cold and up walked Captain Jones.

"Pete, how did you know I was coming to look for you?" said Stoney.

"Now what could an airline captain want with a ground-pounder like me?" asked Jones.

"Let's go into the cafeteria, I want to get breakfast and I want you to examine this case for me. It is Steve's, my co-pilot's flight case. It has been in the storage closet on the Connie since the aborted flight with the Russians and I noticed a strange odor coming from it. I looked at it with a flashlight and it appears to be burned and scorched on the inside. I wanted to get your opinion as well."

"Hey, no problem; I was headed for breakfast myself. Let's get something to eat and I'll look at it. How's the airplane look for departure?"

"Engine temps look OK, and we should have enough fuel to make it to Victoria, B.C., where we'll top off and head to L.A. I am concerned about the winds. Over night they have picked up considerably; we may have trouble getting out of here."

"What's the problem?"

"The Connie has a maximum crosswind capability of about thirty-five knots. That is what the design engineers put in the flight manual. Theoretically that means once the wind exceeds thirty-five knots perpendicular to the runway there's not enough rudder authority to keep the airplane moving on the ground or in the air in a straight line. If the wind blows it sideways it could overload the gear and cause it to collapse, on the other hand, if we make it into the air I might not be able to keep her going straight down the runway and we could be blown into the snow drifts lining the edge of the runway. I'll have my work cut out for me."

"Well, sounds like to me you're going to have to do some serious pilot shit to get us out of here in one piece. Oh well, just another day in the Corps!"

"Assuming we get airborne in one piece, you guys are going all the way to L.A. with us and then you'll catch a flight back to Elmendorf."

"That's the plan. Higher ups don't want any more surprises on this flight. Yep, we'll sit in the back and enjoy the ride. What else can happen, eh?"

Entering the cafeteria, Stoney set the flight case on one of the tables and they walked to the kitchen to get a generous portion of ham and eggs and a large mug of hot coffee. Returning to their seats they ate and continued to talk about the flight to come. Stoney said he was worried about the weather in general, but without access to accurate meteorology reports and graphs he would have to 'wing it'. Once they finished eating, Jones picked up the flight case and started taking things out of it.

"Boy, I see what you mean about that odor, almost smells like burning wires. I can't imagine what could be in here to cause that smell." Jones continued to empty the contents on the table. Everything he took out had that strong smell and several items looked like they were subjected to a lot of heat. Both Stoney and Jones were surprised that whatever had caused the heat hadn't melted through the outside of the case. Once the case was empty he felt down inside and discovered what appeared to be the bottom of the case was in fact a false bottom. Pulling it out he realized it had been subjected to very high heat but whatever material it was made of did not burn. Using his flashlight he peered into the case and discovered the cause of the smell. He pulled out a small incendiary device attached to what appeared to be a control module and laid it on the table.

"Looks like you found the source of our 'electrical fire'," said Stoney.

"Yep, looks like someone wanted to force you to land by faking an electrical fire. Is this really Steve's case or is it possible it was switched somewhere during your trip?"

"It sure looks like his, but it's possible it was switched that morning at the hotel before departure. We all met in the restaurant and the hostess had suggested we leave our cases by the coat rack. It very easily could have been switched then. There would be no reason to suspect Steve would do something like this."

"This control module has a small wire that looks like an antenna. This might just be a radio receiver of some sorts. Yep, just as I suspected, here is a radio frequency crystal," said Jones as he pried the cover off the module.

"Do you think a signal was sent from the ground which caused it to go off at just the right time to force us to land here or could it have been someone on the aircraft with a small transmitter?" asked Stoney.

"Well, it could have been one or the other, however I would tend to discount the passenger aspect. Without proper time, distance and ground speed information it would be hard for someone to know when to set it off. By the same argument, a timer would not have worked either since the perpetrator wouldn't know the exact time to make it go off ensuring you would land here. However, if the Russians had covertly airdropped a small transmitter in the vicinity they could ensure you would land here to be met by their ground team. The transmitter, most likely, sends the signal periodically and after a specified period of time the batteries would run out ensuring it would not be found in the vastness of the arctic. That would be much more reliable than any other method. They knew this was the closest alternate airfield and even I know that smoke in the cockpit is a sure fire way to get an airplane on the ground. It was just icing on their cake that the engine acted up as well; though it was likely just a coincidence."

About that time Lee walked up. "Hey guys, what's up with the flight case? Isn't that Steve's?"

"Oh, hi Lee I thought you were dead asleep. I went out to the bird to get her ready and as I was putting my case in the storage closet I smelled something odd, and discovered it was Steve's flight case. We found this device under a false bottom, looks like this is the source of the electrical fire we all smelled."

"I woke up just as you were headed out the door and decided to go ahead and get up. Why would Steve want to make us believe there was an electrical fire on board?"

"I don't think he did it intentionally, I believe the cases were switched at the hotel, that morning at breakfast," replied Stoney.

"Sounds like the Russians, most likely KGB had someone working at the hotel that made the switch," added Jones.

"I'll be damned, this whole thing was a setup from the start!" said Stoney.

"They sure went to a lot of effort for whatever it is you have on that plane. Can I ask what it is?" asked Jones.

"You can ask, but unfortunately I can't tell you; and yes, they did go to a lot of effort to commandeer her," said Stoney.

"I'm looking forward to a nice safe flight back to L.A. and on that note I'm going to get some chow; back in a minute," Lee said as he walked off.

"You need to alert your 'upper management' about the Victoria thing. Sounds like KGB might have infiltrated your operation. If they've gone to this much effort once, there's no telling what they might do the next time," said Jones.

"Pete, you said it. I'm glad you guys will be with us on the return flight. I'll inform HQ as soon as we get to some secure communications. I really don't want to broadcast this in the open."

"I'm going to make sure the rest of my guys are headed this way. I know you want to get an early start. I'll catch up with you in a little while. What are you going to do with the case?"

"I'm going to put it back on the airplane, it is our only proof. I'll wait for Lee, and we'll see you at the main exit in about an hour. If you see Tyler, please ask him to stop by."

"One hour; see you then," said Pete as he walked off to rouse his sleeping Marines.

I bet the folks at NSA will not be happy about this discovery, Stoney thought as he waited for Lee. *I can see them shutting down the whole program and the worst part is I may be out of a job when we get home.*

"Glad this is the last breakfast here," said Lee as he sat down.

"Why, I didn't think the food was so bad?" said Stoney.

"I have never been a fan of mass produced food, it's always very bland since they fix it for folks who think a little bit of pepper will burn their palates. I have to doctor up the food so much just to get some flavor. No, I'll take a nice sit-down restaurant any day or even my wife's cooking over this. At one time she was a great cook, now she just dabbles in it. We eat out a lot."

"I'm ready to leave as well though I'm grateful we've had hot food and coffee. Guess my palate is not as discerning as yours. I may be from Colorado, but this arctic cold gets down into the bones. I'm not cut out to be an Eskimo!"

"Yep, I'll agree on that one and I can't wait for the Palm trees and sandy beaches of L.A. I hope they'll let us take some leave when this is all over. I could use a week on the beach. If they do, I might just pack up the wife and catch a hop to Cancun. It'll be a cheap getaway since we fly for free and off season the hotels are reasonable. I can just hear the waves lapping on the shore, the cool ocean breeze rustling the trees and taste the umbrella drink in my hand as my beautiful wife rubs sun tan lotion on my back and other 'strategic' places—if you get my drift!"

"Hey, cut it out! All you've done is make me colder! I might just do the same thing except I think I'll head down to San Diego and charter a fishing boat and spend the week out in the Pacific. Just think me, Becky, and a case of rum bobbing around in the waves with no one else in sight. You can keep the umbrellas. Yep, that thought alone and I could almost carry the Connie back to L.A.! Alas, back to reality, we need to get going, that storm is not going to let up. I just hope the cross winds don't keep us grounded. Since we don't have any stews this trip, how 'bout having the cook brew us up a large urn of coffee for the return trip. Bet the Marines would like some as well. I really don't want them messing around with the galley equipment. They might just catch the whole damn thing on fire! I'll see you at the main door in about twenty minutes."

"Can do boss; I'll get a thermos we can keep up front with us as well. With this weather and a so-so co-pilot won't be much time to wander back to the cabin till we get to Victoria."

"Good idea; didn't think about that. I am going to find Jonathan to make sure his folks are ready and to re-brief how we'll handle the front seat duties. See ya in twenty," replied Stoney as he got up and headed out the door to look for Jonathan.

✪

Great! I'll be able to spike the main coffee urn with those sleeping pills I ground up last night and it won't seem odd that the cockpit crew is not drinking from it. I couldn't have set this up better myself. Damn there is one aspect of this caper I hadn't even thought of, what will happen to everyone else on the aircraft? It didn't even cross my mind to get Ivan to promise to return them to the States. There is no way the Russians will let them go since they would tell the world the Soviets have a Northern Star aircraft. I know, I'll write down everyone's name and send an anonymous letter to the State Department after they take us to that island and once the U.S. Government realizes they did not perish in an accident they will force the Soviets to send them home. I feel sorry for what the Soviets may do to them in the meantime, but I have to look out for myself. I do know one thing, Stone is going to be madder and as dangerous as a hornet when he realizes what is going to go down; he'll cooperate with a pistol to his head. Bottom line is the Soviets will have their precious plane and I'll have a lot of money and no more worries at all.

These thoughts made Lee unconsciously grin and chuckle to himself, just as Tyler Noland walked up.

"Hey Lee, thought Stoney wanted to see me. I just got word to look for him here. By the way, what's so funny?"

"You just missed him; he's gone to look for Jonathan. We're going to meet by the main door in about twenty minutes. I was just thinking of sitting on a beach and getting out of this cold; since you're here, would you ask the cook to make a large urn of coffee we can take with us? Stoney doesn't want the jar-heads messing with the galley equipment. We'll also need a couple of thermoses for the cockpit. I'll stop by to pick it up just before we leave."

"No problem, glad to help. Don't worry about picking it up I'll have someone bring it out to the aircraft. I'll see if I can find Stoney after I talk to the cook. Enjoy your breakfast. See you at the main door."

"That's OK Tyler, I don't mind getting it just before we leave; save your folks a trip. You guys have been so good to us, that's the least I can do to help you for a change."

"OK, I'll tell the cook and he'll have it ready. Thanks."

Boy that was close, thought Lee as Tyler headed to the kitchen. *It'll just take a second to pour the powder into the urn and the sloshing around during transport will make sure it dissolves.*

Tom Train was chatting with Colonel Tomlinson and gazing out the large windows when the sleek silver Boeing-707 rolled up to the VIP terminal at Elmendorf AFB. Just as he heard the engines start to shutdown, he saw the stairs roll up to the front cabin door. Several young airmen began opening the baggage compartments and getting ready to load baggage on the big silver bird from carts sitting nearby.

"Well sir, if you're ready, I guess its time to send them on their way," said Tom.

"That sounds like my cue," replied the colonel who quietly cleared his throat and then loudly said, "Ladies and Gentlemen, this is Colonel Tomlinson, if I could have your attention for just a moment." As the room quieted down, Tomlinson continued, "First of all, let me say that I hope your brief stay here at Elmendorf has been a pleasant one. Though it's not the same as downtown London, we have tried our best to make your stay here as enjoyable as possible. On behalf of the entire base I want to wish you Godspeed on the last leg of your journey. If you will head out the door and up the stairs we'll get you on your way as soon as possible."

The passengers all applauded and they lined up and headed out the door and across the ramp to the waiting jet.

"Virginia and Brad, thank you very much for your help over the last few days. We couldn't have accomplished what we did without your help as well. I hope you have a good trip home," said Tom.

"Have you heard any information about Captain Stone and the aircraft?" asked Brad.

"No, I haven't heard from 'Q' or from Washington. The repair crew should have arrived and I would imagine they have completed the repairs by now. I would assume that they are either in the air or soon will be. If I do hear something, we'll try to radio the 707 in flight and ask the crew to pass it on."

"Thanks sir. I'm sure anxious to hear how things are going. Hope you have a good trip home as well. We better get going or they'll leave without us." Shaking hands all around, Brad and Virginia headed out the door to the waiting 707.

As the last passenger exited through the door, Colonel Tomlinson turned to the group and said, "Tom, please pass my hello's to your DDO, I worked with him years ago. Congratulations on a job well done and have a safe trip home. Now, if you'll excuse me, I have a meeting to get to. Major Cooper, I'll see you at the office when you're finished here." The colonel shook hands with everyone and hurried out the door to his waiting staff car.

"Well everyone, well done. I didn't think we could do it but we did. Glen and I thank you on behalf of the NSA and CIA. Katie, I now know why your reputation preceded you and why CIA selected you for this mission. I'll be singing your praises back in Washington."

"Katie, if you don't mind me asking, how did you convince every one of those passengers to sign a sworn secrecy agreement?" asked Cooper.

"Well, Erik, it was a matter of appealing to their patriotic side and a few needed a gentle economic push as well, courtesy of NSA 'slush funds' and that call from the head of British MI-6 didn't hurt at all. Since it was a military call, it didn't break the military exercise scenario we painted for them. Deep down inside, they all are patriotic to their countries. If they revealed what has happened it would damage East/West relations for years to come. The Soviets would capitalize on the commercial spy plane aspect and we would capitalize on the hijacking of a commercial airliner. A stalemate, if you will, that doesn't help anyone. All we did was show them and their bank accounts the light. We ended up paying some of them an equivalent sum to what a publisher or newspaper would pay for their story. Those sworn statements are as good in an international court as well as a U.S., Canadian, Scottish or British Crown Court. If they break their agreement, they have consented to immediate arrest, a closed military tribunal style trial and immediate forfeiture of money and property equivalent to what we paid them. I believe I can safely say this matter will remain buried forever."

"Katie is the best! That's why CIA hired her. She's earned a large bonus as well for her efforts here. Keeping this out of the papers is priceless in terms of National Security and international politics," added Glen Burton.

"Now, if you'll excuse us there is a jet with our name on it spooling up its engines. Major, thank you again for everything and please pass our sincere thanks to the rest of your folks. Without you and your team we could never have pulled this off," said Tom.

"Glad to help and I hope you all have a safe flight home. There's a van waiting to take you to your plane," said Cooper.

"Good bye Erik if you're ever in D.C. look me up. Here's my real phone number," said Katie as she handed Cooper her business card containing a handwritten phone number while giving him a big hug at the same time.

"Thanks Katie, I will definitely do that. In fact, I have some leave coming up, and I've always wanted to go to the Smithsonian. How 'bout dinner and a museum in two weeks?"

"It's a date!"

With their goodbyes said, the group walked out to the waiting van climbed in and headed to the executive jet waiting to take them home. As the van passed from behind a large hanger, they saw the 707 lift off into the cloudy Alaskan sky bound for San Francisco.

The team's luggage was loaded onto the U.S. Government Lear jet and once they climbed aboard, sat down and fastened their seatbelts, the aircraft started to taxi. Within minutes of settling down into those large overstuffed executive seats, all three of them were sound asleep. Tom drifted off, secure in the knowledge that this entire incident would never see the light of day, except in the after action report he and Glen had to write. Once management approved the report, the records section would file it away in the archives for some historian to find, in about fifty years. By then the entire program would be declassified. The last thought he had was the potential for Congressional Oversight to cancel the program based on recent events.

CHAPTER 25

J ust as Lee was finishing his breakfast, one of the guys from the kitchen wheeled out a large coffee urn on a cart.

"Where do you want us to take this?" he asked.

"It needs to go to the main entrance where everyone is meeting. Don't worry about taking it, I'm headed there right now and you guys have done so much for us, I'll take it for you."

"Thanks, we have a lot of things to do to get this place back to normal. We're glad we could help. Have a safe flight."

"Thanks, we'll see you later." Lee took the push cart with the urn and he noticed the kitchen folks had also put two thermoses of coffee on the lower shelf and had added a few baggies with sugar and creamer and a stack of

Styrofoam cups. *They think of everything,* Lee thought as he rolled the cart out into the hallway. He headed toward the main entrance and along the way he passed a door that was ajar. Opening the door, he looked to see if anyone was in the room. Seeing no one, he pushed the cart in and closed the door behind him. Turning on the light, he lifted the top off the coffee urn and poured the powder into the steaming brown liquid. He replaced the lid and he peeked out the door to make sure no one would see him coming out of the room. He closed the door behind him and as he headed for the main entrance, he made sure to jostle the cart to make sure the coffee inside the urn would slosh around and mix up the contents as he walked.

"Oh Lee, there you are. Thanks for getting the coffee. Do you have all of your stuff as well?" Stoney asked as he saw Lee walking toward him.

"Sure do. Let's rock and roll."

"Could I please have everyone's attention?" Stoney said in a loud voice.

The group quieted down and Stoney began to speak.

"If everyone is here and has their things, we're ready to go. However, I would like to make a few remarks to the Marines and the support crew here at airfield 'Q'. What you all have done for me, my crew and the passengers has been nothing short of spectacular. Tyler and his folks have gone above and beyond what anyone could expect. The maintenance crew did an outstanding job of repairing our bird the first time and now the second time. I'll make sure the management at NSA and CIA both know the outstanding work you've done here. To Captain Jones and his Marines, again I cannot express our gratitude for all that you've done as well. We have one more leg to go before this ordeal is over. I know you guys are riding along with us, but I wanted to say thanks so that everyone here could hear it as well. Tyler, I'm sorry for your losses as well. I'll make sure their personnel records reflect their ultimate sacrifice and their heroic efforts. Now, if everyone would please bow their head for a moment of silence to honor those that have died during this ordeal." After a short pause, Stoney continued, "Unless anyone has anything to add, let's get this show on the road; Load 'em UP!"

Turning to Tyler, Stoney stuck out his hand and Tyler gripped it warmly. "Thanks again. If you're ever in L.A. please look me up."

"Glad we were here to help. Have a safe trip home and I'll look you up if I'm ever down that way; so long pal!"

Stoney and the group headed out the door across the ramp and up the stairs into the Constellation. Everyone seemed relaxed; however, the wind was blowing quite hard and it had started to snow. The snow had not been coming down long enough to cause a problem on the runway but they would need to get moving. Entering the cockpit, Stoney stowed his and Steve's flight bags in the closet and even though it was quite cold in the cockpit he hung up his coat and climbed into his seat. Jonathan squeezed himself into the co-pilot seat. Stoney had assigned Lee the cabin attendant duties so he and Jonathan would have to get the big bird started without him.

As Stoney and Jonathan settled down into their seats, Stoney looked out his side window and saw the maintenance guys pulling the stairs away from the aircraft and after that they hurried over to remove the heater shrouds from around the engines. Stoney knew they needed to begin the start up sequence as soon as possible to keep the engines from cooling off.

"Jonathan, if you're settled in let's go with the Pre-Engine Start checklist," said Stoney, his breath forming vapor as he spoke.

The main cabin was no warmer and Lee could see everyone's exhaled breath as he performed the final cabin check and made sure everybody had their seatbelts fastened. He heard the starter begin to whine on number one engine and looking out the window he saw the number one propeller start to turn and within seconds the engine itself coughed to life causing the floor of the cabin to vibrate until the engine smoothed out.

"I know it's cold in here, and it will be for a while, if you guys can keep from burning yourselves during take-off, I'll go ahead and get everyone some coffee. Do I have any takers?"

A chorus of "yes sir" rang through the cabin.

Lee methodically poured everyone a cup and passed out the condiments.

"Everyone will need to stay seated until the 'Fasten Seatbelts' sign is turned off. These winds will cause it to be pretty rough until we get above the storm so just hang on. I'll get the heat running as soon as the engines generate some. Any questions?" said Lee.

"Nope, just tell Stone to get us there in one piece," said Jones.

306

Satisfied his cabin duties were complete, Lee headed toward the cockpit. Just as he sat down, adjusted his seat and put on his seatbelt, the last engine rumbled to life.

With all four engines running Stoney began to taxi to the runway.

"Man that wind is really howling!" Stoney said as he taxied the large plane to the end of the runway. "I hope we can get her off OK, we're probably at or beyond her cross-wind limit. Jonathan let's have the Pre-Takeoff Checklist."

Jonathan started reading the items and both Stoney and Lee replied with the appropriate answer after verifying switch settings, valve settings and other such items. The whole plane was shuddering against the wind. Once all of the pre-takeoff items were covered, Stoney said "Guess we're ready. Jonathan make a cabin announcement and tell everyone to hang on, it's going to be rough."

Picking up the microphone, Jonathan relayed Stoney's instructions and when he finished Stoney called for take-off power and the big Constellation began its roll down the runway.

Stoney turned the yoke into the wind reducing the upwind wing's ability to produce lift which might flip them over. He pressed the left rudder to the floor attempting to keep the nose from trying to turn into the wind. As the aircraft accelerated down the runway he gradually centered the yoke just as the tires broke from the ground and the Constellation became airborne. Without the friction of the tires against the asphalt runway to hold her straight the aircraft rapidly spun to the left putting her nose into the wind and continued moving sideways down the asphalt mere feet above the runway.

"I can just keep her straight down the runway. Soon as we reach fifty feet pull up the gear!" yelled Stoney.

Just then the aircraft began to drift toward the right hand side of the runway and the piled up snow drifts.

"We're getting closer to the drifts on this side," Jonathan yelled.

"Put the gear up—now!"

Agonizingly seconds later everyone felt the 'thump, thump, thump' as the gear locked itself in the up position.

"The right half of the tail is over the snow drift," Jonathan yelled.

"C-l-i-m-b you beautiful baby, c-l-i-m-b," Stoney kept saying as if talking to his girlfriend while attempting to make the aircraft climb through sheer will power alone.

"We're at one hundred feet," said Jonathan.

"And we're clear of the runway and the snow drifts," added Stoney the tone of his voice a little more relaxed.

"200, 300 feet" called out Jonathan, "400, 500, 600 . . ."

A collective cheer went up in the cabin, as the Connie climbed into the low clouds headed to the sunny west coast. As they gained altitude the crosswinds lessened allowing the Connie to turn its nose more in the direction of flight vice flying completely sideways.

"The books all say that couldn't be done," said Jonathan.

"Well, if you had suggested we even attempt it a week ago, I would have suggested a psych eval. The Constellation is one of the greatest birds man ever built and today she proved it," said Stoney.

They continued to bounce around in the thick grey clouds as they sped toward Victoria B.C. Just as they were reaching cruise altitude the rough air smoothed out and the sun began to peek through the tops of the clouds above them.

"Good job back there Jonathan, if you ever want to trade those wrenches for approach plates I'd be glad to help!"

"Thanks boss, but I think I want to keep turning wrenches, way to much excitement up here for me."

As Stoney leveled off at their cruising altitude, Stoney heard Lee say, "Boss, between the coffee I had for breakfast and that take-off, I need to hit the head. I'll be right back."

"Don't take too long, I really want you to keep an eye on those engines," replied Stoney.

As Lee opened the cockpit door and walked into the cabin, the first thing he saw was Captain Jones lying on the floor. Checking around the cabin, Lee confirmed that all of the Marines and the two maintenance guys were sound asleep. Lee knew he couldn't leave Jones on the floor and even though Jones was a 'big boy' Lee summoned all of his strength and managed to get Jones into a seat and strapped down. Since he had no way of knowing how long they would stay asleep he headed back to the cockpit for the next phase of his plan.

Lee looked in the cockpit door and saw Stoney and Jonathan having a discussion both looking forward out the windshield. Stealthily entering the cockpit Lee crept to his console and retrieved the pistol he had hidden there. Standing about five feet behind the center console, Lee spread his legs apart and with both hands held the pistol out in front of him and pointed it at Stoney's head and said, in a loud voice, "Gentlemen, if I could have your undivided attention please."

Stoney and Jonathan turned simultaneously and saw Lee standing behind them with a pistol pointed at Stoney's face. Stoney noticed he was holding the pistol with both hands. Even though the aircraft was in mild turbulence, Lee was using his legs to balance his whole body and was not holding on with his hands. Doing his best not to yell, he used as calm a tone as he could manage and said, "What the hell do you think you're doing Lee?"

"Unfortunately, you managed to thwart Captain Leshev and his band of Spetsnaz troops, but Mother Russia, particularly the Committee for State Security—KGB for you lug heads—still wants this airplane and the secrets it holds. Therefore, it has fallen to me to take matters into my own hands and deliver this aircraft and its contents to Siberia. So, if you will kindly turn to a heading of zero-five-zero degrees we can stop wasting fuel and be on our way. By my calculations, the tanks will just run dry by the time we get to our destination, so if you don't want to walk part of the way you better get cracking."

"I know you've had your problems, Lee, but this is no way to solve them. You know that if we don't show up on time, then they'll send out the search teams again. There is no way you can win," said Stoney who hadn't moved a muscle.

"Captain Stone, you don't seem to understand that if you don't turn this aircraft at once, I will shoot you and then it will be up to Jonathan to get us to Siberia. Personally, I would prefer that you flew us there. The chances of arriving in one piece are much better with you flying. However, either you turn this aircraft NOW or I will shoot you in five seconds." Lee began counting, "five . . . . four . . . . three . . . ."

Stoney turned around in his seat and using the automatic pilot's heading control he caused the aircraft to begin a slow turn to heading zero-five-zero degrees. As he did so, Lee stopped counting.

"Good job captain now, Jonathan, dial in 359 KHz on the Automatic Direction Finder and set it to play the Morse code identifier sound on the overhead speaker so we can hear it. We'll maintain this heading until we start receiving that signal. By the way, if you were wondering about your saviors in the cabin, I pulled the same trick on them that we used on the Soviets. Needless to say, they are sleeping like babies back there. They should stay asleep until we land."

Turning once again to look Lee in the face, Stoney said, "I know you've had money problems Lee, but once Washington figures out what's happened you can be sure the FBI will collect your wife and they'll put her somewhere no one will be able to find her. What good is all the money KGB is paying you if she's not there to enjoy it with you?"

"Not your problem, the KGB has assured me they'll get her out of the country as soon as I deliver the aircraft. It'll all be over before Washington has a clue as to what's happened to their aircraft and crew. They'll have search and rescue on the brain thinking that we've crashed somewhere between 'Q' and Elmendorf. We'll long be in Siberia sipping vodka before they get a clue. Enough talking, you just turn around and fly this plane! Jonathan, keep your hands where I can see them. Oh, by the way, don't try the anesthesia gas trick, if you even think about touching *that* radio panel I will shoot Jonathan."

Turning back to his flying, Stoney's brain was racing to figure a way to take out Lee without getting anyone else killed. Based on what Lee had said, getting help from Jones and his Marines was not going to happen. Lee was standing up but with both him and Jonathan strapped to their chairs there was no way to surprise Lee and try to get the pistol from him. Stoney noticed Lee's pistol was one of the special ones which would not affect the pressurized cabin if it went off. He glanced over at Jonathan who was obviously quite nervous; he was sweating profusely and it looked like his hands were shaking. The question that was swimming around in Stoney's head was, *How do I knock Lee off his feet and get the pistol from him?* Just then, the aircraft lurched as it hit an air-pocket.

Even though they had climbed above the storm and were in the clear, Stoney saw a cloud bank just ahead of them. As he sat there and looked at the clouds racing toward him, Stoney suddenly had an idea. It was about as risky an idea as he could have conceived and he hoped the old Connie had the structural strength to carry it out. As carefully as he could, he began to undo his seatbelt. He had to do it carefully so that Lee or Jonathan wouldn't notice. He had loosened it enough when they entered the cloud bank. Fortunately there was minimal turbulence in the clouds and gripping the control wheel as tightly as he could and using his knees to wedge his legs under the instrument panel, he pressed the button to disengage the autopilot and quickly turned the control wheel completely to the right causing the aircraft to rapidly roll in the same direction. Fortunately Jonathan did not grab the control wheel and Stoney hoped he would keep his hands in his lap. Stoney didn't notice Jonathan grab his seatbelt and tighten it as he realized what was about to happen.

Behind Stoney, Lee shouted "Stone, level this airplane or I swear I will shoot you!"

The aircraft continued to roll and just as it passed the point where Lee could stand upright he pulled the trigger and fired the pistol. The shot echoed throughout the small confines of the cockpit and Stoney felt a sudden bolt of pain from his left shoulder and the glass of an instrument shattered as the bullet smashed into it. Keeping his cool and doing his best to ignore the pain, he continued the roll. As the aircraft rolled onto its side everything not secured began to fly around the cockpit. Somewhere in the back of his mind Stoney hoped everyone in the back was strapped down. Just as the aircraft rolled completely upside down, all kinds of alarm bells began to ring and lights were flashing. The oil system in the Wright-Cyclone engine didn't work when upside down. There was no way for the oil pump to suck the vital lubricating oil out of the oil pan and pump it into the engine since the oil intake was now uncovered and sucking air from inside the oil pan. Oil pressure in the big engines went to zero causing the cacophony of alarms to sound.

As Stoney was trying to keep from falling out of his seat while he was completely upside down, he heard a thud then a sudden yell from behind him. He couldn't look but hoped Lee had bashed his head on the new ceiling and was out or at least dazed. The aircraft continued to roll and was on its way to being right side up again. Just as the aircraft completed the roll, Stoney yelled to Jonathan to be ready to take over when they became level.

James A. Jack

As the aircraft became level, Stoney jumped out of his seat and saw Lee lying in a heap on the floor. He grabbed Lee's pistol and then he grabbed Lee by the shirt collar and jerked him to his feet. Though he saw it, Stoney ignored the blood running down Lee's face as he did his best to ignore the intense pain in his own shoulder and the blood that he felt running down his chest.

He did not know how much damage the bullet had done, he just knew it hurt like hell but he had to ignore it until he got things under control. Lee was groggy from the strike to the head and he didn't fight back. Stoney shoved him down in the chair at the Flight Engineers station.

"Jonathan, engage the autopilot once you turn us back to our original heading. Lee, you will sit very still or I'll shoot your traitorous ass!"

Lee just sat slumped over the engineer's console. While he was watching Lee, Stoney glanced at the engine instruments to make sure his little maneuver hadn't caused an engine failure. He knew that the engines took a beating running without oil circulation he just prayed they would last long enough to get them to Elmendorf.

Once he completed the turn and returned the Connie to its original course toward Victoria, Jonathan turned around in his seat and said, "Captain Stone that was the gutsiest maneuver I've ever seen in an aircraft like this!"

"Take this gun and point it at his head, if he even breathes wrong, shoot him. I'm going to get something to tie him up with." Stoney handed Jonathan the pistol and stepped out the cockpit door. He was surprised to see some of the Marines were beginning to wake up. Based on what Lee had said, he thought that was odd. He walked over to Pete Jones and shook him as he tried to wake him up.

314

"What the hell are you doing?" yelled Jones as he woke up.

"You, my friend have been drugged and I am trying to wake you up. I have a traitorous flight engineer with a gun pointed at his head in the cockpit. Once again, you missed all of the fun!"

"The hell you say, man, damn, I slept through all of the fun? What happened to you? Sit down, let me get a First Aid kit and patch that nasty looking wound," said Jones.

When Jones got back, he helped Stoney take off his shirt.

"You are lucky, that bullet went right through the soft part," said Jones after looking at the wound.

"That's great but it still hurts like h-e-l-l!"

"Here let me clean it up and cover it, you'll be OK until we get on the ground. I assume we're diverting to Elmendorf?"

"Yes, I—just—hope—the—engines—make—it—that —far," said Stoney through clenched teeth.

Just as he thought he would pass out from the pain, Jones said, "Finished; that should hold you for a while. Are you OK to fly?"

"I'll get us there."

When he finished, Stoney slowly put his shirt back on and filled Jones in on the events before he woke up.

When Stoney finished he said "Since all of your sleeping beauties are waking up, follow me and I'll let you have the traitor and you can take care of him while I get us to Elmendorf. I want him off this aircraft ASAP and I can't throw him out the door regardless of how much I want to!"

Jones followed Stoney back to the cockpit. Things were just as he had left them, Lee was sitting there with

Jonathan pointing the pistol at him. He worked his way to where Jonathan sat, and he took the pistol, and handed it to Jones. "Get that piece of trash off my flight deck! Why don't you have him drink a *large* cup of that coffee back there, but don't let anyone else touch it."

Jones took the pistol and yanking Lee out of his seat shoved him out the cockpit door. Lee stumbled and crashed to the floor. Jones grabbed him by his shirt collar and practically threw him into a seat.

Once Jones had gotten Lee out of the cockpit, Stoney took his seat, fastened his seatbelt and looked over at Jonathan. "Little more exciting than you thought this trip would be, eh?"

"Exciting? That doesn't even begin to describe what has been running through my head over the last while. That roll was pure genius, I didn't expect it and I'm sure Lee didn't have a clue as to what you were doing. I'm just glad those Lockheed engineers put a little extra cushion in the stress points on this bird. The mechanic in me is concerned about the engines; they ran for several seconds with no oil."

"I was checking the engine gauges while holding Lee at gun point, and I didn't see anything that looked abnormal. We'll need to keep an eye and ear on them. It wouldn't surprise me if at least one of them has metal flakes in the oil. Hopefully, they will hang on till we reach Elmendorf. By the way how's your sextant work these days?"

"I am rather rusty. I'd feel better if you let me drive while you take a look. With my navigation, we might end up in Tahiti or at least over the Pacific Ocean when we run out of gas!"

"No problem, I can use the practice. You have the airplane; try to keep it straight and level." And once again

Stoney climbed out of his seat. Retrieving Steve's sextant and clock, he climbed up on the small stool and stuck his head in the glass dome. Ignoring the intense pain in his shoulder, Stoney put the sextant up to his eye to take the reading. Standing there looking out of the sight glass, he had a moment's hesitation as he thought of his lost co-pilot and friend.

After he fixed their position on the chart, he had to wait about thirty minutes before he could take another reading. By the time he was ready for the second reading, his shoulder had evolved into a severe throbbing pain but ignoring it once again, he took the second reading. With that reading, he could plot a direction of flight. Drawing a line on his chart he calculated the new heading that would take them directly to Elmendorf instead of Victoria.

"Jonathan, turn to heading two-seven-five degrees and maintain that. Try to contact Elmendorf approach. I am going to step into the cabin and see how that's going. I'll be right back." And with that Stoney headed out into the cabin.

Stoney walked over to where Jones was standing and talking to one of his troops. Lee was slumped down in his chair and appeared to be out.

"Pete just wanted to check and make sure all was quiet."

"Yes sir, Captain Stone, our prisoner is definitely out, and no one is touching that coffee. I thought it was strange when you said to make him drink it, now I know why. I guess Lee didn't use as many pills as we did with the Russians. I'm grateful that we came out of it when we did. The thought of waking up with a Russian Kalashnikov in my face sends shivers down my spine. By the way, I didn't know you could roll an aircraft this big. How's that shoulder feel?"

"Actually, as far as I know it has never been done before. They will have to take this baby apart to check it out completely before flying passengers again. That maneuver puts a lot of stress on the airframe, but the biggest losers are the engines. They are not designed to fly inverted and when we were upside down, they ran with no oil pressure for several seconds, which is an eternity for a large radial. They will have to tear down the engines as well. However, that's a small price to pay for not losing the electronics in the back end. The shoulder hurts pretty bad but I have no choice but to put up with it. I can't take any kind of painkiller and still fly. Jonathan is a good co-pilot but he's not checked out in this aircraft. He can do the straight and level stuff, but no way can he land safely."

"I know for me and the guys, I am sure glad you pulled it off."

Glancing at his watch, Stoney said, "Got to head back up front and get another navigation fix. I'll announce an ETA as soon as I calculate it."

Arriving back in the cockpit, Stoney checked with Jonathan and he took a quick look at the engine gauges. Everything looked OK so he grabbed the sextant and took another reading. He had to really grit his teeth as he held up the sextant to take the reading; the pain in the shoulder seemed to be getting worse as well as getting stiff. After taking his reading he plotted their position and drew a course line starting at the first position reading then through the two positions and continued the line until it hit Elmendorf Air Force Base. Now if the weather would hold they would make Elmendorf in just over an hour and a half. *Plenty of fuel to get there,* he thought as he sat down at the Engineer's console.

"Jonathan, according to my calculations, we'll make Elmendorf in just about an hour and a half. Please make a PA announcement to the cabin. I need to sit and rest this shoulder. Let me know if anything needs my immediate attention."

"Can do boss, do you want me to ask Jones to take another look at that shoulder when I make the announcement?"

"No, just keep on your heading. I am going to sit here a while. Make sure I take another reading in forty-five minutes. Want to make sure the winds haven't changed."

Crossing his arms on the Engineer's desk, Stoney laid his head on them and just heard the PA announcement as he nodded off.

CLANG-CLANG-CLANG

After what seemed like a whole minute of sleep, Stoney was jarred awake by the sound of the engine warning bell. Jerking his head up and quickly scanning the engine gauges he saw that the number two engine oil pressure was zero. Jumping out of his seat he climbed back into his pilot's chair. Jonathan had already started the shut down procedure for the number two engine. With Stoney's help, they managed to shut down the engine and secure it. They had to make adjustments to the other three engines and with the loss of the number two they would lose some airspeed.

"How long was I out?" asked a somewhat dazed Stoney.

"Just about forty-five minutes, matter of fact I was going to wake you just as the engine alarm went off. I have the airplane if you want to take that reading you mentioned."

"Great, let me climb out of this seat and I'll take one more."

Gritting his teeth against the pain, he slowly climbed out of his seat just as the cockpit door opened and Jones stepped in.

"Sorry to bother you guys, but I happened to be glancing out the window and noticed that one of the propellers is not doing much to keep us in the air. What gives?"

"We lost the number two engine; oil pressure went to zero and we shut it down. We can more than make it on three engines, but it will slow us down just a bit. I was getting ready to take another reading and see where we are," Stoney said with a pained expression on his face.

Jones seeing that Stoney's face had become pale and there was more blood on his shirt said, "You don't look so good, is there something I can do to help?"

"I hope I look better then I feel. Yes I'll take the help," said Stoney.

Holding up the sextant he continued, "I need to hold this with one hand and adjust it with the other. Since my shoulder and arm are useless, how 'bout you hold it here while I do the adjustment and take the reading."

"I'll have to get real cozy with you on that stool to reach, but I'll do what I can."

"Just keep your free hand to yourself and we'll be fine!" said Stoney as he tried in vain to sound jovial.

With Jones' help, Stoney took the reading and plotted it on the chart. They were dead on the course line he had drawn and should be close enough to contact Elmendorf Approach Control.

"Jonathan, dial in Elmendorf and see if you can get them on the radio."

"Pete thanks for the help. You're welcome to sit at the Engineer's console for the last bit of the flight."

"Don't mind if I do. Always wanted to see what goes on in the front end of one of these things."

"Captain Stone, I have Elmendorf Approach on the radio. I gave them our ETA and asked to have an ambulance and Security Police waiting for us."

"Good job! Let me get back into my seat and we'll get this bird on the ground before *I hit the ground!*" said Stoney.

"Elmendorf asked if we would like a surveillance approach and I took the liberty of saying yes."

"Under the circumstances, that's exactly what I would've done; we'll make a good co-pilot out of you yet."

"Thanks captain, but I just want to work on them and leave the excitement and flying to you guys. Being able to go home at night and sleep with my wife is good for me. Can't handle this much excitement!"

About twenty minutes later, Stoney contacted Elmendorf Approach and they started the Surveillance Approach into the Air Force Base. This type of instrument approach is much easier on the pilots, since the ground controller monitors the approach and gives vertical and horizontal guidance to the pilot in terms of 'go up, go down, turn left, turn right, etc'. All the pilot has to do is follow the directions and the runway should appear in the windshield at the right time.

The surveillance approach worked out just fine and before they knew it, the big Constellation was coming to a stop at the VIP terminal. The same terminal the passengers had departed from some hours earlier. When the big radials came to a stop, people on the ramp pushed the

James A. Jack

stairs up to the front door just as Jones opened it. The Security Police rushed in first, followed by the medics with a stretcher. With Jonathan's help Stoney stumbled out the cockpit door and lay down on the stretcher. Just as he closed his eyes he saw the Security Police roughly pushing a handcuffed Lee down the stairs. With that sight burned into his memory Stoney closed his eyes and allowed himself to drift off into blissful unconsciousness.

EPILOGUE

USAF doctors patched up Captain Stone at the Elmendorf Hospital. Fortunately his wound would heal with no permanent side effects and no impact on his flying career. After his doctor released him from the hospital the USAF flew him to Washington, D.C. where he met with the heads of the intelligence services.

While hospitalized, representatives from CIA and NSA thoroughly debriefed him so the directors already knew the story; however, they wanted to personally thank him for his efforts to keep the sensitive equipment out of the Soviet's hands. They also asked if there was anything the U.S. Government could do to say thank you.

He requested a customs clearance to import one of the new British MGB-RV8 sports cars even though it did not meet U.S. car specifications. They were more than happy to "pull some strings" to make it happen. Several months later the car arrived at Stoney's house in Durango. The government assured Stoney they would arrange for him to have a job with any airline when he decided to start flying again. Stoney said thanks, but had decided to take several months off and travel around the country with Becky in that brand new sports car.

NSA, CIA, the Congressional Intelligence Committee and the President's National Security Adviser all agreed to shut down the Northern Star Program. They also directed the destruction of all of the Northern Star aircraft since it was impossible to extract the surveillance equipment.

APA put all salvageable parts, such as engines and avionics, up for auction allowing them to recoup some of the original investment. The company dissolved itself and all of its financial assets went back to the U.S. Treasury. Since it was a private company with no public stock, no one noticed that it just faded away. Many of the pilots and flight attendants went to work for other airlines and continued their flying careers.

The alternate airfields were all abandoned and the personnel transferred to new jobs within the intelligence arena.

All of the Northern Star Program funds transferred to a new U.S. Government agency known as the National Reconnaissance Office (NRO). One of NRO's jobs was to perform similar functions as the Northern Stars, using newly designed satellites.

Dieter Kauffman as well as Tom Train officially transferred to NRO and within months of the last Northern

Star flight, NASA successfully maneuvered the first submarine detection satellite into polar orbit.

A special court convicted Lee of hijacking, attempted murder, espionage and treason. During sentencing the judge gave him a choice of life in prison or loss of citizenship and deportation to the Soviet Union. He elected life in prison with no chance for parole.

Just after the trial, his wife divorced him and after their final meeting with the divorce judge she was seen driving off with a much younger guy in a Mercedes convertible. Lee, in shackles, climbed into the prisoner van and headed back to federal prison.

Captain Leshev and his Spetsnaz troops did make it back to the Motherland and just as Leshev had feared, they all received immediate transfers to Siberian border stations.

Some years later, Leshev received a transfer from his Siberian exile and a promotion. Spetsnaz needed officers to lead raids against the Afghani insurgents, the Mujahadeen, so the newly minted major received orders to go to Afghanistan to assist in those efforts. Through chance, he met a CIA operative who helped him defect to the U.S. Some weeks later, after a harrowing journey across the Pakistani border, he was on an airliner headed to Washington D.C. complete with a U.S. passport and an escort. Upon arriving at Dulles International Airport, he was whisked away to a CIA safe house where Katie Fuller debriefed him.

During their conversations, the story of his adventures in the Arctic came up and it was then that Katie realized just who he was. Months and many debriefing sessions later, the newly minted Mr. Mark James, a new member of the defector protection program, received a new identity, a house and a well paying job to live out the rest of his life.

The General Secretary, of the Soviet Union, wanted to send Colonel Sikovski and Admiral Ninsky to exile in Siberia as well. He thundered through the corridors of the Kremlin for days bellowing about the colossal political headache that would have resulted from a successful capture of the aircraft and its crew.

Moreover, dealing with the fallout from the capture and transfer of a squad of Spetsnaz troops from an American Air Base in Alaska back to Russia did nothing to lower his blood pressure. He repeated more than once that if Comrade Stalin had been in charge he would have had them shot in the courtyard but fortunately for them, cooler heads prevailed and they quietly disappeared into retirement after giving their assurances that no one would ever know about the project.

All of Flight 28A's passengers returned to their normal lives, though several of them had large checks to deposit.

Lightning Source UK Ltd.
Milton Keynes UK
UKOW02f1932120115

244381UK00001B/9/P